Fresh Cuts

The Breaking Volume

Edited by Jack Feril

CHOPHOUSE
BOOKS

ISBN: 978-0-9969744-1-7

Compiled by Joan Reginaldo

Edited by Jack Feril

Copyedited by Catherine Hill

Published by Chophouse Books

Acknowledgements

—✺—

For my wife, No Young Sook. Happy Anniversary!
I'd like to thank Joan Reginaldo for her tireless support and all of the
other Fresh Cuts writers for inviting me to participate.

—*Robert Bevan*

For all the on-again, off-again writers.
This is my first published story and I want to thank the following
people that got me here. First, to everyone in the Black Hats Writing
Group. Whether it's luck or fate, something brought us together and
I'm thankful for it everyday. Thank you Joan for being tough on my
writing. Thank you Dean for all the risks you are taking to help us
writers succeed. Hugo and Saman, thank you for being good friends. I
enjoy the long drives and good stories. Finally, to my family, thank you
for your never-ending support. Christina, Sheila, Tiffany and Angela, I
know I can be awkward but thank you for being there.

—*Ernest Ortiz*

For Futurehusband and Grimlock. You make me more human.
Thank you to the Black Hats of the Bay Area Writers Group.
You make me more me.
And thank you to Robert Bevan. You are the balance of both.

—*Joan Reginaldo*

For the White Hawk and the Little Wolverine.
Thanks to Chophouse Books, Black Hats, and Robert Bevan.
You guys are all right.

—*Jack Feril*

To Caffe Romanza, thank you for being our Secret Lair, panini place, and coffee den since 2010.
—*Black Hats of the Bay Area Writers Group*

To the writers and poets of TIBU where Dean was incubated... like an infectious disease.
—*Dean Fearce*

Contents

On *The Girls*–

Jack is the writer you always strive to be. Ever since I met him in 2011, I noticed no matter what genre he writes in, he can deliver a story that tugs at your heartstrings and makes you question your morals during ambiguous situations. He is the reason my writing has improved in recent years. What I loved best about *The Girls* is that Jack delivers his usual excellent balance of character development and well-paced tension. There is always that gray line at the edge of our feet, daring us to cross it.

—*Ernest Ortiz*

P.S.: Dean Fearce said this scary creepy ghost story hooked him by the eyeballs…*slide-thump*…*slide-thump*…and yanked until they bled.

The Girls

Jack Feril

━━━◥◣◢◤━━━

THIS HOUSE WAS SMALLER than the other six houses we've lived in over the past three years, but it felt like it could be the one. I rolled over on my side. My sister and I were sharing a room again; with all the moves, my parents could no longer afford a three-bedroom.

"You think this is the one?" I whispered across a gold river of dust motes as the last beam of sunlight died between us.

"I hope so," my sister whispered back. She sounded tired.

A bony hand broke through from the darkness of her side of the room and reached for me. The room was so small, the space between the beds so narrow, I barely had to reach over to touch her hand. She was a year older than me, but shorter, smaller, slight and fragile. Like the act of *living* took so much energy, she barely had any left for growing. At sixteen, she looked like she was twelve. At fifteen, I could probably buy cigarettes at the corner liquor store without getting carded. My hand engulfed hers. I gave it a squeeze, then pulled my hand back under the covers. It was a cold night for fall.

Though it was toasty warm under my soft worn blankets, I couldn't fall asleep. Usually, I grabbed precious sleep wherever I could—at school, waiting in line, on the drive to and from soccer matches. But it was a terrible irony that the best chance I had for a full night's sleep, the first night in a new house, was also usually the night I had insomnia.

Completely wrapped up, even with my layers of blankets tucked under me, I shivered, listening to all the strange groaning and creaking and rustling noises. I wish my parents had been able to afford to rent a newer place, like one of those apartments we drove by to get to the town's only Catholic church. Old houses had too much personality, and sometimes our personalities clashed.

Tonight though, the noises weren't too ominous or inexplicable. And the next thing I knew, my phone's alarm was blaring.

I opened my eyes to the disorienting landscape of the room. Moving boxes were stacked where my desk was supposed to be. Sacks of winter coats and snow suits, unnecessary now that we were in California, were piled high inside an unfamiliar closet. I shook my head to clear away the memory of my room three moves ago and resigned myself to the house of now.

"Shelly," I said. "Get up. We're gonna be late for school."

There was no answer. I had a heartbeat-skipping thought that maybe it was over. Maybe last night was the last night of having to keep moving. But then there was the sigh of sheets on skin, the sigh of a yawn, and I sighed. Not one of relief, not one of disappointment. A shameful mix of both.

"Want the shower first?" I said.

"No," said Shelly, pulling on a pair of grass-stained sweats. "I took a shower a few days ago."

Six schools. Six "new student" days. Shelly might've given up, but I was still interested in actually having a social life. I showered, put on some lip gloss, and got ready in record time, having unpacked my lucky jeans and favorite red sweater last night. Mom dropped us off at the high school just as the warning bell rang. Before she drove away, she called my name. Shelly was already shuffling toward the office. I looked at my mom and her insomnia-bruised eyes, pale slack skin, prematurely graying hair. She gave me the usual unspoken task. I gave her the usual unspoken promise.

———— ᙍᙍᙍ ————

The day went smoothly. Invigorated by the first large block of uninterrupted sleep I'd had in months, I signed up for two clubs and hung out with some girls on the soccer team. Told my parents all about it at dinner.

"How about you, Shelly?" said my mom. She'd unpacked most of the kitchen while we were at school. We were smushed in what the landlord had generously called a "breakfast nook," which was a sore replacement for the dining room in our original house.

"It was okay," Shelly said.

"Just okay?" said Dad.

Shelly took a deep breath then smiled. "It was better than okay. There weren't any…issues at all."

We all looked at her, probing that smile for weaknesses. It held up and we all relaxed.

Afterwards, Shelly and I did homework on top of some stacked boxes in the tiny living room while our parents went to their bedroom. I heard their TV come on. Shelly had on headphones and was murmuring French responses.

Je suis, tu es, nous sommes.

Pretending to work on my calculus homework, I listened to what my parents were watching. A reality show? Really? Then I realized they were fighting and the TV was on, loud, to cover their voices. But they kept talking during silent moments. I heard snatches of the fight. About the house. Money again. Surprisingly, our future. No, *my* future. College. And the giant elephant in the cramped, tiny house: my sister.

When Shelly and I finished our homework and went to our bedroom, they were still fighting but tiredly, softly, like they were only fighting because it had become routine and they had nothing else to fill their evenings. They moved from the fact that my dad should never have quit his cushy, high-paying job at Taraya Tech to the fact that my mom should never have married an atheist.

As I tucked myself into my blanket cocoon, I said, "Did you really have a good day, Shelly?"

"Yeah," she said. "I'm feeling okay. I think everything's gonna be okay."

She wasn't asleep ten minutes when she was proven wrong. I was doing my usual nightly vigil and I heard the sound, so familiar it was almost comforting in the terror it evoked. The *slide-thump, slide-thump* sound of someone large, limping through the house. An impossible sound because the entire house was carpeted, and it was a tiny house, with one short hallway.

Still, that *slide-thump* came closer and closer to our closed and locked door.

I pulled the covers up and over my face, waiting for the inevitable, knowing that no matter where I went, it would find me, and I might as well stay in bed. At least I didn't pee myself anymore.

The lock on the door clicked. My blankets flattened as the opening door made a breeze in the room. The temperature plummeted and I was paralyzed by the cold. It passed too quickly; feeling and sensation unfortunately returned. Even in my blanket cocoon, I could smell the scent of vomit and shit. It still made me gag but I no longer threw up.

I felt its presence enter the room, heard that *slide-thump* limp up to the space between our beds. Then the end of my bed lifted up about a foot. Then it dropped with a bone-shaking crash, like the carpet beneath it had turned to stone. Then up again. Then crash. Over and over.

As it continued, I felt something heavy and wet on my chest. I managed to roll over but the weight stayed on my upper body, crushing me against the bed just hard enough to make breathing difficult. I wanted to scream but I didn't, couldn't. Biting my knuckles helped. My knuckles tasted like tears.

"Stop!" my sister said. "Just stop! Please stop!" She screamed and screamed and screamed. Whatever The Presence did to me, it seemed to do two-fold to her. Her bed rose several feet and crashed so hard, I thought it would shatter. She was pressed so deeply on her bed, she nearly disappeared into the mattress.

This went on for what seemed like the entire night. But when it stopped and I looked at the clock, hoping sunlight would soon stream through the curtains and banish The Presence, only half an hour had passed. The Presence would leave us alone for a few minutes. Just enough time for exhaustion to push me over the brink of sleep. Then it would start again. Sometimes there would be scraping all over my back though I was supine against the sweat-soaked mattress. Sometimes there would be the feeling of water gushing over my face. Sometimes the feeling of something lodged in my throat, choking me, or hands contorting my arms and legs. Over and over, the whole night through.

No prayer could stop it. No cross in the room, nor sheets washed in holy water could ward it off. Nothing stopped it except moving, and that bought us a day or so, a week at most, as if it had to track us down, find us. Find Shelly.

By unspoken agreement, we all knew it came for her.

———— ∞ ————

The next morning was like every other morning of my young adult life. I don't even know what it would be like to have a normal morning. I imagine most teenage girls don't have to peel layers of stinking, slimy blankets off them. They're probably not stiff and achy, sometimes in so much pain their mom has to half-carry, half-push them as they shuffle to the shower. They probably don't get called in to the nurse's office the fourth period of their second day at a new school.

"They're concerned about you," said Nurse Graham. "That's all.

Don't be worried or scared. Mrs. MacEnroe said you could barely keep your eyes open during group work."

Took my sleep-deprived mind a long moment to remember who Mrs. MacEnroe was. Ah, second period Calculus.

"It doesn't look bad on you if you want to tell me you'd rather not be in that class," said Nurse Graham. "Trust me, most seniors couldn't hack it. You are doing fine for your age."

The convoluted way she talked would've bothered me if I'd had the energy to be bothered, but her voice was soft and the room was warm and smelled like a combination of Vick's mentholated rub and Pantene shampoo. Her curly brown hair looked freshly washed and glossy in the pulsing florescent lights. She pushed her gold-rimmed glasses up the thin bridge of her nose.

"If it's not the class, then please, tell me how we can help you," she said. "There are so many problems you kids are facing, despite all the technology your generation has been blessed with, maybe even because of all that technology there's..."

I tuned her out easily. Her soft voice was nothing compared to the *slide-thumps,* the unholy inhuman shrieks, my sister's whimpering, and the terrible crying coming from beyond our open door. Our parents, kept out by an invisible barrier, saw and heard everything that happened to their girls.

On Nurse Graham's cluttered desk, she had one framed photo, and it was one of those freaky-looking 3-D sonograms. At the horizon of her desk rose the considerable bump of her pregnant belly. She kept trying to reach across it and her desk to touch me, maybe take my hand. I squeezed my hands into fists, wanting to draw every aspect of myself to the black hole in my center. At the same time, I wanted to let her hold my hand while I told her everything.

But that would kill her.

Of course we'd sought help when *things* first started happening. My mother the Catholic had called in a priest to bless our house and the guest house and even the pool house. That priest was murdered exactly a week after my mother told him why we needed a house blessing. Strangled. Same thing with the shrinks, the parapsychologists, the young and hopeful representatives from every major religion. Dead, dead, dead.

I never saw the bodies or photos of the bodies but I'd met them when they were alive. I'd shaken their hands. In the beginning, I'd believed them and hoped with them and wanted them to save us. Save me. But the more we asked for help, the more people we lured to their deaths. I could imagine how they looked, dead in their beds, faces swollen from the pressure, and their eyes, red from broken capillaries, staring back at me.

Though Nurse Graham looked perfectly capable of dispensing Ibuprofen and bandaging minor wounds, I doubted she could help me with this. And I didn't want her elfin face and the naked mole-rat face of her unborn child added to my macabre mental memorabilia.

"…your sister, too," said Nurse Graham.

I focused on this. Like a practiced abuser, The Presence left no inexplicable bruises on visible skin.

"What about Shelly?" I said.

"She seems to be having the same…problem as you. At the very least, but it *is* a significant part of your health, both of you don't seem to be getting enough sleep at home. Now, part of it can be excused with moving cross country—"

"That's it. That's why we're so tired. Moving."

"About that. Six moves in three years. That's a lot of moving for a non-military family." She tapped a thick blue folder on her desk with my name on it. My academic file. The other thing that followed me from move to move.

"It hasn't affected my grades at all."

Nurse Graham puffed out her cheeks, blew out the breath in a mint-scented gust. "You can say that again. If you beef up your extracurriculars, you could graduate a year early with better-than-decent prospects."

"Could you help me with that, Nurse Graham? I would so be grateful if you could help me with that."

She was shocked speechless. Then, "It's not really my area. You would actually need to go to the school counselor if you wanted to do something like run for a student council position—oh, but that's over! Missed it by two months. I suppose—"

"The soccer team," I said. "I want to be on the varsity soccer team."

"But the tryouts were last month."

"I know. But I heard you and the coach are pretty tight." I'd heard no such thing but I was gambling on them not being mortal enemies. "Please," I said. "It would mean a lot to me. And it would look good on my college application if I could have one consistent thing through all those moves."

"It would. All right. I'll talk to Coach Park."

"Thanks." I got up to leave.

As I shrugged on my backpack, she said, "You can go for now, but I'll be calling you in soon to finish this."

"Sure."

"And if it continues, if it gets worse, I'll have to take measures. Up to and including calling CPS to do a home visit."

"Understood," I said with my hand on the door handle. "And it won't be necessary."

"That's what I like to hear."

From the door, she looked like she was about to be swallowed by the clutter.

———∞∞∞———

Nurse graham meant well but we were too far gone. No one could help us. At first, it seemed like my parents were fine asking for help from anyone who would listen, fine with killing the whole damn world if it would save their family. But the deaths of those trying to help us, the *murders*, started being too frequent and we were at the nexus of too many clusters. Moving became a necessity as well as a hopeful chance to lose the thing. Roger and Amanda Franco were *persons of interest* in two states.

The only ones who could help us were us. And my parents were running down. They knew *normal* and they wanted to get back to it no matter the cost but they were spinning their wheels, wasting their fuel on ruminating and arguing and pointing fingers—mostly at each other, sometimes God, and one time, when dad was drunk, at Shelly.

It was up to me now. I could see it in their dim eyes, lit by a candle at the end of an ever-lengthening tunnel. I could see it in my sister's eyes too, the light in them so dim they were probably just reflections from my own gaze.

What could I do, though? I had no money. No job to get money. Barely any energy for school, let alone the amount needed to find and keep even the most menial job. All I had was an iPad so old it didn't use a lightning cable. I stole it from a classmate in the city before this one. I had no money for a data plan so I could only use it wherever there was free wi-fi. Usually Starbucks, but I think my parents found the only city in America that didn't have one. Ironically, it had a boba place. One of those small Asian tea shops where they sold sweet milky iced tea with tapioca balls.

I "borrowed" some money from kids at school to buy one of the drinks and get the wi-fi password, which they changed daily and only gave out to customers.

I got my drink and took the table farthest from the door, which was also farthest from the counter where the workers would keep track of how long I'd been here. Sipping the cold, refreshing drink, I turned on the iPad and logged into their wi-fi. Then I opened my password-protected note-taking app. The "password protection" probably wouldn't hold up to an experienced hacker or whatever they want to be called now, but at least a random person couldn't open it and see what looks like an unsettling emo notebook of copy-pasted "Magic" recipes that used moonlight and "dew off a honeybee's wing," lists of demon names from several religions, and "Protection Spells."

Most were from questionable sources that also conveniently sold the ingredients for the magic recipes and protection spells. I had dismissed them before but when things started getting worse, and people that tried to help us kept dying, the snake oil suddenly didn't seem so snaky.

I tried all the easy ones first. Brick dust around the house, and I even put it at the threshold of our bedroom and around our beds. Smudge sticks made of sage grown with tears from a virgin, harvested in the light of a full moon, rolled on the thighs of a virgin, and lit by a virgin. That one was big on the virgin thing, which was easy since both Shelly and I were virgins; we didn't neck in the woods for fear of falling asleep and having The Presence show up and kill our dates, and we didn't bring guys home for the same reason.

My very long List of Hope was full of strikethroughs and had dwindled down to the last few choices. Dangerous alternatives. It was no small matter to nail the first fleece of a spring lamb, soaked in the blood of a Catholic priest, to our bedroom door. And I doubted my parents could now fund a jaunt to the Vatican nor arrange a quick meeting with the pope and five cardinals. I crossed those off, as well as a few others: eat a feather from six-hundred-and-sixty-six black birds, drink a tea made from fragments of fallen stars, have sex in the shadow of a jackal, etc. I was left with three possibilities if I stretched myself.

One of them I could try in a few days. It required menstrual blood.

Another, I could try if all else failed. It wasn't as drastic as all the blood and sex and bloody sex possibilities I'd crossed out. Still, I wanted to keep it for last if I could.

The third one I could try tonight. My own special little idea. I would need Shelly's help but I'm sure she'd be up for it.

I slurped up the tapioca balls from the bottom of my cup as I looked up a few details on the internet. Then I packed up my stuff and took a bus to three addresses I got online. An Indian clothing shop, a used sporting goods store, and a Catholic church.

By the time I got home, it was dark. Mom gave me a hard time for coming in that late, but it sounded scripted, like she didn't really care but needed to keep up pretenses. After dinner, after brushing our teeth and washing our faces, I sat on Shelly's bed and told her the plan.

"We can't see it, but we can feel it, right?" I said.

Shelly nodded.

"That means it has mass," I said. "So that means we make it so we *can* see it. I couldn't get a hold of that colored powder Indians use for that color festival they do, but I managed to get this." From my backpack, I took out two cellophane packets of hot pink cloth with gold embroidering. The cellophane crinkled as I opened one of the packs and unraveled the cloth to a long rectangular swath and draped it over the foot of her bed.

Shelly smoothed a hand over the shiny fabric. I opened the other cellophane pack.

"How did you afford this?" she said softly with awe. Then she repeated it in a voice hard with suspicion.

"How the hell do you think?" I said. "I stole them. I went to the store and asked for the colored powder and they didn't have any. Then I asked if I could use their bathroom. I waited until another customer came in. While she was being helped, I put these two in my backpack."

"But…why?"

"We're going to throw these on The Presence." Saying it out loud, calling it by the name we gave it when we were younger and too afraid to think of anything else, made it seem like some silly childish Boogeyman thing.

"Why these?" said Shelly. "You didn't have to steal them. We have sheets."

She kind of had a point, but I hadn't decided to go through with this plan until this afternoon, and I didn't want to come back for sheets and leave again to get them blessed, nor did I want to hold it off until later.

Whatever. It was done.

"I got these blessed by a Catholic priest," I said. "Blessed, sanctified, sprinkled with holy water and held over incense. The whole shebang." The priest knew me and my mom; we'd gone to church the day after we'd arrived in this city. I'd told him I was having trouble adjusting to the move and it would help me a lot to feel the Lord's embrace—as in, the blessed fabric—while I studied.

She rolled her eyes and sighed.

"It's gonna work," I said. "And then when we have The Presence covered and we can see it, we'll bash and smash it!"

From under my bed, where I'd stashed them as soon as I got home, I retrieved two old baseball bats from the used sporting goods store.

"You steal those too?" said Shelly.

"Wouldn't fit in my backpack. I worked out a deal with the manager. He said I could have them on account of them being so old no one would pay to use them. In exchange, I have to vacuum the store and help sort the donations and trade-ins on the weekend. He said I could have whatever doesn't sell if I keep coming in on the weekends."

"Nice gig," she said, not really meaning it.

"Thanks," I said, feeling the same. Then I grinned. "I had these blessed too."

She chuckled. "Bet you did."

"I told the priest, while he had everything out anyway, might as well, right?" I held one out to her, handle side out.

She held it weakly. It almost dropped on my foot.

"This'll work," I said.

"Yeah."

"Why don't you believe me? Why can't you just... Why can't we just try this."

"Try. How many things have we *tried*."

"A lot. And if this doesn't work, we try something else. And something else after that. We keep doing it until something works because if something drew it to us, then something has to repel it. Or destroy it. Or whatever. Okay?"

"Fine."

It rankled me that she would be so defeatist, so apathetic about this whole situation when she was the target of its worst attacks. To avoid a screaming match, and eager to try my plan, I got into bed. Didn't tuck myself into a blanket burrito this time. I had the hot pink sari wrapped around my right hand and the bat tucked against my left side. Over and over in my head, I practiced what I would do, just like my coach back home used to tell us. Envision the kick. The rest is you following through.

So I envisioned myself leaping up as soon as the *slide-thump* got close enough. Leaping up and throwing the cloth over the sound. Then reaching down for the bat and whacking away like a kid with a sugar rush and a vendetta against piñatas.

Lights were turned off. Mom and dad creaked into their bed. The house settled down. I listened for that *slide-thump* eagerly and it occurred to me how demented it was to eagerly anticipate the thing I'd dreaded for so long. And I doubted my plan. Of course I doubted any part of it would succeed. I was a fifteen-year-old girl trying to succeed where so many adult experts had failed. But they hadn't been this close, I reasoned to myself. They had all been theorists.

In theory, an exorcism would've driven it away. *In theory*, going vegan would've put it off our adrenalized sweat. *In theory*, conducting a séance and politely asking it to leave us alone should've made it leave us alone.

The theorists meant well, but most of them hadn't lived long enough to actually see what happened to us at night. The others…they lived just long enough to confess they hadn't one-hundred-percent believed us.

Well, I believed in its existence. And since it existed, we could fight back. We could give as good as we got.

Every night if we had to. No more lying down and taking it.

My sister dimmed the lights, jumped into bed, then huddled under the covers.

The first *slide-thump* happened almost immediately, weakening my resolve. It seemed to come from very far away. My entire body was rigid and attuned to it. I strained to hear the sound under the tempest of my own rushing blood.

Slide-thump…slide-thump…slide-thump. After what seemed like a day, it was finally here. The doorknob glinted as the door swung open on silent hinges. In the dim light, I saw nothing come over the threshold but I knew it was here when my breath fogged in my face and the vomity sewer stench filled the room.

Unraveling the cloth from around my fist, I saw Shelly moving out of the corner of my eye.

"Wait," I whispered through gritted teeth.

The coldness came closer and closer until it felt like I was standing in front of an open freezer. I wanted to make sure it was close enough to catch the cloth but if we waited too long, it would have a hold on us for the rest of the night.

I felt a shift in the air, a press of warmth then frigid cold, like something had passed in front of my face.

"Now!" I yelled, leaping up, throwing the brilliant sari over the space between our beds. It fluttered a long way down and my heart sank with it; I had missed!

But then it settled on an unmistakable topography of head and shoulders. It was shorter than I'd thought. About my height. But broad side to side, thick all around. My sister's cloth came down too as The Presence swayed unsteadily, like it was surprised.

"Now, Shelly!" I yelled, swinging my bat with all my might.

I struck its head so hard, the force of the rebounding bat jarred my shoulder. If I'd struck a person, that person would be dead or at least floored. The Presence was still upright, but the swaying took a wider arc. I swung again, aiming for its neck, and heard a crack as my bat struck Shelly's bat.

"Keep swinging," I yelled.

I jumped to the other side of my bed so I could strike The Presence from behind. It felt wrong. I would be weaker with a less-practiced left-handed swing. I should've made Shelly do it. Her swings toward The Presence's front were not as targeted and not as forceful as mine.

Where I stood, swinging my bat, I could see our parents beyond that invisible doorway barrier. Mom was cheering us on. Dad was launching himself against the barrier, yelling, "Hold on! You got it! Keep going!" as if I was running a marathon.

Shelly and I kept striking that thing but it wouldn't go down. It was dazed and spinning wildly, but it wouldn't go down. We'd struck it a dozen times, two dozen, three dozen, but it wouldn't go down. It would outlast us.

I hadn't planned on that.

And it would be angry.

We had to end it. Now!

"Harder!" I yelled at Shelly.

She was barely lifting her bat. In her eyes, I saw that she'd already given up, that she didn't see the significance of how much we'd just accomplished.

"Come on, Shelly," I said, growling with disappointment and the force of my swing.

Something came up from the beneath the vibrant saris and an invisible force gripped my bat. It yanked. I was gripping the bat so hard, the force nearly popped my shoulders out of their sockets. The Presence swung the bat easily with me on the other end. I held on because I knew if I let go, that blessed weapon would be used against me.

"Help me, Shelly," I screamed.

She dropped her bat and ran for the door. As soon as she touched it, she flew back, repulsed by a blast of frigid air that swept the room. Her back struck the opposite wall, followed by the crack of her head. Dizzy, she slid to a crouch.

She looked vulnerable. The Presence thought so too. It released my bat suddenly. I stumbled and slipped on the bat Shelly had abandoned as she abandoned me. I landed hard on my butt and my left wrist twisted under my weight.

I watched in horror as the vibrant saris slid off The Presence. It was invisible again, but only for a moment, because I saw where its hands might be as Shelly was suddenly lifted up and pressed against the wall. She clutched at invisible arms. It was fascinating watching her throat shrink beneath powerful, invisible hands. I knew where The Presence was, and it looked like I was too far away for it to do anything to me, or it was concentrating on Shelly because she was the weaker of us.

Silently, I grabbed my blessed bat and stood up. I tiptoed to them. If The Presence was watching me, it didn't show it. It didn't let up on Shelly's throat. Her nightshirt rolled up and her chest started to shrink too from the compression of an impossibly large hand. Shelly gasped in breaths.

I estimated where The Presence's head would be. As I lifted the bat, I caught a glimpse of our mom. I saw the unspoken task. I nodded my unspoken promise.

I raised the bat up over my head and swung down with the force of my love.

My sister's head crushed in like an aluminum can.

Abruptly, she fell to the ground, released.

The sewer and vomit smell evaporated as warmth returned to the room.

Dad rushed in and, keening his grief, cradled Shelly against his chest. Mom took me into her arms and hugged tight until I saw stars. I felt weak. The blessed bat slipped from my grip and banged against my ankle.

"You know what you need to do?" Mom softly demanded of Dad.

He wiped the back of his hand against his wet face and nodded. "Yeah." Then he looked at me. I expected anger or hatred but all I saw was the emptiness of my sister's eyes. As he stood with her in his arms though, I saw that his eyes were not quite so empty. There was determination in them. And, finally, hope.

Over my sister's body, he kissed Mom's forehead.

"Wait," I said.

I took one of the blessed saris and wrapped Shelly's head with it so the wound wouldn't drip all over the house. It wasn't bleeding much anymore anyway. Most of it had gushed up onto the ceiling and left a ragged red ribbon along the wall. I kissed both of Shelly's eyes and wiped away her tears. They were still warm. They had mingled with mine.

"Bye, Shelly," I said.

When Dad was gone, Mom and I cleaned up the blood. She asked me how school was going. I told her what Nurse Graham had said about me graduating early if I really applied myself. But I should stay the whole four years, do more sports and extracurriculars to get as many scholarships as I could, seeing as how we were not as financially secure as we had been before...well, before.

Mom gave me a quick hug and said it would all work out with the insurance money.

On *Spiffy One Up*–

Dean and Jack sat across the table discussing the contents of what would become this book, *Fresh Cuts: The Breaking Volume*.

"Got some older stories, could resurrect those," said Dean. "Might work with some cleanup."

"Good," said Jack. "Spiffy one up."

"Spiffy one up," Dean said, "sounds like a good title."

Thirty seconds later, Jack had laid out the plot of this story, and it's a spiffy one. Jack R. Feril has a gift for storytelling. This is one of Dean's favorites.

—*Dean Fearce*

Spiffy One Up

Jack Feril

~~~WW~~~

...static...

...static...

YEAH, I GOT IT. Kept falling off my lapel. You can start recording now. It's been on? I just want to reiterate that the money is not mine and we're very glad you're here. That's all I wanted to say before we formally begin.

...

It was one day before New New Year's Eve, which we still cele-brated on that lonely piece of rock on account of the old folks were keen on keeping up with Earth-1 traditions. The last rush of customers already come and gone and we was counting down minutes to when I could officially lock the front door. That's when that goddamn 'spector came in, shaking the red dust onto our just-vacuumed floor.

He had on one of them white inter-moon traveling coats. Looked new. Picked up the light. Wasn't yet dulled by the ubiquitous atmo-spheric dust, as fine as ground cinnamon. Keeps gunking up our O-filters. I gotta keep requisitioning new parts and pieces and those don't come as timely as I'd like them to. One time, Davey and I had to wear emergency O-tanks while we was doing the welding. That's a work hazard. We coulda been blowed up.

Anyway, you make a note of that, kid.

...

Lemme see the note.

...

Good job on that. Make sure you underline how *necessary* the *timeliness* of it all is.

...

What was that?

...

Come again?

...

Yeah. Yeah. I was getting to that part.

So that guy comes in. Young fella, once he took that fancy white coat off and hung it on the coat peg after I asked him to. Weren't none of us raised in no barn, I said.

"Yes, Sir," said that fella. Pale as a Popolos whore.

They like 'em that way. Pale. On account of it being so sunny all the time. Makes the women look dainty and fragile. No, they don't look like our kind of women. Think of a kangaroo, paint it yella, and put scales up in its hooey. Sharp serrated scales that'll skin ya faster than a fishmonger on juice. It ain't pretty, by God. I been on Popolos long enough to see e'ry kind of man come in with a willy so red and raw they beg Doc Pinang to just cut it off.

...

Yeah, I'm getting to it.

That pale young man with baby-soft cheeks and short blond ringlets, he comes up to the counter and starts asking Davey questions like he's afeared of me. Won't even meet my eye. Don't bother me none. I do take a while of getting used to on account of my size and missing ear and my prossy hand and leg. Jorn-mining ain't for the soft.

...

What's that now? Why not— Well all my family's dead! Light-speed travel wasn't what it is now. You need to brush up on your Theory of Relativity, son.

I stayed because my friends are on Popolos. They're still hale and mining, and TarayaCorp set Davey and me up with that nice store and them homey little pods in the back. It'd be a service to the community, they'd said. We'd be helping out our friends and their families, they'd said. Davey and me, what else would we have done anyway? It was good to be useful. So we stayed.

We stayed, and we run that TarayaCorp outlet, and yes indeed, our friends and their families are grateful for that…that little touch of luxury e'ry now and then.

We put up with the occasional visit from TarayaCorp reps to broaden their franchisee.

When that pale fella in his slick new traveling coat come in, that's what Davey and I thought he was. A TarayaCorp rep, come to show us some new pneumatic mouth or self-lubing prossy. Now, it's not uncommon for a rep to request a…a sample of our wares, and usually we'd oblige, but this fella… He was so young, he still had gills. He comes up to the counter sweating into his collar and looking around like he's gonna get caught lookin' at a nudey mag.

"They sending them younger 'n' younger," Davey said to me, soft-like but the pale fella heard and took umbrage. He showed us his mining badge.

Kelly Vanger, IGS. Inspector of General Systems.

"What kind of name is Kelly for a man," said Davey.

"Hush now, Davey," I said. "We're talkin' to the new boss of half of Popolos."

"Yeah," said Kelly, looking a little more solid, a little more glad to be here.

"What can I do for you," I said to him.

"Can I uh, can I uh see your catalogue," he kind of muttered.

Davey laughed and slapped the counter hard enough to make the glass eyes roll in their little oily sockets. "We ain't got no catalogue," he said.

"We ain't got nothin' to rent out, period," I said. "It's the day before New New Year's Eve. E'ry last one of our models is out on a date. E'ry last one'll be gone for the holiday."

"Come on," said pale little Kelly-boy. "You gotta have a spare back there or something."

He rubbernecked, tryna see into our workroom. We had the lights off on account of it being almost New New Year's, and power gets kinda shady on holidays what with e'ryone baking and making calls to the multi-Earths.

"I said we ain't got none," said Davey.

"Look," Kelly-boy said, "I'm really in a bind here. I haven't seen my wife for two whole months. Can't you just give me...I dunno, give me anything you got back there. I don't even care if it has a head as long as it's got the uh, the other parts."

Now this fella was complaining about not having seen his wife for two whole months, when I had fellas comin' in who hadn't seen theirs for a year or more. Some of my friends hadn't even *touched* their wives or husbands for five years. Five years!

This guy, this Kelly, takes a credit crystal out from under his shirt and waves it at Davey like he's some kinda Houdini tryna hypnotize us.

Make a note so you can look that up.

"I'll make it worth your while," said Kelly. "Name a number and I can make it happen."

He dropped the credit crystal in Davey's hand. Davey handed it to me. The crystal clinked against my prossy palm. I scanned it with my prossy eye. Info came back. Millions of bona fide credits on it, but they were TarayaCorp credits. Wages for the staff that supports the miners. The receptionists and secretaries, the packers and shippers, the cooks and barkeeps. This guy, this Kelly, was willing to spend someone's hard-earned wages just so he could get his rocks off.

It made me angry but it also made me kinda leery of him. If he was willing to do that and we denied him, what would he offer next? By the crazy hopscotch way he was looking between me and Davey and the prossy lips we had on display, I figured he wouldn't stop. Couldn't stop. Might start threatening us with all sorts of corporate red tape, bind us up tighter than our size Double-Aught Anuses.

"Okay, okay," I said. "I'm telling you true that we didn't expect anyone to come in on the day before New New Year's. We have rented out all our models, basic to luxe. There ain't nothing here but parts and some broken biddies we're fixin' to scrap and melt."

"Well can't you put some parts together for me," said this guy, this Kelly. "I'll take anything. Honestly, I'll take mismatched boobs, no anus, no eyes, bald. Whatever."

"As long as it's got a hooey," said Davey.

"Well yeah," said Kelly. "That's the best part."

This guy's never tried the size A-4 lips on a D-20 mouth.

"Anything you got back there," said Kelly, "except man parts."

Now, I ain't one to judge. I can code e'ry kind of program to feed into e'ry kind of model. Want someone who'll suckle you from six breasts, diaper you and burp you? There's a model for that. Want someone with four feet you can suck? There's a model for that. Want someone who looks like your old grammar school teacher? As long as you got a picher, there's a model for that. What we ain't got, we can build. For an extra fee, I can sculpt and Davey can build to any spec. Any spec.

But it'd been a while since we got someone like this guy, this Kelly. I don't mind catering to a simple palate, but it's like asking a chef to make you toast.

Davey chuffed and said, "I don't think we got enough woman parts to make a whole body without some man parts."

"Like what kind of body parts are you talking about," said Kelly.

"We got more leftover man parts than woman parts," I said, "on account of some *inventory error*." I shot Davey a look. "Off the top o' my head, we got a pelvis, coupla penises, size Y-18 hands, ZZ-20 feet. Most of the body parts can go with either sex, to tell you truly. We get guys that come in askin' for K-10 penises over B-16 labias all the time. There's even a new model, the Vaganal. Only comes in letter sizes for the diameter because the length goes in the vagina and out the anus, or vice versa."

Kelly turned as pale as his traveling coat.

"Can you make it look like a woman?" he said.

"We could make it look like your wife," I said. We got a lot of wigs and a bunch of extra faces, on account of it costs extra for the really realistic ones.

Kelly looked at the clock on our wall above our *Dainty-Dainty* brand foot sample case.

"Not my wife," he said quickly. "I'll take a brunette if you have one. I don't care if it has man parts but please no penis. And I'll give you an extra five kilo-credits if you can rush it. I gotta get back to the dock for the last ferry to Gadley Basin."

That gave us less than an hour. I was tempted to make him wait, miss that ferry, hole up in one of the hotels down the road. But that was me being petty and he would've spent more of those wages.

"All right, we'll spiffy one up for you," I said.

"But Boss," said Davey, looking like he was fixin' to throw pale Kelly out into the fine red dust.

Now Davey, I love him like a son but he tends to run his mouth and his temper's shorter than a day in midwinter. I squeezed his shoulder and pushed him into the workroom with me. I closed the door before turning on the lights. Didn't want to let Kelly-boy see exactly what we had. It was a modest space and most of the silver-edged cabinets and backlit hooks were empty. I was telling true when I said we'd rented out all our models. All that was left were rusty or broken limbs with torn plasti-skin, melty eyeballs, crusty wigs, the stiff plastic lips I'd told Davey to throw out but he kept saying later, later, I'm saving 'em for a Art Project.

"He's the new boss of half our friends and their kin," I said to Davey. "We won't be doing ourselves, or them, any favors by treating him unkindly."

I opened our oldest cabinet, wood instead of steel, and beheld the dusty face of a Raphael Madonna.

"Not Ruby," said Davey.

I'd carved Ruby's face with my own bare hands, you see. And Davey, when he'd been given to me as an assistant, well, I trained him with Ruby. Every body he first put together, I made him use Ruby's face, so he would learn and develop a respect for the human form, learn and respect the divine and necessary release of sexual tension.

"Why, Boss?" said Davey.

"Because I trust her to do right by us," I said.

For when I turned her on, there was an intelligence and wisdom in her dark brown eyes I know I didn't program. Truly, part of her was always on, always listening, because unlike the newer models, she had to be kept plugged in and *dormant* or her battery would drain and she'd lose all programmed positions and conversation matrices.

"Hello, Father," she said. Maybe I imagined it but I swear she was chiding me for leaving her asleep so long.

"Davey, get some parts and put a body together for Mr. Kelly Vanger while I fix Ruby's hair and makeup," I said.

"Sure, Boss," Davey said sullenly.

Neither Davey nor I talked while we put Ruby together. He did the best he could with parts scavenged from the dump crates. He screwed an A-4 left breast and a D-10 right breast onto a thin man's torso. I helped him saw a Q-17 penis off an old pelvis, which we screwed on under the torso. He managed to find matching female legs but mismatched arms. One very muscular and short, one very thin and long. A pair of Y-5-12 hands. Larger than Davey's hands. Davey put all the odds and ends on then draped everything with an ECE5B6 skin.

"Lasers on, stay clear," he said and flipped a switch. Blue lasers from the ceiling passed over the skin sheet and the skin melded with the Frankensteined body—

...

Sure, I'll show you some time. Just call in advance so I can be sure to have one ready for you, otherwise you'll have to wait while I put a body together and all that.

...

It's too expensive to just run the machine for a small piece. I'd rather do a whole body that's been ordered, on account of if I ran the skin-lights for e'ry looky loo, the power bill would go up. Next thing you know, Corporate's breathing down my neck, requisitions take a dive, and models start costing more than a week's wages.

...

No, it's okay. It's a fascinating thing to see and I'll gladly show you but like I said, let me know in advance.

...

Uh-huh. Uh-huh. Now Ruby, she's different. And it was extenu-ating circumstances. I'd like to remind you that we told that guy, that Kelly, that we done run out of almost e'rything to put together the usually requested models with the usually requested parameters. He had us pissing up ropes, as far as I'm concerned, and I think Davey and I were very accommodating.

Very accommodating.

I told you I made Ruby's face with my bare hands.

…

Yeah, back when I had both hands. You can't do that kind of fine detailing with a cheap-ass prossy like this. I carved her face with my bare hands. I programmed her personality too, after my own dear Ma and my six sweet baby sisters and e'ry sharp-witted, slick-tongued woman I e'er loved on e'ry Earth I e'er touched toe to.

…

Yeah, you could say that. She was kin to me. Like a daughter. My family…

…

Well, if you'd stop innerupting me! God Almighty!

So with one eye on the clock, Davey squared Ruby's body and I checked and re-checked her face and crystal processors and programming and lube levels. Check, check, and check. Got her head onto her body, put her in one of the protective water- and dust-proof robes, and led her out to that guy Kelly.

Boy, what a face on him when we brought her out. Like he'd just seen a pan of hot steaming shit. And he still wanted to stick his willy in because it was still body-temperature. Then he looked up at her face and he smiled the smile of a man you'd kill for touching your sister.

I can tell by your face you don't know what I'm talking about. That used to be the way of the world, far, far long before you was born, so maybe don't pay it no mind right now. Maybe just take my word for it that that guy Kelly gave me the heebie jeebies something awful and if I didn't feel responsible for the psychological and emotional well-being of an entire forsaken planet, well…

Davey ran that guy's credit crystal through and finalized the transaction while I explained some finer points, just in case, but that guy Kelly, he busted into my explanations and said he knew how to run a model.

"Even one as old and *janky* as the one you're giving me," he said.

"Ain't no one said anything about *giving* you Ru—"

I almost said her name but I caught myself. It felt... Now don't laugh, but her name felt sacred. Like if I'd told that guy Kelly what her name was, he woulda wrecked it too.

"Fine," I said, "but you surely need to see this part. This here's the emergency shutoff switch, all right? You see where my finger is behind her ear? Look closely because once I take my finger off, looks just like skin and hair."

He looked, nodded, looked at the clock, and took her shoulder. For the slightest moment, I swear she hesitated. But it coulda been just rusty gears or a loose crystal on her motor-board. Made a mental note to check it out on her return.

That guy Kelly pulled her out of the store and Davey and I, we watched her disappear into the swirling red dust.

. . .

. . .

. . .

What was that? Sorry, I was just thinking. About that moment. It was like watching a tooth sink into a pool of blood.

. . .

I blame my Pa. Ma was the breadwinner, she was gone most days, helping to build one of the first Black Hole stabilizers. Pa took care of us, schooled us in the classics and neo-classics and astral-classics, me and my six sisters and three brothers.

. . .

'Course I miss them. We kep' in touch. I got reels and reels of

vid-phone conversations in my bunker. I play them for Ruby and Davey
sometimes, when business is slow 'round Second Christmas.

...

No, that wasn't the last time I saw Mr. Kelly Vanger. He returned
Ruby the very next day. I tell you truly I was surprised that she looked
the same as the moment she left. The protective water- and dust-proof
robe was wrapped around her exactly the same way, 'cept it had some
dried jizz flaking on the sleeves.

Davey and I had a good laugh about that. I'm not ashamed to say
it. You put down on your notes that Davey and I, we ne'er e'er poked
fun at anybody about the state of the models when they got returned.
Some folks are just big, or clumsy, or they got different *needs*. Davey and
I, we learn from that and we make provisions. Like Ol' Lady Langstrom,
standing order of two well-hung models with size S-17 breasts, every
Saturday at noon. Davy and I learnt that we had to double-layer the
skin on the buttocks, because Ol' Lady Langstrom, she's a biter.

I tell you true, on a planet this small, with a population this dependent on each other, nothing stays a secret for long. But no one ever
learns it from us.

So I hope you see the significance of what I've told you, how open
and honest I've been about this guy Kelly's proclivities when it comes
to the business he's done with me and my apprentice.

That was the beginning of a long and strange relationship he had
with us. He would come to the store right before we closed like he was
trying not to be seen by the neighborhood folks. I imagined him sitting
in his Cloud Cruiser, peering at his watch in the crimson light of the
setting sun. He would come in and request Ruby.

...

About every other week at first. Then more often. He'd come and
ask for Ruby, and at first, I'd deny him, tell him that we had stockrooms

full of models now that the holidays were over. And I'd remind him that Ruby was an ancient model, not really under warranty no more, so we couldn't be held liable for any injuries obtained during the course of use. We reminded him that that New New Year's Eve deal was just for that night, on account of the fact that we hadn't had anything else to give him then. But he always asked for Ruby.

Not even on a new body. He wanted the exact same rusty, mismatched, creaking parts we first put together. Davey had trouble remembering what parts they were but that guy Kelly, he knew, down to the off-sized toes. We even had a dramatic turn when Davey forgot and threw one of the arms into the melter. That guy Kelly almost jumped into the fire to get it. We held him back. After he saw that it was gone, that it had melted and could no longer be distinguished from the other old parts being recycled, he let us sit him down. He shook so badly, he chipped his front tooth.

That's how I was sure it was that guy Kelly when we came upon the body. That chipped front tooth.

So at first, we tried real hard to dissuade him from asking for Ruby and her Frankenstein body, but he insisted to the point of offering to pay thousands of credits. TarayaCorp credits, remember? The money that was to go to the hard-working support folks for the TarayaCorp miners. So I relented. We gave him Ruby. We gave her to him so often, we just never took her apart no more.

She was like his drug.

He came back again and again, spending all them TarayaCrop credits that coulda been someone's groceries or fuel money.

It got to the point that she would just come out from the workroom at the usual time that he came to fetch her. On her own.

...

No, I tell you truly! I'll swear on anything. I told you she was special.

She knew. She learnt. Don't try to understand it because if I can't, you haven't a prayer. I'm not saying that to be pretentious. I'm saying that because there are more things in space and time than are dreamt of in your philosophy. Shakespeare. Look it up.

At first I thought Davey was sending her out, but he wasn't. I asked. Then I thought it might be some kind of short or hiccup in her programming. When I looked at her codes, they were as I'd left them.

I asked her once, when she came out and that guy Kelly hadn't shown up yet, I asked, "Why do you come out for him, child?"

She told me it was on account of advice she'd heard me tell one of the customers: "When fate runs to meet you, face forward and meet it head on."

I told her, quite angrily, "that man is not your fate!"

She looked at me then, with that something-knowing shining in her dark eyes, and she stared at me like she was willin' me to read her mind.

I could not.

Though I seem to be made mostly out of metal like her, I'm still half man. Half human. Not privy to interstellar mysteries. The more she seemed to be human, the less human she was. The nadir of the uncanny valley.

And that was the last night we saw that guy Kelly.

About a week or so later, you probably have it in your notes somewheres, we all volunteered for the search party. Of course the authorities checked his pod first. Gary Gregson, over at the water farm, said we should check out the pod too, in case the authorities missed something. Gary's thorough like that, and I like him for it because he's keen but respectful about it. He's saved e'ry person's butt at least once when it comes to crossing Ts and dotting Is on corporate contracts.

So a bunch of the older folks and I, we went over to that guy

Kelly's pod off Second Street. Looked like a normal ol' bachelor pad to us, which was weird on account of him supposedly having a wife. I remember he mentioned her that New New Year's Eve eve that we met. Though there were feminine traces here and there, we'd heard neither hide nor hair of Mrs. Kelly Vanger.

By feminine traces, I'd like to remind you I had sisters. I know a tube of lipstick when I see one. But it was nearly brand new. There was a toothbrush on one side of the sink, but the bristles weren't as worn out and splayed as the one we presumed to be Kelly's on the other side of the sink. There was a dinner set for four, but only one set of dishes had chips and silvery streaks left from silverware.

And a fine layer of red Popolos dust coated e'rything.

We conferred upon ourselves and came to the conclusion that Kelly had either been playing love nest with one of the locals, or his wife had come and abruptly left for some reason. Left quickly enough to leave her satin slippers, her lipstick, and an array of decent but completely unnecessary fancy jewelry.

Now who, in God's vast universe, leaves their slippers behind?

We found her body under the pod. We'd only thought to look when we couldn't get over anybody leaving their slippers behind and Gary, thorough as ever, found a shovel in the kitchen pantry. What would a paper-pusher need a shovel for? Wasn't like he could plant anything in the fine red Popolos dust anyway.

Took us a few hours to find the burial site, another few hours to dig her out of it. The wind was blowing somewhat fiercely and filling the hole as quickly as we could excavate.

Mummified is what she was. Completely and utterly. Buried alive, is what Doc Pinang said, on account of she found red dust in that poor woman's lungs. Doc Pinang said Mrs. Vanger must've died right after she got home because she still had her Epi-Solar shuttle ticket in her pants pocket.

The ticket read that she'd gotten to Popolos a few weeks after New New Year's Eve.

I broke away from the crowd then, because I'd pieced together some stuff. Just hypotheticals about what might've transpired, and since my business, Davey, and Ruby made cameos in those hypotheticals, I wasn't about to share them with anyone right there and then.

I shuffled away—

...

I *know* I shuffled on account of it being windy and the dust was all riled up and in my eyes. Made it hard to see more than a pace or two ahead, so I shuffled to keep from smacking headfirst into a wall.

As I shuffled, my foot caught on something. Looked like a piece of pink cloth. I bent over, rubbed it between my fingers, and some of the pink came off to be dust. The cloth was white. Reminded me of that water- and dust-proof robe we wrap the models in, like the one Ruby wears to meet that guy Kelly. And that got me to thinkin' about that first time I met Kelly Vanger. He'd been wearing a white traveling coat, slick like the one that'd snagged my foot, like it had wanted to be found, and it had wanted *me* to find it.

We dug him up too. Didn't need an autopsy to know that guy Kelly had died recently. Still had his hands around his pecker, which came off when we pulled him out, on account of us not being careful and pulling him up by his arms.

Since none of us really liked him much, we didn't feel no qualms about placing bets on how he died. On a planet that small and forgotten, we learnt to make our own entertainment. Not that often that we come across a "Mysterious Death" so we thought we'd roll on it. Seeing as how I was most familiar with him, though, I opted out of the betting and I was made to hold the pot.

The betting was broken down into three categories: accident, foul play, or suicide. Then those had subcategories: manner of death, weapon, etc. Most money was put on foul play on account of him being found buried and such, so bets placed on accident and suicide paid out almost tenfold.

Doc Pinang, who wasn't allowed to bet on account of her being the final judge and jury of that guy Kelly's fate, said he swallowed his own tongue. Now, that ruled out foul play and suicide. Had to be an accident.

But then they got to arguing about the possibility that maybe, just maybe, he had been engaged in some kind of auto-erotic asphyxiation. There's models for that. That kind of ruled in suicide again. Accidental suicide. Then another theory came about. Well, more of an old folktale rather than a theory. Someone said that if a person were submissive enough—again, there's models for that—or under some kind of hypnosis or something, they could be made to swallow their own tongues.

That ruled in foul play again.

So you see, I told true when I said I was glad you alls have come to investigate the mysterious death of Kelly Vanger. That considerable sum of money you found in my store belongs to the folks here, and we would be grateful if you could help us figure out who won that bet.

On *The Woods*–

Joan's novelette, *The Woods*, with its quirks and superstitions is a complex mélange, her special recipe of charming, haunting and unsettling; a fondue pot where the clash of class, gender, sexuality and east vs. west melds together in an unexpected delight of the senses. Like watching an open heart surgery, Dean is both tumescent with ardor for the Filipino culture and horrified by the consequences of indulging in too much of their fine fare. Read, enjoy and bon appetite!

—Dean Fearce

The Woods

Joan Reginaldo

THE FLIGHT FROM CALIFORNIA to the Philippines is about sixteen hours. It's considered non-stop because we don't get to disembark from the plane while it refuels, but we stop at Honolulu for an hour.

I tell you this because time is elastic. Sixteen hours on solid ground usually flies by, at least when you're my age. For a teenager on a crowded plane though—breathing the stale recycled air redolent of farts and vomit; with a mysterious crying baby roaming the cabin; with turbulence jostling us around like a 7.2 earthquake, understandably skewing the fart-to-vomit ratio in favor of vomit; with the recurring but jarring thought that if the engine malfunctioned, we would plummet to shark-infested waters below—those sixteen hours crawl like purgatory years.

And yet I would sell my soul to get those sixteen hours back. I've thought about it a long time, and I can now say they were my last hours of peace.

Noah and I, we were best friends practically since we were zygotes. Kindergarten. We always had to line up next to each other. Ocampo, Ortiz. For eleven years, he followed me around. Not a shadow or echo, but a reflection. In many ways—all the ways that counted, anyway— he was the opposite of me. Pale to my darkness, pliant to my rigidity. Don't think one of us was popular while the other wasn't. But when he entered a room...

There I go on a tangent again. Please excuse the dithering of a tired old man.

The sixteen hour flight.

Last time I felt peace. We were sixteen. Our bodies were hard from JV soccer. We had all the hormones and energy of meat-fed boys and thirty-two inches of legroom to use them in.

"Charlie," he whispered, elbowing me. "Can you ask the stewardess for a blanket?"

"It's ninety-fucking-degrees. What the fuck do you need a blanket for?"

He didn't say anything. He looked like he was holding in a fart, but I suspected it was a different type of *emission* he was after. I tried not to look, but of course that impulse to check, perhaps to compare, overrode everything.

The topography of Noah's full-blown chub made it look like he was smuggling a military-grade flashlight in his jeans.

I scooched away as far as my seat would let me and screeched "what the fuck?" that earned a disapproving head shake from my mom two rows forward.

Noah leaned in, whispered, "So I was reading this Playboy article on why mile-high club—"

"No," I said. "You're not going to...I'm not..." Couldn't seem to get past *What the fuck.* We'd joked about having boners, about rubbing them out so quickly during breaks between classes that it hurt more than felt good, about ducking into changing rooms at the mall and stuff, and I'd seen his dick plenty of times before, having been raised together as closely as brothers, but never in this kielbasa-sausage stage. And yeah, I'd watched my share of free internet porn but those had been men. *Men,* not boys like us.

Noah clutched my arm. His grip was hot. Couldn't help but try to remember where I'd last seen his hand, what it had been doing, but I'd been absorbed in reading a paperback. This was before smartphones got prevalent, you see.

He kept talking about that damn article and his breath was hot and stale in my face.

I peeled his sweaty hand off my arm. "Just shut up about that article. I don't care what some assholes on Playboy said."

In the scuffle, the tip of his dick had managed to push itself out of his waistband. It stared at me with its weeping blind eye.

"Goddamnit!" I yelled. The echo of my own voice shocked sense into me and I could finally take my gaze away from his dick to his hurt little red-cheeked face. Embarrassed more than hurt. Shocked maybe. Wary of the possibility of Air Marshals and the just-as-equal possibility of a terrorist who didn't need the aggravation of two teenage boys yelling, I took a deep breath and willed myself into a normal position in my seat and said, "You need to take care of that the way everyone else does."

"Huh?" said Noah.

I hooked a thumb over my shoulder and pointed down the aisle at the lavatory.

"Aw man, lookit that line," said Noah.

"Fine. I'll just tell the stewardess you need a blanket so you can masturbate under it." The word *masturbate* felt awkward in my mouth, as unpracticed as I was saying the technical term for it.

Noah rubbed a hand over his face. "Fine," he said. "Let me out."

I did, bowing like a caricature maître d' as he unfolded himself from his seat, inched into the aisle, and stretched a moment before ambling to the lavatory line. Took him about half an hour, enough time for the drink cart to come and go. While he was gone, I got dead set to ignore him; making a big deal of it might encourage a habit. Also, despite my family's yearly vacations overseas, I'd never done it on a plane and I didn't want him to know. But as I stood to let him into his seat, curiosity made me ask, "Well?"

He sat down slowly, dazed. I spared a thought for the elderly couple in the row before us but both were snoring softly through cheap rattling dentures.

"Did you take care of it?" I said, curiosity waning.

"Uh, yeah," he said.

"And?"

"And it wasn't anything special."

I suspected he was baiting more questions so I didn't say anything else. I opened my book to signal that the conversation was done. Noah took his tray down from the seat in front of him, opened a bag of peanuts, but sat there gazing at the sparse, pube-kinky white hairs on the top of the old woman's head.

Reading my paperback became impossible when his leg started bouncing, hitting the underside of his tray. The frenetic thumping was all I could hear, drowning out even the doppler of the mysterious roaming baby. I don't know why his thumping leg was so annoying to me. Maybe, like the telltale heart, it signaled my undoing. Noah was my responsibility on this trip, the first trip he'd ever taken out of the United States, to a country where he didn't know the customs let alone the language, despite claiming he was one-fourth Filipino whenever there was a chance of gaining something from it.

If something had happened while he was jacking off, if he required medical intervention while I was being prudish and stubborn and he got sick or died because of it, I'd never forgive myself for letting a situation snowball into ruining our family vacation.

"You're being weird," I said. The closest I would get to *Are you okay?*

He clenched and released his fists a couple of times, cording the muscles in his forearms. "Feels weird," he said.

My curiosity piqued again. Maybe he did it wrong and I wanted to know so I could tease him about it. Not cruelly. Okay, with just enough patience and cruelty to use it when it benefited me the most.

"Want me to get my mom?" I said, hiding a schadenfreude grin.

When he didn't respond, I got up and pretended I was going to fetch my mom. I took my time and if it came to it, I'd squat down next to my mom's seat and ask her some trivial details about the trip.

"Charlie!" he whispered up the aisle when I was only a quarter of the way.

I came and sat again, one hand on my paperback to signal how bored I was with the situation. "Well?"

"I couldn't do it," he said. Then nothing.

I thumbed the corner of my paperback, ruffling the pages with impatience.

"So I was in line," he said, "and then this woman asks me for help. Built like a brick house. Solid. And stacked, y'know? With…" he glanced at the seats in front of us, where the old people were still softly snoring away, "with *tigo bitties*. Her kid wanted something from the overhead bin but the lady couldn't reach it she was so short. So I'm helping her. Trying to help her. The kid wanted some toy in a plastic bag behind a bunch of carry-ons and it's tough because my boner's all up in her face while she's sitting down and I'm thinking of her mom and her mom's…*tigo bitties* and I'm, like, hoping I'm not gonna just *bukkake* all over that little kid…"

A strange mixture of arousal and laughter was bubbling up inside me as he was talking. Had to dig my fingers into my thighs to stymy my own burgeoning boner and to keep from guffawing at what was obviously a trying time for my friend.

"…And then just as I'm about to say fuck it and leave, the kid says 'Thanks, *kuya*.' That means big brother, right?"

I nodded.

"So all of a sudden, kid's calling me *kuya* and…and I'm having these really weird and inappropriate thoughts about our *mom* if I was this kid's big brother. And this thing bursts on my chest and it feels hot, and I look down, scared I blew my load all over myself, but my boner's deflating so fast it hurts. I think that's what happened. I spooged *in* myself or something."

I stopped trying to squeeze my thighs and started pinching my forearms under my tray, trying to distract myself with enough pain to counteract the nearly overwhelming desire to laugh.

"Do you think I should see a doctor to make sure I didn't, like…" he shrugged, "like, burst my pipes or something."

"What the actual fuck."

"The high altitude!" he whispered.

"It's just blue balls, nerd."

"Uh, no."

"Yeah. It is. It just feels different because of the high altitude, not being able to get up and walk it off, and the fact that we're fucking talking about it in the middle of a goddamn plane."

His face got red and he didn't say anything until his face became that usual milky white color of a baby's cheek. He had such a boyish face. Naive, not ignorant. Made me kind of annoyed, actually, impatient for him to grow up and catch up with the rest of us cynical bastards. Even at sixteen, I'd already felt the sting of heartbreak and the cynicism that comes from repeated disappointment. Mostly because of Noah. But I think that's what best friends are for.

I checked my watch. Noah caught the motion, asked, "How much longer."

I bit back the retort that he could check his own goddamn watch, exactly the same as mine because my mom had given *him* the same watch on *my* birthday. "Just seven more hours. We're past the hump."

He giggled. "Hump."

"Want to borrow a book?" I said.

"Nah." He secured his tray in its upright position, bent down, and retrieved a stack of comics from his backpack under the seat.

Within minutes, he was asleep and drooling on my shoulder. I pushed him aside and got up to use the lavatory. On the way, I searched the aisles for the woman "built like a brick house" with a little kid. Almost missed her; she and her kid were huddled against the window, covered in one of the plane-issued dark-blue blankets, asleep. I continued on, used the lavatory, made uncomfortable by my own wilting erection and some sudden turbulence that made the plane pitch and sway like a small boat on open water. I'd taken my Dramamine though, so I didn't throw up, but I got piss all over the inside of the cramped bathroom, which I halfheartedly tried to wipe away.

By the time I made it out, the flight attendants had cut the lights for night-time flying so passengers could get some sleep. In that darkness, it was hard to find my way back to Noah. Everything looked different. I was annoyed and scared for some reason. Darkness always made me scared. Still does.

The plane kept bobbing and pitching a little, like aftershocks. Despite the lights on the floor demarcating the aisle and the dim lights along the ceiling, marking the exits; despite the murmurs and snores and snorts, that freaky crying baby, snack packages crinkling in the distance, all sounds muted somehow by the darkness; despite the various stale recycled-air scents, the old-people ointments, the trying-too-hard perfumes and colognes; I felt completely isolated, sensory-deprived.

I spied a seat without an elbow on the arm rest. Probably mine. The distance seemed doubly long and getting longer as I gripped seat-backs to stay upright while I made my way back in the swaying darkness. I was sweating beads by the time I got to the row. And there was Noah, slumped across the arm rest we shared. He was half into my seat. I pushed him aside with mild irritation, still somewhat nervous of my whole ordeal and confused as to why I felt the way I had. I'd made this trip several times and never had that reaction.

Noah woke when he reached an upright position. I daubed at my sweat with the bottom of my shirt.

"You okay?" said Noah.

Didn't think he could see me in this gloom. All I could make out of him was his human-shaped form laid back on his chair in an attitude of unconcerned repose. A mix of emotions toppled in me like dominoes: resentment that he should feel so at ease on *my* family vacation while I was probably about to die of some kind of plane-induced psychosis, envy that he'd gotten to see the woman with the *tigo bitties*, anticipation of having two whole weeks of mostly unsupervised fun in a different country, and touched that he would be concerned about me.

I wanted him to suffer and rejoice too, so I brought up his recent failure.

"I couldn't find that woman," I said.

"Huh?"

"The woman you told me about, who needed your help with a bag or something? From the overhead compartment? The one with the kid who called you *kuya*?"

Finally, he nodded, said, "Oh yeah. Wait, what? Whatta ya mean you couldn't find her?"

"I didn't see anyone who matched the description of 'built like a brick house, and stacked.' Jeez. Look for yourself." He half rose in his seat, scanned the rows behind us.

"What the fuck," he whispered. "There was a woman. I swear to God."

"Coulda been a ghost," I said.

"Fuck you."

I shrugged. "We're in plane full of superstitious Filipinos, on the way to the Philippines, one of the most superstitious and haunted countries on earth. It'd be completely understandable if you saw a ghost." It was completely illogical and I never would've attempted it in daylight. But, in the darkness? It just made things more plausible, even to me. So I continued.

"You should be very careful who you help," I said. "Be wary of who you talk to. They might not be alive. And if you talk to a ghost…"

"What?" he whispered.

"Listen. *Kuya* means older brother. But people use it with any guy who's older than they are. It's kind of manipulative. If you use *kuya* or *ate,* older sister, it kind of compels the person you're talking to into helping you. Like how your sister pouts and you let her watch those godawful cartoons."

"That kid kept calling me *kuya,*" he whispered, sinking into his seat.

"If you do anything for a ghost, they'll haunt you forever," I said, feeling better for scaring him, feeling worse for feeling good about scaring him.

"Are you sure you didn't see them?" he said, half rising again.

I was getting bored and irritated with his gullibility. "You're making it worse looking for them. I mean, they already made a connection to you. Stop calling them back into the living world."

"You're fucking with me."

"Hey, I'm not the one who's prolonging this conversation. The best thing to do would be to stop and pretend it didn't happen. Don't ever bring *it,* or this conversation, up again. Especially in the Philippines. Especially to old people." I added that last part to prevent him from telling on me to my mom.

"Why old people?"

Scrambling, best reply that came to me was, "Old people are already near death. The older someone is…well, the line between life and death gets blurrier. So…yeah. Don't talk to people about this. You know, like my mom and dad and stuff. Just keep it between you and me. Don't bring it up again until we're back in California. Okay? Can I get some sleep now?"

"You're totally fucking with me," he whispered but he believed me more than he believed himself as he said it. I could tell.

The first thing that hit me as we debarked was the heat. No matter how much the airport tried to gradually acclimate visitors to the oppressive tropic clime, with collapsing tunnels on the tarmac and air-conditioning blasting so ferociously it almost scalped people, there was just no way to avoid the hot humid air leaking in like warm wet fingers.

Noah and I put our sunglasses on, kept them on while we all rushed toward our connecting flight's gate. By rushed, I mean we walked at a pace suitable for the *lean forward* culture of California. We were like champion sprinters in the very much *lean back* culture of the Philippines. We boarded the much smaller plane heading to Camarines Sur and hoped our luggage made the transfer.

During the hour-long flight, my mom handed me a small bundle wrapped in a white handkerchief embroidered with her initials, SNO. Keeping it low on my lap, half covered by my left hand, I thumbed back a corner of the handkerchief. It was a colorful roll of Philippine pesos. One hundred one-thousand-peso bills, roughly the equivalent of two thousand United States dollars. But it would still buy much more in the Philippines than the equivalent amount in California; I could buy a beachfront mansion for about a hundred thousand USD.

Well, technically I could buy the *mansion*. Foreigners aren't allowed to own land in the Philippines. Though by blood, I was a hundred percent Filipino, my paperwork and mannerisms were as American as Tesla coils. The way I talked, walked, held my head—all alluring qualities to terrorists and kidnappers, or so I was told, repeatedly, by my dad as he diligently photocopied our passports and mailed the copies to the family lawyer, the Philippine Embassy, and to our most trusted family members on both sides of the Pacific.

My mom nudged my arm to get my attention. She had a second handkerchief-wrapped bundle, and she gestured for me to pass it on to Noah. I weighed it in my hand as I did, wondering if it had the same amount, and feeling a little annoyed when it felt like it did. He took it with a questioning look. I showed him mine, thumbed up the corner again, and his eyes widened.

"Calm your tits," I said softly, so only he could hear. "It's just two grand stateside."

I peeled a thousand-peso note off my roll and tucked it into my shorts pocket. The rest of the money I carefully rewrapped in my mom's handkerchief and shoved into the bottom of my backpack. I piled empty granola bar wrappers, my barely-used shaving kit, and my sweatshirt on top of it. Noah copied me and finished just as the announcement came on that we were arriving at the Camarines Sur airport.

That was a generous name for the small paved strip and terminal building the size of a house.

As we debarked, I could see my uncle on my father's side at the little fenced-in enclosure that served as both arriving and departing gate. With him were three cousins about our age. There would be more cousins at my uncle's house, where we would be staying for two weeks.

After some overenthusiastic greetings, my mom and dad pointed out our bags and the cousins and my uncle took up a suitcase in each hand then led us to the *jeepney*, the half-Jeep, half-bus vehicles used for public transportation but available for private hire. Unlike the *jeepneys*

I'd ridden in on previous visits, this one didn't have the round-eyed, smooth-hooded face of the classic American Jeeps left over from World War II. Nor was it painted bright neon or pastel to draw attention and customers. This *jeepney* had thin headlights and a sharply peaked M-shaped hood, giving it a sinister mug. It was painted black, but dust gave it a matte brown cover like toad skin. Along the brow above the windshield, where usually the owner's name was hung, was a hand-painted wooden placard of black letters on amber-yellow background: Private Use Only.

I remember all this because of the driver. He was younger than my parents, older than my cousins and I. He wore black plastic-rimmed sunglasses and a chauffeur's hat but it felt more like he was mocking us with it than using it as a sign of servitude or respect. He didn't help with the bags, which made my uncle and dad share a look I read as an understanding that no one was to tip him.

That driver never took his glasses off. He forced a smile as we all climbed in. Noah and I had to duck to avoid the low roof. He sat next to me. We faced my uncle and cousins. It was an awkward ride trying to avoid eye contact without looking like we were trying to avoid eye contact.

My uncle pointed out the local sights and yelled their names and explanations over the honking horns as we puttered along the narrow roads. We made the requisite *oohs* and *ahhs* but Noah seemed more interested in the slums behind the new houses and boutiques like skid-marks on silk panties. Having sat in the middle of the plane, he'd missed the view from above as we approached Manila, missed the sight of the floating shantytowns neighboring Manila's skyscrapers, the border of one-room houses made of corrugated tin and tarp clinging to the shore like the oily ring around a bathtub.

Even I found it difficult to understand how such barefoot poverty could exist within blocks of well-heeled gated communities.

We left the city proper and headed out to the rural areas, where my dad's family owned several hundred hectares of rice plantations and banana and mango tree orchards. The air cooled but grew more humid as the road entered an area thick with parasitic balete trees, trees that spread by attaching to another tree, growing and feeding on it, then suffocating or crushing the host tree.

The sounds of the city receded, leaving a silence soon filled with my uncle and parents talking about how the last rainy season had impacted the farms, if any houses had been flooded, what needed repairs. I adjusted my sunglasses and sat far back in my seat to keep my knees from bumping my cousins' knees. I was almost the exact shade between their dark knees and Noah's pale ones.

Dense forest sometimes gave way to little fields growing yams or maybe ginger, dotted with caribou as big as cottages and cottages as small as caribou. We passed through a couple of areas I could swear used to be more rainforest but now had incipient neighborhoods with cookie-cutter American-style houses and apartment buildings and long rows of shops attempting to be strip malls. There was even a McDonald's at one of them, two shops away from a Jollibee.

Nearly an hour later we finally headed down the long winding driveway, perhaps an old caribou trail, to my uncle's house. Two stories, but sprawling on a high foundation to protect against flooding. White walls, brown roof and trim. Large windows. And all around the yard were tiny tents made of two sheets of plywood. At each tent was a glossy, dark-feathered cock. Each cock had one foot chained to a tiny stake on his territory so he couldn't kill the other cockfighting cocks on the property.

"How many do you have now?" I asked my uncle in English.

He ducked his head in mock humbleness and said, "Oh, maybe a hundred or so" in Tagalog.

I understood the national language and several words in a few local dialects. I just never bothered to learn how to speak it.

Noah and I checked them out while my uncle and cousins brought our luggage up to our rooms. More cousins poured out to help. More Aunties and Uncles, *Titas* and *Titos*, came out too. Only a few were actually related to me. Several were just from the neighboring areas, keen on meeting the American relatives of the family that owned the land they work.

"Oh, *pogi pogi talaga!*" cried my *titas* as they remarked on my handsomeness and likeness to my dad.

Dutifully, I turned my cheeks for kisses and pinching, making sure Noah did the same. Finally we got to the elders who, slower than the *titas* and *titos*, have come last. I removed my sunglasses, nudged Noah to do the same.

"*Mano, po,*" I said to the closest elder, practically the only Tagalog I've learned how to say, asking for her blessing. I held my hand out, palm up, to my *lola*, my grandmother. She put a thin, wrinkled, liver-spotted hand on top of mine. It was cool and dry as a corpse hand. I bowed and pressed the back of her hand against my forehead. There were eight other elders, but two of them were maids. I repeated the request for the blessing and the bowing and pressing of hand to forehead with all of them except the maids, Grace and Concepcion. I said hello to them, made them giggle when I shook their warm, calloused hands.

Noah bowed too quickly, thunked the elders' bony knuckles against his forehead, caused a commotion when he tried to *mano po* Grace and Concepcion but his smile was genuine and warm and the elders forgave his clumsy manners as eagerness.

"Thank you for inviting me into your home," Noah said.

The elders, who have forgotten most of their grammar school

English, or who had never gone to school at all, smiled politely and gestured for us to go into the house. My parents had already disappeared to check on what needed to be fixed or renovated, added to or subtracted from. I called it my uncle's house because he and his family lived in it, but technically it belonged to my father, not the eldest child but the one my grandparents had believed would be most successful. And since it technically, on paper, belonged to my father, my mother treated it as hers too, poured money into making it as pretty and expensive-looking as our California homes.

So the first floor, the floor used for entertaining guests, the floor people would see and talk about, was fine and luxurious with marble floors and chandeliers and cherry-colored wooden chairs with delicate carved backs; white gossamer curtains that should have billowed and danced in the breeze but hung limp with humidity and oil from sweaty hands; mirrors, so many mirrors that some were turned face to the wall as a guard against spirits who sought to trouble the vain—these would be turned face out while my mother was here; shelves and shelves of hardbound books my mother shipped to the Philippines in her quarterly *Balikbayan* boxes, along with the Hershey bars, Spam, and jars of Nutella from Costco.

American fiction almost no one here could read, and no one here had time for.

"Do you want to eat?" one of the *titos* asked me in heavily accented English.

"In a little bit, *Tito*," I said. "We're gonna lie down for a few minutes."

The *titas* and *titos* murmured amongst themselves as they slowly crossed the room, excusing my refusal with the fact that I was tired, the flight was long, it was too hot for my American blood, what do you mean American blood? He's an Ocampo! Regardless, it's too hot for his friend, yeah, his friend is very American, what did they say his friend's last name was, Ortiz, isn't that Filipino? We'll ask the mom, oh you ask she's so abrupt…

Their voices died as they entered the hallway toward the kitchen, where the women would drink Cokes and gossip while the men went into the back yard to smoke and drink beer.

My mother cared less about the second floor of the house, where no casual guests went, and it showed. Our sneakers squeaked on the plain dark floors polished to a luminous shine with coconut husks. The hallway was lit by sunlight coming in through skylights overhead and windows, open to let the rising warm air escape, between the rooms. There were no pictures or paintings on the plain white walls, only large wooden crucifixes between dark brown doors, all shut except for one near the end on the left.

"How many bedrooms are there?" Noah asked.

"In this part of the house, I think there's six," I said. "I don't know how many there are total. I tried to count when I was a kid, but people move in and out, they turn bedrooms into storage rooms, then some of the old people can't use stairs anymore so storage rooms become bedrooms."

"If you had to guess."

"I dunno. Seventeen. Twenty maybe."

"Wow. I didn't know your family was that loaded."

I ushered him into our room, shut the door, and turned on the little window-mounted air conditioner between the two twin beds. It chugged twice then hummed and cool air blew on my face.

"They're just rooms to sleep in," I said. "Think of it like a monastery or something. It's not like the states where how many rooms you have is a sign of how rich you are. Here, if you need another room, you just build it with whatever's around. They don't seem to be so anal about zoning and shit. And if you live in the country, there's room to expand.

Fuck, build a house with forty rooms." I toed off my sneakers and threw myself on the starched white bed closest to the door. "You'll have to rebuild half of it after the next typhoon anyway."

"Good point," Noah said. He chucked his backpack in the corner and threw himself on his bed next to a large cherry-colored dresser. "Hey Charlie?"

"Yeah?"

"Where's the bathroom?"

"It was the first door on the right, coming in from the stairs."

"Is there—"

"Yes, there's toilet paper. If you developed a vagina and want quilted two-ply you can ask my mom for one of the rolls she brought from home."

He rose off the bed, clutching his stomach. "It's, like, a real toilet, right? Not just a hole in the floor?"

"Real toilet," I said.

While he was gone, I looked around for mosquito tents. I wanted to put them up before it got too dark and the bugs would be drawn inside by house lights. My uncle's family didn't use the tents. Mosquitos left them all alone. But they seemed to love me and my milk-and-sugar American-raised blood. No doubt they'd suck Noah dry. Or worse, give him some life-threatening nearly-eradicated third-world disease. I searched under the beds, in the wardrobe on my side of the room, in each drawer in the dresser on Noah's side of the room. No sign of the gauzy white material. One of the maids would know.

I paused by the bathroom, knocked on it, told Noah I was headed for the kitchen, and received a grunted "Fine" in response.

The twittering conversations ceased and every dark head swiveled as I padded into the kitchen. My mom was holding court among the *titas* and female cousins of marrying age. I appreciated some of the looks

I got from both sets.

"Mom, where's Grace?" I said.

She gave me a blank look and turned confused eyes on one of the *titas*.

"Grace," I said again. "The maid with the long gray hair? She was wearing a blue apron today?"

"Ah, Grace," said one of the *titas*. "She's outside getting the chickens for dinner. Do you want me to get her?"

"No, *Tita*. Don't get up. I'll find her." I left through the back door toward the rear yard.

The sun was already touching the tops of the balete trees. The wind coming from the forest was wet and smelled of decaying leaves. My uncle's household didn't keep food-chickens in a coop but rather let them roam around to mate with the cockfighting chickens and eat grubs and wild seeds to keep them healthy and, in turn, keep the family healthy. I'd been in the forest many times but always with my dad and either a family member or a local boy as guide. I was sure I could find my way around, but I hesitated.

The trees grew such that voices echoed strangely and at a different pitch. In this area of the world, the inclement weather didn't involve an insulating layer of snow but rather torrential rains and fierce winds that could bend a palm tree almost in half. This led to a ground soft with decaying vegetation, and in some areas, fallen vegetation could coat deep ponds or exaggerate the shore of a lake. If the sudden plunge and drowning didn't kill you, a lurking crocodile could. Or one of fourteen venomous snakes. Or leeches, centipedes, scorpions, rabies-riddled bats.

There could indeed be wild animals. Or the *capris*—some kind of forest-dwelling entity—that locals always warned their kids about. Or terrorists and insurgents who had moved further north than reported, and I would be kidnapped and held for ransom.

"Grace?" I called into the woods. "Grace?"

"Grace!" yelled Noah, who joined me in the gloaming. He'd wet his dark curls and smoothed them back. Now he looked like a fifties movie star. "Who's Grace?" he said between yells.

"One of the old maids," I said.

In the gloom beneath the tree canopy, Grace appeared like pollen motes coalescing. Her long hair was more white than gray now. Still, she had aged better than my relatives. Even with the sun behind her, I could discern the resolute jaw of my childhood, the fine cheekbones as sharp as the keels of starving birds, the intelligent dark eyes probing back at me. In her left hand swung two fat hens by their feet. Their heads flapped loosely on broken necks. In her right, she gripped the end of a burlap sack with several round, heavy things in it.

When she was close enough for me to catch a whiff of her salty sweat and talcum powder, she said, "*Ano po ang gusto ninyo?*" She asked what we wanted, in a formal way that hurt me a little, but I should've expected it given I was sixteen now. More man than child. In the Philippines, at least.

I took the sack from her and swung it on my back.

"Grace, this is my friend, Noah," I said. "Noah, this is Grace. If you need anything, just ask her and she'll tell you where to find it. Speaking of which, I couldn't find the mosquito nets for our beds."

Grace gestured for us to follow her back to the house but we took a circuitous route that brought us near the pig pens. Concepcion, the other maid and Grace's cousin through several entanglements and lineage knots, was mucking out one of the empty pens. Her features were similar to Grace's, but less pure, like seeing Grace through a greasy glass. Grace clucked her tongue and muttered, "Idiot girl," in Tagalog then louder, "The sun is setting. It's almost time to light the first candle."

Concepcion glanced at the sky and nearly tripped on her mucking rake in her haste to finish.

"Leave it for tomorrow morning," said Grace.

"I have a lot to do tomorrow morning," said Concepcion. She flicked her gaze towards me and Noah, added, "This would be done now if I hadn't had to help take in all those bags. So many bags for one family—"

"Charlie can understand you, remember?" said Grace.

Concepcion closed her eyes for a moment and bowed her head. It was awkward. I didn't know what to do or say.

"We can maybe help you," Noah said.

Grace gave him an appraising look. "No. It's getting dark."

Noah searched the ceiling over the pig pens for light fixtures. Finding none, he shrugged. "It don't matter. We'll work fast, bring out flashlights or uh, lanterns or something."

"We don't work at night," Grace said in a tone I recognized as one retort away from spanking. My ass stung from the very threat of it.

Noah reached for the mucking rake. Grace gave me a look similar to the look my mom gives my dad when she thinks he needs to grow a pair and *do something*. She was right, of course. No way could she try to take the rake away from Noah, a male guest, nor intercede between him and another servant.

Using the heavy burlap sack to knock Noah and Concepcion apart, I took the rake from both of them and leaned it against the pen gate just as the sun's last beam struck a pane on the house, flashing the world red. It struck me as ominous. A warning to get Noah under control.

"What the fuck, man," Noah whispered to me. "I was just trying to help."

"Hey man, if this was back home, I'd let you clean the entire fucking house if you wanted to. But here, we have to leave well enough alone."

"What's the big deal with letting me help? Seriously, dude, I'm not gonna mess up your precious pig garage or…yard or… whatever it's called."

I put a hand on his shoulder to calm him. "Listen. You're jet-lagged, you're hungry, you're tired. Just leave it alone. Don't mess with Grace and Concepcion," who were listening so intently behind me, I could practically feel their stares like centipedes crawling along my nape. "They got a system. They got some rules that are important to them. Just a few, so you can remember, okay? No working after sunset. No throwing rocks. No cutting down plants or hurting any of the animals in the woods around the house, all right?"

"You're creeping me the fuck out."

I snorted, punched him in the shoulder. "It's local superstition. Don't mess with it, okay? It's cultural stuff. We don't laugh at that, right?"

We were good Americans. Politically correct to a fault. Noah nodded and said, solemnly, "I get you. Sorry, Grace. Sorry, Conception."

"Concepcion," I said, correcting him.

After a few tries, he got the pronunciation right. Grace told Concepcion to get dinner started, handed her the chickens, and had me give up the heavy burlap sack. Rather than just tell me where the mosquito nets were, Noah and I had to follow Grace to a cupboard in the hall of the servants' quarters and then she insisted on helping me put them up. While we unfolded the nets and oriented them to match the beds, she grilled me about my past year in Tagalog mixed with untranslatable English words, a mixture known as Taglish. And I would reply in English, always English.

"When do you go to Stanford?" she said.

"It's not even time to apply yet," I said.

"You'll get in," she said, with the surety of one who is merely reporting on the time.

Grace fetched a pair of folding chairs from another room, and using them, we started tying the little ribbons of the mosquito net to small hooks in the ceiling.

"You're not doing those drugs, are you?" said Grace

"I do pot sometimes at parties," I said.

Noah frowned a little at my confession but I wasn't worried. Grace had kept worse secrets for me.

Grace clucked her tongue. "As long as you don't do anything stronger. You remember what happened to your *Tito* Joseph."

"Yeah, yeah, I remember. What about you, Grace. You ever try weed?"

She ducked her head and I caught a glimpse of how alluring she might have been when she was younger, and I felt sad that she'd spent her life serving my extended family.

"Oh, don't ask me those things," she said.

"You're evading."

"You have a girlfriend yet?"

"Still evading."

When she didn't come forth with a response to the pot question, I set it aside for later. "Nah, no girlfriends."

"How about your friend?"

I couldn't tell if she was asking if I was attracted to Noah, or if I knew if Noah had any girlfriends. "It's not really *girlfriend/boyfriend* over there, Grace. We just call it 'hanging out.' So even if you're dating someone, you just say you're hanging out with them. Only seniors call each other that. Some of the college kids, I guess. I mean, probably when we're, like, in college or something, we'll say stuff like—"

"You're using safe sex?" she said, with the *safe sex* part in English, which made it kind of funny.

Noah laughed. I managed to choke mine down with a grin.

"Yeah, Grace," I said.

"Good," she said.

We finished tying our last ribbons then stepped back to check our work. Each twin bed was isolated in its own gauzy, white, rectangular mosquito net. And just like when I was a kid, Grace blessed the net to protect me from the house-bound spirits, the *duwendes,* the reasons why she had the rule of "no working after sunset" for fear of disturbing them as they made their nightly rounds. Funny how I still believe such a flimsy material would protect me from ghosts.

That night after dinner and our nightly going-to-bed rituals, as Noah and I tucked the ends of the mosquito nets under our mattresses, he thanked me again for inviting him on my family vacation. I heard a *but* dangling in the darkness between us.

"Go on," I said.

"It's creepy as fuck here," he said.

"You get used to it," I said and yawned. "Just a different…way of life." Though I'd slept some on the plane, and technically it was about six in the morning in California, I felt heavy with sleep. I was surrounded by the mosquito net glowing white in moonlight, moving in and out with the pulses of air from the air conditioner like I was inside a giant white beating heart. I imagined the movement was caused by spirit hands gliding over the soft cloth. They wouldn't hurt me. They could, but they wouldn't. Grace had blessed our nets and I was diligent in following her rules. This, I was sure, protected me.

I drifted farther and farther from the glowing whiteness.

"—arlie. Charlie. Hey, Chuck."

That woke me fully. He knew I hated being called Chuck.

"What, Noah?"

"Why don't they just install lights outside? So the maids can uh… Look, I'm not saying the maids should work as much as you want them to, it just seems silly to stop if you want to finish something. Like, maybe they made up that *rule* about not cleaning after dark because they want to make sure you don't make them work too late. I mean, it's not really like there's spirits that'll go apeshit if you're sweeping a fucking hallway or something..."

I sensed his fear coursing below his rambling and turned to face him, but he'd melted with the darkness. A disembodied voice.

"Noah," I said gently until I broke through his night terror. "Listen. It's just superstition and boondock logic. Are you listening?"

"Yeah," he said.

"The reason you shouldn't work at night is because electricity is unpredictable in rural areas. Brownouts are common. If you don't stop what you're doing when the sun sets and there's a brownout, you could get caught in pitch blackness and you could hurt yourself or someone else. That's why you shouldn't work after sunset. Just safety stuff."

"And the throwing rocks?"

"That's pretty fucking self-explanatory, don't you think?"

He was quiet a moment, then chuckled. "Yeah. Yeah. And don't hurt anything in the woods is probably so people don't touch poisonous things or pick fights with bears."

"Technically there aren't bears in the Philippines but yeah. Strike that—there's something called a bear-cat, but those are farther south. They're like sloths. Don't worry about them."

"You promise there aren't evil spirits just waiting for me to fuck up?"

He was starting to annoy me. So childish. So afraid. So trusting and utterly dependent on what I said, not what he could figure out for himself. I didn't respond because I wanted to see what he would do. Cry? Get up and stagger towards the light switch?

"Charlie?" he whispered. "Chuck? Hey, Chucky?...I guess you fell asleep?...One of your cousins is hot. I think I'm gonna ask her out...I'm uh, gonna mess with her...I'm gonna do her out by the chicken tents...I guess you're really asleep."

His bed thumped with kicks. A sheet slid out from beneath his mosquito net, fell in a pool of moonlight on the floor.

"So fucking hot," he said. Minutes later, he was snoring.

I debated whether or not to play a prank on him but I couldn't think of any good ones. Noah's bed creaked and the snoring died down. Must've changed position. Now I could hear the crickets chirping, the owls hooting, the bats squeaking, the muted murmur of voices from different parts of the house. A harmonious blend of nature and civilization. I drifted off but woke with a start when I heard the high-pitched scream of a fox, so similar to a woman's scream. When I slept, I dreamed more than thought the memory that there are no foxes in the Philippines.

———— ⊗∞⊗ ————

I woke coated in sweat and tangled in damp sheets twined tightly enough around my legs to make my feet turn purple. The room was hazy with smoke.

Wood fire from the kitchen. Someone had turned off the air conditioner and opened the window, probably to save on electricity, probably thinking we'd wake up early enough to shut the window before the air turned hot. No such luck for two boys on summer vacation. It was probably noon, judging by the color and clarity of light outside. I woke Noah, we showered and dressed, then I took him downstairs, hoping to have a quiet brunch and a day of exploring the rice plantations and visiting with some of the old tenant-farmers. I'd overheard two of the *titos* talking about new tenant-farmers who were experimenting with home-brewed liquors.

But the long kitchen table was occupied by my dad and three men I didn't recognize. The tension among them was enough to occupy every seat. At the head of the table was my dad. To his left was a white man, American. His blond hair was gelled back in frozen waves. A sheen of perspiration coated his sunburnt face. He used a white handkerchief to wipe his forehead as he and my father listened to a Filipino man in a suit, younger than both of them, sitting on my dad's right and pointing at a map with a butter knife.

A fourth man sat at the other end of the long scarred expanse. A priest in cassock. He was as young as the man speaking but the expression on his face, contempt, aged him. He didn't want to be here but something kept him in his seat. My dad?

No. Grace. He gave her fearful looks as she hovered in the background, stirring shrimp and sausages in frying pans on a stove with no fire, drying dishes that were squeaking because they were already dry. Distracted, she beckoned us to her and handed each of us a plate of food. I wondered why she should care about this conversation when she'd never cared about the family businesses before. Then I heard it.

"...bulldozers to move clear the thick stumps," said the white American. His words were rushed but not excited. East coast jabs.

My dad shifted in his chair.

"We'll send some men in with machetes first," said the young Filipino-American. "To drive the animals further south. If you sell the land to me—"

"You don't need to make any decisions now, Nando," the priest said in English, using my dad's nickname in the village. Then in Tagalog, "What about the tenant-farmers? I haven't heard any provisions for all those people who depend on your family."

My dad nodded and expressed the sentiments in English.

The American mopped his forehead and leaned forward to tap the map. His ring finger was a fat red sausage, engorged by the tropic climate. "We would pay their relocation expenses, of course. And

Mr. Ocampo, with this land cleared, there would be space for a state-of-the-art hospital. Schools, even. You could build a legacy that would help your community as well as your family."

My dad reddened at the implication that he *wasn't* helping the community now.

The priest pushed off the table and stood but my dad beat him to it.

"Are you saying that because I live in California, that I'm out of touch with my community here?" said my dad.

The American hooked his collar away from his neck for a second, leaned back in a defensive manner. "Now I'm not—"

"Are you thinking because I live in America, because I raise my son to be an American, that I would quickly embrace American money and American progress?"

The American and the young Filipino-American looked at Noah and me where we leaned back against the kitchen counters, but there was no doubt I was my dad's son. The height gives it away, and the vaguely Chinese sharpness in our cheekbones. I gave them a cool nod and continued eating my rice and *longanisa* sausages.

If my dad asked my opinion, I'd tell him he was a fool to even consider selling the land these men wanted when there was perfectly good but unfarmable land west of that location, and closer to a major road too.

The land these developers wanted was a gibbous moon into prime farming territory. Libmanan was famous for rich, fertile soil and a steady supply of water to support rice farming. Our tenant-farmers lived on the land they worked and paid our family rent in rice. In times of plenty, everyone prospered. When times were leaner, they depended on us to get them through it, and we depended on them to help us defend the land against anyone or anything that threatened it.

On the rare occasion my dad had to make a decision about the land, being the absolute head of the entire clan, he always consulted with the eldest tenant-farmers, and always with the heads of the village families who would be directly affected. When the power lines went up, when a monsoon had flooded one of the main canals, when marriages had to be negotiated between tenant-farmer children, the parties of interest would always be invited to the house for *merienda*, priests and ancestors' spirits would be consulted, and plans were hatched over fried plantains and steamed yams. More often than not, negotiations or planning lasted until dinner and ended with beer and cigarettes on the back patio.

There were no tenant-farmers here now.

Don't sell. Don't sell. Don't sell.

I readied my answer in case my dad asked my opinion.

"What do you think?" he said.

My mouth was full. I held up a hand to indicate I had a reply.

"I think you should do it, Mr. Ocampo," said Noah.

I almost choked on my sausage.

Around the kitchen table were a mix of expressions—anger, surprise, happiness, greed.

"If the money's good," said Noah, "it would help modernize every-thing. You could install lights all around the outside of the house, all along the livestock pens, up and down the roads. Your maids wouldn't have to use lanterns outside if they wanted to finish something or whatever, I mean… Modernizing is always a good thing, right?" He sought the room for approval.

At sixteen, an American sixteen, he was more boy than man.

I tried to keep my face blank when my dad nodded as if he were considering that exact same thing. By the time the bolus of food had slipped into my esophagus and I was able to speak, my dad and the other men had resumed their conversation, backs to us, shutting us out, shutting *me* out.

I flashed on the memory of the one time we went to Disneyland and Noah had been too short to ride the adult rides so I'd missed out on three quarters of the park.

Appetite left me. I put my plate in the sink and headed towards the back door. Noah followed me.

"Charlie," said my dad. "Your mom said don't go too far. You have to be back in time to greet everyone for the dinner she's throwing."

"Sure, Pops," I said.

We put our sunglasses on. We left through the kitchen door and I immediately started sweating. My shirt stuck to my back, my shorts stuck to the insides of my thighs, my loafers felt like I'd pissed in them.

Someone whistled from a second story window. Two of my cousins, waving and asking us to wait. They were a brother and sister from one of my uncles, and they were okay so I waited.

A few minutes later, Maribel and AJ came out the back door. Maribel was a year younger than me, fifteen, but already a great beauty. Baby powder whitened her neck. Taller than most Filipinas, not as fat, and I hoped she didn't get married right away and start having kids because she was pretty smart. She could have an actual career as something other than the voice at the end of a help line.

Her brother AJ was a year older than us, two years older than her, but not as tall because he had scoliosis and the top of his spine curved like a candy cane. But he was kind and funny, and he used to walk me to the sweet shop in the village when I was a kid.

"*Kuya*, did they finish talking to your dad?" Maribel said in Taglish.

"No," I said. "They're still in the middle of it. I was going to take my friend to meet some of the old tenant-farmers. Want to come?"

"Yeah," said AJ. "We can go to the Riveras' house and check out their home brew setup."

"You idiot," Maribel said to him. "*Tita* wants us to pick up the *lechon* for tonight."

"Jesus Christ!" I said, "How many people are coming?" I doubted we would be hosting enough people to justify roasting an entire pig.

AJ laughed. "From the way your mom describes it, we're expecting everyone within a twenty mile radius. Do you want to come? We could use the help moving it."

"Yeah, sure," I said. "Noah, you want to come with, or stay here?"

"What are we picking up?"

"A *lechon*. Whole roasted pig the size of a ten-year-old."

"Uh…sure. Are we going to uh…carry it all the way back between the four of us?"

"We getting a *jeepney*?" I said to Maribel and AJ.

"I think it's already here," said Maribel.

A cold dread cemented my breakfast. Noah and I followed the siblings around the house. The cold dread spread through the rest of my body, froze my face in a grimace as I saw the same matte black *jeepney* from yesterday. The same cocky driver, sunglasses on and chauffeur hat askew, was inside and leaning an arm out the window.

He greeted Maribel and AJ in a friendly but polite manner. To Noah and I, his smile twisted into a smirk. I wanted to ask what his problem was but in the heat, decided it wasn't worth the effort. Best course of action would be to fetch the pig and come right back.

We all piled into the back. It was roomy without all the luggage so we all sat sideways and stretched our legs on the seats, feet to feet. The drive took only ten minutes into the village. I smelled the roasting meat of the place before the *jeepney* rolled into an alley between two tiny restaurants. Chickens scattered before us. We passed the rear doors of a little general store, a bakery, a fruit and veg shop, and came to a stop next to a small building with a large walled yard. Smoke billowed from a corner in the yard. AJ got out and we followed him to a paneled wire gate manned on the other side by a barefoot preteen girl with a sooty face.

AJ told her we were picking up an order. Her little hand crept up to the gate locking lever but stopped when she saw Noah and me. Wait here, she said.

"The fuck was that?" I said to AJ.

He shrugged. "I don't know what's going on. She never did that before."

"She looked at me and Noah. They got something against…" And then I realized there were probably things going on behind the wall that we shouldn't see. Someone had taken great pains to erect the ten-feet-high cinderblock wall, the only such wall for miles around. Probably had to do with animal rights or something Americans would get huffy about. I pulled one of the gate panels down and peered into the yard. Couldn't see much except the hard-packed dirt ground, and a thick wooden table with stainless steel bowls filled with dark, glistening masses beneath a buzzing cloud of flies.

A large hairy man wearing nothing but a plastic blue apron appeared, startling me into jumping back. He motioned everyone away from the door. When we were far enough back, he opened it and started shoving out, head first, the bronzed dead pig.

"Take it, take it!" he said gruffly in Tagalog.

I scrambled to grab ahold of it but it was huge and slick and greasy and hot. Hold it like a football? Cradle it like a baby? Then I grew aware of laughter all around.

"*Kuya, kuya*, there's a board under it!" said Maribel. "Grab the handles."

Sweating through my shirt, with my sunglasses sliding down my nose, I groped under the glistening bronze pig for a handle. My fingers grazed something that felt like a greasy bicycle handlebar. I grabbed it with one hand, pushed my sunglasses back up as they slipped off my face.

"Ready, everyone?" said AJ.

The four of us, AJ, Noah, Maribel, and I carried that damn pig on its bier like pallbearers carrying a child's coffin. We loaded it into the *jeepney* then climbed in carefully treading around the edges of the pig. The *jeepney* driver looked back at the *lechon*, then at us. He raised his sunglasses over his head. His expression was inscrutable. Staring but not seeing. His eyes were of normal shape and dark brown in color, but they were rimmed in black like he was wearing eye liner. That, along with his smooth cheeks and narrow chin, gave him an attractive androgynous look.

"Where to now?" he said to AJ using formal speech.

"Home," said AJ.

Once home, AJ passed me some coins to give to the driver. About a hundred pesos. For some folks around here, that was wages for a couple of days. I gave AJ a questioning look over my sunglasses. He nodded at me to pass the money forward. As I did, a capricious thought flitted through my mind. I took a thousand-peso bill from my wallet and added it to the coins.

"*Kuya!*" Maribel whispered at me and shook her head.

I held the money out to the driver. His eyes were once again hidden by the sunglasses. His lips were neutral as he took the money.

"Can you help us bring the *lechon* in?" I said.

"Sure...*po*," he said, adding the title of respect in an uncertain tone, like I was as inscrutable to him as he was to me.

The four of them lugged the pig into the kitchen while, behind the *jeepney*, I stretched and flapped my shirt to cool my body. Only the driver came back out. He thrust his hand out. Then yanked it back. Belatedly, I realized he was trying to shake my hand. I held my hand out and waited an awkward long moment until he took it. His hand was hot, still slick from the grease of the *lechon* board.

"Thank you for the tip," he said stiffly.

As he walked towards the driver's side, I said, "How do I hire you again?"

He stopped but didn't turn. Sweat rolled down my temples.

"Your car is clean," I said. "And you drive smoothly. My friend gets car sick. When we go sightseeing, I'd like to hire you for transportation."

He climbed into the *jeepney*. I thought he was leaving because he started the engine. Then he got out and handed me a business card. Odd for a *jeepney* driver to have one.

"If you want to hire me," said the driver. "Call that number before eight A.M. on the day you want to hire me."

The card had uneven edges, like it was cut from the blank part of a wedding invitation. On it, in blue ballpoint, was just a phone number and "Carlo" written in cursive. No company name.

"Hey," said the driver, Carlo. "How old are you?"

"Sixteen."

"Your friend?"

"Same."

"Close enough. You want to come to a party?"

Probably meant close enough to the Philippine drinking age. "When?"

"Tonight."

I wanted to agree, but, "My mom is hosting a dinner tonight." Immediately, I regretted mentioning this; he might expect me to return the favor and invite him to my mom's party.

He shrugged. "It's very near. Just two miles that way." He pointed at the woods behind my uncle's house. "It's in a clearing at the edge of the woods. Just young people like us. Three are old enough to be chaperones."

They were big on that—formal courting and chaperones. Vestigial chivalry from Spanish occupation ironically coexisted with modern day random rutting; kids lied about fucking, lied about pregnancy, lied about abortions, and the adults would rather believe the lie than actually talk about sex.

"Maribel and AJ are coming," said Carlo.

That did make me feel safer. "All right. What time?"

"Nightfall."

"Jeez. Be more cryptic about it."

He smiled, shook my hand again and his hand was hard, grip tough.

Then he was gone. I looked at the woods he'd pointed to. Even in the middle of the day, the space beneath the dense canopy of the balete trees was in perpetual twilight. The ground was littered with a thick layer of mouldering leaves. There might be crocodiles in the hundreds of little streams and leaf-covered ponds. There could be snakes. And that was just the creatures people knew about. Every year, dozens of new species were being discovered in and around the over seven-thousand islands of the Philippine archipelago. That's only counting creatures that people could perceive.

Maybe I wouldn't go to the party. It was enough to accept the invitation. If asked, I could say Noah didn't want to go.

———— ✸✸✸ ————

My mom's dinner party was scheduled to start at five but per "Filipino time," no one actually showed up until six—the Espiritus—who were still considered early. Around seven o'clock, more guests started rolling in: the Anunciacions and Domingos from the south, the Reyeses and Villaluzes from the north, and a bunch of lesser-knowns from all around. By the time I finished meeting everyone, I smelled like a sick cocktail of talcum powder, Spanish perfumes, and Johnson's Baby Cologne—the poor man's perfume. My forehead felt raw from all the rings I'd pressed against it for blessing. Though it was a cool night, the fancy downstairs rooms were hot and stuffy from all the bodies packed in.

Thirty minutes after the crush, my mom finally descended from her bedroom. She was wearing her largest jewels. Alone, they were almost tasteful. Together all at once, they looked gaudy and fake. But she always had to impress, and boy were they all impressed. At least, they pretended to be. She did her hostess round of air-kisses and hugs. To her face, everyone fawned over how young she looked, how pretty her dress, how luxurious her jewelry. As soon as she passed, it was like a tide reversing. People drew away into clusters to cluck their tongues about her extravagance and ostentation.

It was one thing to be comfortable, maybe even rich, but such existence belonged on TV *teleserye*. Not in real life. Not close enough to touch. Not here in person, unwilling to help anyone for fear of being unable to help everyone.

We bowed our heads as my mom led the prayer.

"Dear Lord, we thank you for the bounty you have blessed us with, and for the fortune you have bestowed on us, and for the good health of my family and our good friends. Thank you, Lord. In the name of the Father…"

The room was alive with flurried hands doing the sign of the cross, alive with mutterings about the *bounty* and the *blessings* and the *fortune* and *good health* being rubbed in their faces.

The envy, resentment, and falseness grew suffocating. Filipino delicacies and desserts I would have gorged on tasted strange and plasticky. But I ate that damn pig and went back for seconds. I could barely draw a full breath because of how full I was. The heat, the farts, and the acrid sweat riding the cloud of noxious perfumes were making it worse.

"You don't look so good," said Noah.

"I just need some air. You coming?"

"Yeah. Sure."

I stumbled towards the nearest exit, which was the hallway leading to the kitchen.

Grace and Concepcion were sitting at the table. Grace was eating a simple meal of *sinigang* and rice. Concepcion had a plate of party food. She saw me looking at it and blushed and bowed her head.

"It's fine," I said.

"*Ano po,*" said Grace, rising.

"Really, I don't need anything. Maybe…could you make some tea for me? My stomach doesn't feel so good. Maybe that ginger water? That always seems to help."

"Just sit down," she said. "It will be ready in a minute."

There was a pile of julienned ginger on a cutting board next to the stove. She didn't even have to fill the kettle, only light it, as if she'd expected stomachs from all the rich food which most of the guests would not be used to. The back door creaked open. AJ peeked in.

"There you are," he said. "You ready to go to the party?"

Christ! I'd forgotten I was trying to avoid them until I knew for sure they'd left.

"What party?" said Noah.

AJ gave me a funny look. "You didn't tell him? Ah jeez, I keep putting my foot in my mouth."

Maribel squeezed her head in too. "Come on, *Kuya*."

The honorific tugged on me. I resisted. "I'm not really feeling it tonight."

"You sure?" said AJ.

"I'll come," Noah said.

"It's in the woods," I said, hoping to play on his fears that were so vivid and terrifying last night.

"*Near* the woods," AJ said to him. "Just stay with us. You'll be fine."

Noah looked to me for confirmation of this. I wasn't about to say anything bad about AJ and Maribel so I just shrugged.

But if anything happened to Noah, if he got so much as a splinter, my parents would hold me responsible.

"Okay," I said. "Do you guys have a lantern?"

AJ waved a big military-grade flashlight. "All ready."

I herded Noah outside. In the darkness of the rear yard, facing the even darker woods, I hesitated.

"Go have fun, *anak*," Grace said from the doorway. "You spend too much time with the old people."

"If my parents ask…"

"I'll tell them you're with AJ."

"Thanks, Grace."

It wasn't until we were beyond reach of the house lights that I heard the kettle's forlorn whistle.

———⁂———

No darkness I've experienced since could ever equal the absolute darkness of that night. AJ's flashlight beam was a bright sword cutting through a black void. The brilliance of it made the area surrounding us so much darker. And in that darkness would come twinkling pairs of eyes from above, disappearing when AJ shone his light in their direction.

Though it was slightly cooler in the forest at night, it was no less humid. I felt like I'd swum in my clothes and they were taking forever to dry. Blisters were starting to form on the backs of my heels. Everything quieted at our approach, resumed their nightly chorus after we passed. The fighting cocks were all tucked into their little wooden tents. And though I'd walked these woods hundreds of times with my dad, I recognized nothing now. Shadows formed by AJ's flashlight made everything larger and looming and more ominous.

"Are there gonna be a lot of girls there?" Noah asked.

"Should be," said Maribel. "I invited all my friends."

"Are they as hot as you?"

I elbowed him in the ribs. Maribel laughed. AJ shook his head.

The silence after that was heavier. I wanted to say something, make some noise to break the spell descending on us, but I couldn't think of anything to say except talk about how anxious I was.

Then AJ's light flashed on something large and sharp.

"The fuck is that," I said. "Back, to the right."

AJ slowly swung his beam. The end illuminated only a piece of the hulking machine but I'd recognize a bulldozer blade anywhere. The fear and surprise gave way to anger. I grabbed the flashlight from AJ and swung the beam around. Sap and moisture still glistened on the trunks of decapitated trees like diamonds caught in folds of yellow cloth. Most of the tree trunks were still rooted to the ground. But gathered at the sides of the bulldozer were the ones uprooted to make a trail into the area.

Even though a patch of forest about twelve feet wide had been cleared, I still couldn't see the sky for the surrounding balete trees looming in like they were grieving over their fallen brothers and sisters.

"Cool," Noah said slowly.

I shoved him, light swinging wildly into the forest canopy. "Don't say that! It's not *cool.*"

He looked at me with hurt in his eyes. "I mean it's cool to see progress. Don't you think it's cool? Progress?"

"This is not land to *improve,*" I said to Noah. "It's not mine, not theirs," I pointed at AJ and Maribel. "We're just the caretakers. Progress is all well and good, but it doesn't have to be everywhere. It doesn't have to mean expansion. It doesn't have to be here."

"But your dad said they could clear it and build those offices here. He told me at the party. That's...why everyone was invited. Didn't you know? So he could tell them the final decision."

The flashlight slipped from my grasp. Inexplicably, I felt betrayed.

Maribel picked up the flashlight and handed it to her brother. "Come on, there's nothing we can do about it right now."

I felt them tugging on my clothes but I didn't move until Noah took me by the arm and dragged me after them.

"I'm sorry," he said morosely. "I don't even know why I'm apologizing but I feel like you're mad at me."

I was, and he made me madder for apologizing without knowing what he was apologizing for, the weak idiot. But at least he was trying to make me feel better.

"I'm mad because you should have said something when my dad told you the news. I'm mad because...because I'm your friend. You should know me so well that when I'm not around, you can speak for me, protect my interests like I protect yours."

He gave a shallow chuckle. "'Protect my interests'...You sound like your dad. I didn't know it meant that much to you. If I'd known...You never said anything about it."

Even I couldn't understand what had come over me in the short time we'd been here. But then, thinking about it, it wasn't new. The feeling had always been in me like a tension, releasing only when I was in the woods.

There was a warm light coming from up ahead. We approached it and the sound of voices, laughter, and guitar music reached us. Soon, there was no need for a flashlight. We entered a small glade bathed in the yellow light of a large bonfire. Around it were dozens of people about our age, sitting on small plastic stools, upended metal trashcans, even some laundry hampers, whatever they could bring from home. They yelled greetings when they saw us emerge from the forest.

Someone older than most of the partyers beckoned us closer to the fire. He gave up the plastic stool he'd been sitting on to Maribel and sat cross-legged on the picnic blanket next to it, gesturing for me and AJ and Noah to join him on the ground.

"Glad you came," he said.

I recognized the voice and the mouth. Carlo, the *jeepney* driver. A surly grunt hello was all I could manage.

"Pistol!" Carlo said to a boy a few seats down. "Pass me that jug."

A glass gallon-jug was hefted, person to person, until it reached us. The amber liquid inside was murky with floating bits. It looked like urine from a diseased person. Smelled like it too.

"Home brew," he said. "From one of the new farmers over there." He nodded towards an area deeper into my family's territory.

I relaxed a bit. Those were the new tenant-farmers I'd heard about, the ones who were experimenting with home brew, and here was the result.

"Is it any good?" said AJ.

Carlo grinned. "Tastes like sewer-water but it gave me a decent buzz."

AJ tilted his head back and took a swig. He coughed and sputtered.

"God, it burns," he said, passing it to Maribel.

Maribel took a healthy gulp. She hid her reaction but her cheeks turned red.

"Well?" I said.

"Tastes like rice-water that's gone bad," she said, voice raspy. I took the jug. I tilted my head back and concentrated on swallowing without tasting. It worked, and I was pleased that I'd been able to drink the most out of it so far.

"Well done," said Carlo.

"It's okay," I said. "Noah, want some?"

"Hell yeah," he said. He drank. And drank. And drank, draining over half the jug. Only reason he stopped was he had to come up for air.

I took the jug so he wouldn't finish it all.

"That's good stuff," he said.

Carlo gave him a cold look. "Yeah, that was for everyone. *Baboy ka!*"

I laughed. Though I'd forgiven Noah, it felt good to hear someone insult him, felt good to laugh at him.

"What?" said Noah.

AJ, laughing too, managed to get out, "He called you a pig."

Noah poked his nose flat with his index finger and snorted like a pig. This set off another round of laughter. People around us were looking over. Noah snorted at them too. They laughed. He got up and snorted at everyone around the fire, pausing to grunt and snort and roll on the ground in front of groups of girls. Everyone was laughing by the time he made it back around to take another swig from the jug. We'd all been drinking from it. It was more backwash than liquor. He finished the few tablespoons left and smacked his lips.

Maribel, who'd been waiting for a turn from the jug, screamed her outrage. Noah took off running and she went after him. I was laughing so hard, I could barely see them through my tears glowing with bonfire flames. The alcohol made me hot, but the heat was within and not uncomfortable. My head felt like it was barely attached to my body.

Noah came back and huddled behind me.

"Save me!" he wheezed out. "Save me from your cousin."

"Hey, I'm siding with her," I said. "You shouldn't have finished the bottle."

"Ugh, you're right! I don't feel so good."

Maribel yanked him off my back, threw him on the ground, and sat on his stomach.

"Oof!" he said, "I'm gonna throw up on you."

Maybe she didn't hear. She leaned forward and wrapped her hands around Noah's neck. He was twice her weight, could've knocked her off no big deal, but he was weakened by booze and laughter. Maribel shook his head as he batted at her. I laughed and laughed, riding the spinning top of the world, laughed until I saw him cop a feel. That sobered me up some.

"Hey now," said AJ. Maybe he'd seen it too.

Maribel tried to get off him but Noah caught her by the wrists and pulled her back down. "Where ya going?"

"Let her go, Noah," I said.

"I'm jes having fun," he said.

Maribel kept trying to get up but Noah held her wrists firmly. Her hair clung to her cheeks with sweat. The two of them looked disturbing and oddly erotic at the same time.

"Let her go, Noah," I said again, more forcefully. Surprised myself with the quavering anger in my voice. The world bobbed and pitched as I rose to my feet.

"Jes leave us alone," said Noah. "Ain't no thing going on."

AJ knocked my arm, gave me a look I took to mean, "Either you do something, or I will."

I was now ashamed of Noah, and it pleased me to be ashamed of him, to have him brought down to a level below me so I wouldn't keep feeling so...jealous. I peeled Noah's fingers off Maribel's wrists. Freed, she leapt up and ran to her friends.

"You're embarrassing me," I whispered harshly to Noah.

My spit flecked his face but he hooted with laughter. "God, god, what a...what a rack..."

I picked him up by his shirt. "Let's go. Say goodbye to everyone."

"But the party's jes getting started," he said.

Was it? I couldn't tell how much time had passed, how many times he'd actually gone around the bonfire, how much we'd had to drink. Everything was clear from one moment to the next, but in between things were hazy, like my memories were mirages shimmering over the fire.

There were three jugs on the picnic blanket. Three empty glass jugs. I didn't remember drinking all that. I didn't remember drinking any of it, actually. Still, everything was clear and logical and the most logical thing to do was take Noah home. The pig was drunk and making a fool out of Maribel, AJ, and me. A fool out of my family.

"Let's go," I said to Noah. "AJ, can I use your flashlight, and you and Maribel can have some of the locals escort you back?"

"Don't worry about it," he said. "We'll just come with you. It's getting late anyway."

He pointed up. I could now see where the trees ended and the sky began because the sky was a few shades lighter. Dawn was coming.

"You sure?" I said.

"Yeah. Maribel, let's go."

"Thanks for coming," Carlo said.

"Thanks for inviting us," I said. "It was…fun, I guess? Did I have fun?"

Carlo laughed. It was a nice laugh because it felt hard-earned. "I'll walk you guys back to your house."

"No need. There's…four of us."

"The fact that you couldn't remember how many people you came with means I should walk you back."

"But—"

"My ride is parked near your house anyway," he said. That sounded like a lie but I was already past caring whether he came with us or not.

We entered the woods. It was a morose silence compared to the yells and laughter of the bonfire party. Morning mist rose to the height of our knees, made me wary of stepping on a snake or crocodile or into one of the hidden bodies of water. Ahead of me, AJ and Maribel both picked up fallen balete tree branches and tapped the ground to make sure we avoided those things. Beside me, Noah listed side to side like a ship on choppy water. A few times, Carlo, behind us, had to straighten and steady him so he wouldn't go off into the woods.

Maybe half way home, maybe less, Noah clutched my shoulder.

"I'm gonna throw up," he whispered. His breath smelled like fish preserved in rubbing alcohol.

"Do it," I said.

"I don't want them to see," he said, nodding at Maribel and AJ's backs. "I've em-... embar-...embarrassed you enough...as it is."

Carlo whistled for AJ and Maribel to stop. "Go behind that tree," AJ said to me, pointing at a balete tree wider than the others. Its girth would easily hide Noah, me, and a Volvo. I took Noah to the tree. Halfway around, beyond reach of the light, we had to feel our way in the darkness, shuffling our feet slowly to avoid tripping.

As soon as we were completely blocked from Carlo and my cousins, I said, "Okay. Let'er rip."

The end of that very short sentence was covered by the sound of Noah vomiting. My eyes had grown used to seeing without the flashlight, and the sky was bright enough for me to see Noah bent over, vomiting chunks. Some splattered against my shins, left scalding trails as they slid down into my loafers. Nausea welled up in me, overflowed, and I threw up too, spinning to avoid hitting the tree with my vomit. I heaved until it was just dry heaves. My head ached from the pressure of throwing up. My throat burned from stomach acid. I wiped my mouth with the back of my wrist and turned around to ask if Noah was done.

A horrific face met my gaze. Skin brown and boiled like toad skin, eyes as yellow as bile, hair a writhing mass of grubs and centipedes, teeth sharp and black and glistening. A hot stream of piss shot down my legs.

The creature was big enough to embrace Noah from behind. It's arms were dark and thick and corded with so many veins they looked like they were covered in tree bark.

"Charlie," Noah said, whimpering. "Help. Me."

I was frozen with fear and indecision. I screamed. My voice seemed to evaporate with the mist; sound didn't travel far. I screamed again, for AJ, Maribel, Carlo. No sound of running feet answered me. No cries of outrage or horror. Frustration gave me strength enough to overcome my fear. I dared not touch the creature. Instead, I ran around the tree to Carlo and my cousins, angry that they hadn't come.

They were gone.

The forest was completely empty and seemed undisturbed. The sky was brightening above. Still no sun, but it was almost here. I knew, somehow, that we just had to last until daylight. The creature, whatever it was, would surely disappear like the nightmare it was. But I had left Noah alone with it! I ran back to the tree and forced myself behind it. The thing was still there with Noah trapped in its branch-like arms.

With a last yell for help, a last plea for AJ or Maribel or Carlo to come, I launched at the creature and tried to pry its arms off Noah. The arms were indeed branches and they were growing, fusing together around Noah's chest. His feet were lodged in what looked like a knot of roots. The roots grew and fused together too, growing upwards to fuse with the branches growing downwards, growing no matter how much woody pulp I tore away with my fingers. I clawed the thing, wearing my fingers to the bone, screaming Noah's name, crying for help from people who would not come.

Noah kept whimpering my name and I could barely understand what was going on, what was happening to him, to us, as the dawn came and the forest was lit with bright gold beams of hope.

The creature groaned and I thought it would retreat to where it had come from but it started to sink into the soft forest floor. And Noah sank with it.

"No!" I said. "No, no, no!" I pulled and pulled with my bloody fingers. Pulled on whatever I could reach of Noah. His elbow, his shoulders.

"Charlie!"

His shirt. His ears.

"Charlie!"

His hair.

"Char—"

Noah was completely underground. The creature's head was still above the leaves. It looked at me. Smiled a smile of mixed emotions. Victory, regret, sadness.

I grabbed hold of its head and my hands disappeared in a mound of centipedes and decaying leaves. Weary of the effort and overcome by the horror, I sank against the tree and let my thoughts sink into nothingness. Just as the darkness closed overhead, I thought I heard the whoosh of a flock of birds changing direction and a voice whispered, "…the wrong one."

———— ∞∞∞ ————

That night lasted longer than any other night of my life. I thought I spent the following day passed out nestled in the roots of that wide balete tree because I woke to the chill of evening. The sun was just setting. Red beams made the backs of my eyelids glow like the red panes of a stained glass window. I didn't open my eyes for a long time because I knew it hadn't been a dream and I was still in the woods and why hadn't anyone come for me yet? The scent of our vomit wasn't that sour anymore. I could smell wood warmed by sunlight, banana leaves, the tang of some small decaying creature. I could hear the susurrus of creatures moving within the canopy. It was peaceful but my head throbbed, my scabby fingers ached, and my throat was parched. I could wait for them to find me or I could attempt to go home.

Going home turned out to be the better choice. It was easy to find the faintest of trails once I stepped out from behind the tree. I even saw the bulldozer on the way back. It was smaller than it had seemed in the dark. With its bright yellow paint, it looked quite harmless. Cheerful, even. Then I came to the cocks in their cockfighting tents. Soon I smelled the scent of wood fire and frying bananas.

Following the trail, it seemed a matter of minutes and I was back in my uncle's rear yard with the pig pens on my right, the door to the kitchen ajar straight ahead. It was so quiet and still in the yard, I thought I might still be dreaming. At the threshold of the kitchen door, I paused to let my eyes adjust to the dimness.

"Oh, dear God," someone said. My mom. She was hugging me. I couldn't breathe because of her perfume but I was too weak to push her away. Then I was in my dad's arms. Then I was being pushed into a chair and there were Maribel and AJ.

"You!" I yelled. It came out a rasp. Someone put a glass of ginger water in front of me.

"Where have you been, *Kuya*," said Maribel. "We've all been looking for you for days."

"Days?" I said. As I drank the ginger water, I narrowed my eyes at her to show how much I believed it. But her face was swollen with crying and her eyes were red-rimmed and bloodshot. AJ looked worse. His face and arms were covered with scratches and cuts. Some were so deep they required stitches.

"I was so scared for you," said AJ. "When you disappeared on the way back, I was scared you were eaten by something, or kidnapped!"

"What do you mean when I disappeared? You guys were the ones who just left me and Noah."

AJ and Maribel exchanged a look of confusion.

"He had to throw up and I told you guys to just go behind the tree," said AJ. His voice rose in volume as he started to get defensive. "I didn't tell you to…to run off or play hide and seek!"

"You're right. I'm sorry, *Kuya*."

The word had its intended effect. It diffused his defensiveness and he deflated in his seat. "I shouldn't have let you out of my sight. You both had too much to drink. Anybody could have had the advantage over you in the states you were in."

Maribel patted his shoulder.

"Where have you been?" said my dad. "Where's Noah?"

I clenched the glass, now empty except for dregs of ginger, as I tried to speak but thinking about what happened to Noah made it hard to breathe. The room spun. The sound of breaking glass pulled me to my senses. Dad was carrying me to one of the sitting rooms. He laid me on a sofa but I pushed myself up, afraid of falling asleep again and waking up in the woods.

There were two strangers there too, standing behind everyone.

"The sooner we get the details from him, the sooner we can continue the search for the other boy," said the woman.

"Charlie," said my dad. "Can you tell us what happened to you and Noah? Take your time."

I didn't take my time. The entire thing spilled out of me like the ginger water had loosened my tongue, like someone else was saying all those strange and terrifying things. The strangers, who I later learned were Filipino-American private investigators flown in by my parents, took note of everything. I remember thinking they would scoff at the idea that a *creature* would take a boy in the woods. But they must have been steeped in Filipino lore, respectful of it. When I was done, they thanked me and told me they would do everything in their power to find Noah. Only to Grace, only when my parents and cousins had left the room and I was pretending to be asleep, did they utter the name of that creature. *Capri.*

They did search for Noah for a long time. My parents flew in Noah's parents and survival experts and more Filipino-American detectives. They called in government favors. The community got involved in a way it hadn't before, or has since. The search took so long, in fact, that the Americans who wanted that land got tired of waiting for it to be released as a crime scene and moved on to another juicy piece of real estate.

Instead of two weeks, we spent months there, combing that trail to and from where the party had been. Neither AJ nor I could pinpoint the exact balete tree we stopped at. Nor could we find that *jeepney* driver to corroborate our stories though I dialed the number he gave me dozens of times. Out *titos* took us to the tenant-farmers who were experimenting with the home-brew but they used dark glass jugs, not clear, and their drink tasted like fermented fruits, not the harsh fermented rice-water we'd had that night.

When my family and Noah's parents returned to the states, we had a memorial service. I went back to school. They gave me grief counseling. I was told that it was normal to hear Noah's footsteps behind me, to feel like if I could just spin around fast enough, I would glimpse him disappearing around a corner or behind a column. It was a symptom of grief along with hearing his voice or even the familiar roar of his car coming up my driveway, or to wake, and for a few seconds, plan my day with him in it.

I felt none of those things. Instead, I looked forward to our next vacation to the Philippines and a visit to the woods behind my uncle's house where a new tree waited for me.

On *Cockfightin'*–

Robert and I met on a writing forum around 2009, when he was just starting his first book in what's become a popular series: irreverent tabletop gamers piss off their game organizer who punishes them by magicking them into the game world as their low-level characters. What I like best about his stories are the clever plot developments, flawed but endearing and relatable characters, and daringly bawdy humor. He inspires me to take chances with my own writing.

I've worked with him for every sequel and almost all the short stories and I'm constantly amazed by how much trouble his characters get into, then astounded by how they get out of it. Two of my favorite new characters in the series are featured in Cockfightin'.

—*Joan Reginaldo*

Cockfightin'

Robert Bevan

⟨⟨⟩⟩

"IT'S GETTING DARK, DENISE," said Randy, back up against a tree, holding a longbow in one hand and a ready arrow in the other. "We best be getting back to the city."

He could barely make out Denise's short, broad form as she paced in the clearing, but he could hear her heavy footfalls. "I can't think in there," she said. "Too many freaks walking around with feathers and fur, got tentacles and shit coming out of their faces. It's like the goddamn French Quarter."

"But I can't see in the dark like you can."

"Then get the fuck out of here," said Denise. "Ain't nobody asked you to come along."

Randy shook his head. "I can't leave you out here alone. It's too dangerous."

Denise let out a hollow, fake laugh and stalked closer. "So you here to protect me? Oh, that's rich. Listen, Randy. The day I need some fat-ass fucking queer to protect me is the day I turn in my gun and badge."

Her words were meant to sting, but Randy grinned from ear to ear as he stood up.

Denise narrowed her eyes at Randy. "The fuck you so happy about?"

"I ain't fat no more." He flexed his pecs and abs, which were nicely defined under his open vest. "Take a look at these abs!"

Denise shook her head. "Randy, you must have been slapped in the head by one too many cocks. Them abs ain't no more real than my vag n' titties. We's in some kind of Matrix type thing. Now cut that shit out."

I can't think while you's doing all that calendar model shit."

Randy stopped flexing and sat back down on his log. "What you got to think so much about?"

"What you think I got to think so much about?" said Denise. "I got to find a way to get my man parts back and get my ass back home."

Randy frowned. "A lot of them folks back at the Whore's Head been here a long time. I think if there was a way to get back home without Mordred and them dice, they would have figured it out by now."

"Please. Don't one of them Obama-lovin' faggots got the sense God gave a bucket of coon piss."

There was no responding to that. Randy swapped out his bow for his sword; he soon wouldn't be able to see anything until it was close enough to stab anyway.

"Winners don't quit," said Denise. "And quitters don't win. My daddy taught me that."

"Didn't your daddy run off with Miss Jolene from the Swap-N-Save?"

Denise glared at Randy. "That ain't the point."

Randy felt bad. He shouldn't have brought up Denise's daddy running off on the family. Maybe he could smooth it over.

"How is your daddy these days?"

Denise turned away and shrugged. "Fuck if I know. Last I heard they was settled up in a doublewide out near Picayune, growing weed and breeding Rottweilers. Jolene let herself go to shit after having two more kids. She already had three from two previous marriages."

Randy smiled. "So you got some brothers and sisters. That's nice. I always wanted a little sister. Closest I got is my cousin Ronnie."

"Goddammit, Randy. I don't give a fuck about your cousin Ronnie. I was making a point. Winners don't quit. Quitters don't win." Denise spun around, eyes wide. "Hot damn, Randy! That's it!"

"What's it?" Randy didn't expect much to come from Denise's

sudden burst of optimism, but it was nice to see her happy for a change.

"They said this is a game, right? It's so simple. We win the game, we get released."

Randy frowned. "I don't think it's that sort of game."

"What sort?"

"The sort where you can *win*."

"How do you mean?"

"The way my cousin Ronnie explained it, there's no end to the game. You just keep playing."

"What the fuck kind of horseshit game can't nobody win? Your cousin Ronnie's a retard. You mark my words. We stay out here long enough, and some little elf or some shit's gonna walk out of them woods and give us a quest or ask us a riddle or whatever, and when we solve the puzzle, we'll get sent home. That's why those cowards back at the tavern been stuck here so long. They got no gumption. They got no drive. They got no— FUCK!"

"Denise!" cried Randy. "What's wrong?"

Denise swatted at her neck. She pulled out a dart and held it in front of her face. Her eyes crossed as she stared at the tip. "What the fuck is— Son of a bitch!"

A second dart was sticking out of her forearm. She plucked it out and threw both darts on the ground.

Randy brandished his sword at the darkness. "I don't see nobody! Where are they?"

"They're everywhere," said Denise, stumbling around in a small circle trying to keep her balance. "They're some ugly little fuckers." She shouted into the darkness, "Come out and face me like men! You fuckin' Pygmy sons of—nyaaaaarrrrr…"

The third dart hit her in the forehead. Denise dropped to her knees, then fell on her face. Fortunately, she landed at a slight angle, and avoided driving the dart deeper into her skull.

Randy looked at Denise, unconscious on the ground. They were both screwed real good now. He did the only thing he could think of. Swinging his sword wildly, he screamed and charged at the edge of the clearing.

He hadn't made it three steps when he felt a bunch of pricks on his chest and abdomen. They smarted something fierce, like horsefly bites. Then the pain started to fade. Then everything faded.

———— ❈ ————

Consciousness returned slowly and confusingly, like Randy was coming out of a particularly powerful dream. That had to be it. This whole Caverns and Creatures situation had been a big, vivid dream.

There was cheering all around him. Had he fallen asleep watching the WWE? Shit. Had he been jerking off? If grandma caught him like that again, she weren't going to buy that "I was only moisturizing it" line a third time. Terrified, he opened his eyes.

"Randy!" said Denise. She was still a dwarf. "Wake up, you lazy sack of shit!"

Randy sighed in relief. "Thank the Lord."

"What the fuck's wrong with you? We're in some serious shit!"

Randy blinked a couple of times, then took in his surroundings. They were in some kind of circular pit, about the size of a basketball court. The sides were rough stone, about fifteen feet high, with barred cage doors at regular intervals. If he had a boost, he might be able to climb out, if not for the hundreds of little gremlin-critters hootin' and hollerin' at the edge of the pit.

Wherever they were was underground, with tree roots poking in through the ceiling. All that appeared to be keeping them from being buried alive was a shoddy-looking network of haphazardly placed wooden beams that Randy wouldn't have trusted to hold up a tent.

The fact that the only sources of light were torches attached to those wooden beams didn't make Randy feel any safer. But given their current situation, he didn't expect he was going to live long enough for the beams to catch on fire.

"What is this place?" asked Randy.

"A temple to some foul goblin deity," said a voice behind Randy and Denise.

Randy scanned the shabby cavern for any hint of religious statues or paintings. "This don't look like no temple I never seen."

"Who the fuck are you?" Denise asked the tall, bronze-skinned elf who had just made his presence known.

"My name is Ferrik," said the elf. "I am a prisoner here, the same as you."

Randy bowed his head politely. "I'm Randy. It's a pleasure to meet you, Ferrik."

"Best not get too familiar. It will only make things harder when it comes to our final trial."

"Final trial? What do you mean by—"

"Are you fucking kidding me?" said Denise. "I think that one's about to take a dump right here in the goddamn pit."

Randy and Ferrik looked in the direction Denise was indicating. Sure enough, one of the goblins was squatting over the edge, his ass facing them. One by one, little black robin egg-sized pellets fell out onto the pit floor.

"Hey now!" Randy shouted. "That ain't right. This is a place of worship!"

The shitting goblin failed to respond. At least, until a hatchet flew into his back. He screamed as the rest of his load squirted out of his ass, spraying the floor with a splatter of black shit, which he then fell into. The other goblins roared with laughter, which Randy found very inappropriate.

Fortunately for Ferrik, who was jogging up to fetch his hatchet, the goblin landed face down.

"Goddamn," said Denise. "That elf boy don't fuck around."

Unfortunately for Ferrik, the goblins at that part of the pit took advantage of him getting too close to the wall and urinated on him.

"Now that's just rude!" Randy shouted, but there was far too much laughing and howling for anyone to have heard him.

Ferrik took his hatchet and fled the golden showers as swiftly as he could. He was smiling when he returned.

"If I should die this day, at least I can do so with the satisfaction that I took one of those devils down into the abyss with me."

"It weren't nice of you to axe a man in the back," said Randy. "Especially while he was choppin' a log. But for the life of me, I can't think of why they'd take us prisoner and leave us armed. I mean, they took my bow, but it seems irresponsible on their part to leave us our weapons."

"They know I wouldn't risk losing my hatchet just to bring down one of their number. I took a calculated risk just now. But without weapons, none of us would survive the first two trials. That may be enough to temporarily sate the bloodlust of their wicked gods, but the third trial is their favorite, so say those who've walked the path."

"This is it!" said Denise, once again uncharacteristically cheerful. "Ain't this exactly what I told you, Randy?"

"You mean what your daddy said about quitters never winning?"

"No, Randy, you dumbshit! This stuff about three trials Bugs Bunny here keeps rattlin' on about. This is how we win the Caverns and Creatures game. We'll be back home in no time flat!"

"Unlikely," said Ferrik. "The third and final trial is combat to the death between whomever of us has survived the first two trials."

Well that wouldn't do at all. Surely if they all stood together, they could find a way out of this. Solidarity was the answer. This elf feller seemed like a nice, reasonable person. And Denise may be mean-spirited, but she and Randy went back a ways. She didn't have it in her to just up and kill him.

"That's some cold shit," said Denise. She shrugged. "Well, Randy. I'm sorry it had to end this way."

"What?"

"As am I," said Ferrik. "May your spirits find eternal peace as you reunite with your ancestors."

Well, shit.

The crowd along the rim of the pit grew quiet. Part of the circle broke formation. Something beyond Randy's field of view was rattling its way toward the gap. A larger goblin, about half again as tall as any of the rest, did some sort of half-strut/half-dance toward the edge. Clusters of bones hung from his elbows and genitals like wind chimes, which is what was causing the rattling sound. He shook his arms and thrust his pelvis to make the bones rattle rhythmically. Randy could tell it was well-practiced.

When he had finished showing off, the goblin chieftain—as Randy assumed he was—stopped. The bones stopped as well. They didn't rattle on for a while like wind chimes are wont to do. They just flat out stopped. That part of the demonstration impressed Randy most of all.

Figuring he had nothing to lose, Randy cleared his throat. "Excuse me, Mr. Chieftain?"

Something hard struck him in the left temple. A small, round stone landed at his feet. "Son of a—" He took a breath to compose himself, then looked at the crowd of goblins in the direction the stone had come from. "That really smarts!"

One of the goblins pointed at him. "You speak not to the High Priest of Bog' Rozgoth until spoken to!"

The High Priest raised his hands. The bones didn't make a sound. He had a mouth full of pointed, crooked teeth, but his smile somehow reminded Randy of the kindly old grandfather that he'd never had.

"The blessed may speak." He looked directly at Randy. "Children, do you speak the goblin tongue?"

Ferrik stepped forward, his hatchet quivering in his fist. "I would sooner fill my mouth and ears with the ejaculate of Bog' Rozgoth himself, than with your vile language!"

Randy and Denise shared an uncomfortable glance. Randy found he was able to pick out which goblins understood English when he saw them sharing similar glances. Even the bones hanging from the High Priest's genitals stirred a bit as his smile faltered.

The High Priest addressed his congregation in a language that sounded like Hitler with a mouth full of bread. Whatever he told them made them all laugh. Not hard and rowdy like when one of their own got axed in the back and died in a puddle of his own shit, but more like how the congregation laughs when the priest makes a joke in his sermon that wasn't all that funny. Randy supposed that was appropriate here.

Still, the High Priest seemed to enjoy the forced laughter of his flock.

"What's so funny?" Denise demanded. She could dish it out all right, but she had a mean temper whenever anyone poked fun at her. "What did you say to them?"

The High Priest grinned. "I told them we are among common people. We must speak in their common tongue."

Randy shrugged. He'd been called far worse. Several times that day.

The High Priest raised his eyebrows. "Are you familiar with the

Three Trials of Som Nakur?"

Randy placed his hand on Ferrik's shoulder. It was time to start building up that solidarity. "My *friend* here told me all about your trials. You can throw all the lions and bears at us that you want, but when it comes to the third trial, I refuse to shed the blood of my friends. What do you think's gonna happen when the three of us refuse to fight?"

The High Priest grinned and raised his arms in a wide shrug. "I cannot see the future, child. I can only predict. Judging by the way your friends are gauging each other right now, I predict you will die second, and swiftly."

Randy glanced back and forth between Denise and Ferrik, who did indeed seem to be sizing each other up. "You two knock that shit off!"

Ferrik jerked his shoulder out of Randy's grasp. "I warned you not to get too familiar. The gods be praised if even one of us lives to see the light of day again. You may choose to prove your worth to them in combat, or you may choose to die a fool. It matters not to me."

"Don't you listen to him, Randy. I think what you're doing is very noble."

Randy put his hand to his chest. "Why thank you, Denise. I never thought you—" A possible ulterior motive for Denise's uncharacteristically kind words occurred to Randy.

The creaks and groans of moving metal echoed throughout the underground chamber.

"What is that?" asked Denise, her voice thick with fear.

Ferrik was much calmer. He twirled his hatchet once, then gripped the shaft tightly. "The first trial. It begins."

Randy pulled his sword awkwardly out of its sheath. "Where's all that noise coming from? I don't see none of them gates moving."

"A second set of gates are being opened, behind the ones you see," said Ferrik. "If the tales I've heard are true, worgs will be inserted from the rear, so that they may be released simultaneously."

Denise gripped the shaft of her axe with both hands. "I don't know what any of that shit means. What the fuck is a worg? You ever have one of them inserted in your rear before, Randy? Does it hurt?"

Randy sensed Denise's stupidity was genuine, and that she wasn't just taking another cheap shot about him being queer.

From behind Randy came a barrage of barks, howls, and snarls. It was either a pack of wild, rabid dogs, or the single biggest wild, rabid dog in the world. Not knowing which he would have preferred, he turned around to discover that he would have preferred the pack. The snarling, slobbering beast clawing against the bars was almost as tall as he was, up on its hind legs. On all fours, it was at least as tall as Denise at the shoulder. The sword in Randy's sweaty grip felt less like an instrument of self defense, and more like a means of delivering a spiteful, yet forgettable "Fuck you" to the creature that was about to devour his body and soul.

Randy thought about how he was never going to see his grandma again and choked back a sob. "At least we ain't got to worry 'bout fighting each other."

"Despair not," said the elf who was planning on murdering him. "We'll take them one at a time."

"Them?" said Randy. He turned around, and sure enough, there was a second giant black wolf staring at him with red eyes. This one wasn't snarling or howling. It just stared. There was something like intelligence in those eyes. Something cold and calculating.

The High Priest addressed his eager audience in their own language. Not being able to understand what was being said, Randy couldn't make any kind of guess as to how much time they had left.

Randy looked to Ferrik for advice. "Which one should we go after first?"

"The wild one seems the most dangerous."

"Uh-uh," said Denise. "I bet on enough dog fights to see what's going on here."

"You are an officer of the *law*, Denise!" said Randy. "How could you—"

Ferrik held a finger in front of Randy's face. "Time is running out. Let the dwarf woman speak."

"It's an old trick," said Denise. "They'll starve one of them dogs to the point of batshit madness, make him sound all fierce and ferocious, raising the odds in his favor. But they'll bet on the other dog, who's stronger on account of he's been properly fed."

"It would be wise to concentrate our efforts on taking out the weaker of the two as quickly as possible."

Randy shook his head. "I don't like the idea of turning my back on that quiet one. There's something sinister about him."

"I agree with Randy," said Denise.

"You do?" Randy and Ferrik replied.

"Now if we was to throw that pup something to munch on, say, a dead goblin for instance, he might be so hungry that he don't pay no attention to us until we take care of his friend."

Randy was shocked. This was a new low, even for Denise. "It ain't bad enough we killed that poor little guy in the most humiliatin' way possible, but now you want to feed his body to a wild dog? That's just—"

"Brilliant," said Ferrik. He bolted off toward the dead goblin before Randy could raise any further objection.

By the time Ferrik reached his target, the High Priest was reaching a crescendo in his speech, and the goblins were beginning to cheer. Randy had a sinking feeling that their time was up, and subsequently had a change of heart about their plan. If it was the one they were going to go with, they'd better get on with it.

"Hurry up!" Randy shouted at Ferrik. "It's almost time!"

His last word was drowned out by the screech of the gates being raised and the roar of the goblin crowd.

According to the logic of the plan, Randy and Denise should probably have been charging at the quiet worg's cage in order to get in one good stab as soon as the gate opened. But they stood back to back, frozen in fear, in the center of the pit.

The dead goblin's body soared over Randy's head, and Ferrik ran for the quiet, sinister worg's cage.

The sinister worg's eyes, however, were fixed on Randy. As soon as the gate opened wide enough, it bolted out toward him before Ferrik could reach it.

"Turn around, Denise!" said Randy. "It's comin'!"

Randy stood his ground, waiting for the worg to come to him. Dodge first. Attack next. That was his plan.

The worg lunged for Randy's face, as he had a feeling it might. Randy ducked and spun around, sword ready to swing. But the beast collided with Denise, catching her off guard as she turned around, knocking her to the ground.

Denise dropped her axe and throttled the worg's throat with both hands as it snapped its jaws and slobbered on her face. She tried to kick it in the junk, but couldn't quite work out the angle.

"Hurry up and stab this motherfucker!" said Denise.

Randy jabbed at the worg's side with the tip of his sword. He hit its ribcage. If the worg felt it, it didn't show any sign. Randy would have to stab a little harder to penetrate.

Denise was losing the struggle. The worg snapped closer and closer to her face. "Goddammit, Randy! What the fuck was that?"

"I'm sorry!" said Randy. "I just ain't the violent sort."

It was time to get violent. Denise needed him. Randy took the hilt in both hands, pulled back, then shoved his sword as hard as he could into the worg's side. "Hiya!"

The worg howled and convulsed, startling Randy and jerking the sword out of his grip.

Denise used the distraction to punch the beast in the face, freeing herself to reach for her axe.

Randy, faced with the split-second decision between grabbing his sword again, or jumping on the prone worg, chose the latter option. He did a diving elbow drop, flattening the animal just as it was getting to its feet. He felt at least one bone crunch beneath him.

The worg struggled to free itself, and Randy could feel it was about to succeed. He made a desperate attempt at a chokehold, but only managed to stick his arm in the worg's mouth.

The pain in Randy's arm was all that existed. No goblins. No worgs. No noise. Just teeth tearing into his flesh, grating against his bones. Randy shut his eyes and struggled to not pass out. He wanted to yank his arm away, but the worg's jaws were locked on it.

And then it let go. Randy's senses came back to him slowly. First the cheering of their goblin audience. Then the taste of his own sweat. Then the odor of dog breath and urine. He opened his eyes. Judging by the wet patch on Denise's crotch, the urine smell was coming from her.

Denise and Ferrik stood over the dead worg, their faces splattered with the same blood that still dripped from the blades of their weapons.

"Thank you," said Randy.

Ferrik kicked Randy's sword across the ground toward him. "You fight like a crone. Next time, use this."

"All right." Randy was barely listening, his attention still fixed on the searing pain in his arm.

"Stand up," said Ferrik. "We still have one more worg to kill."

Randy looked over at the other worg, the one that had seemed so wild and vicious. It's back was to them, and it was wagging its tail as it happily munched away at the goblin's insides. That poor goblin was in a sorry state. The worg had dug in through its belly, which was torn wide open with blood and guts and intestines and shit sprawled out all over the place. It looked like the goblin had swallowed a hand grenade.

"At least that part of the plan worked."

"He will have eaten his fill soon enough," said Ferrik. "We must strike now."

"Just give me a second to tend to my arm." He closed his eyes, whispered a little prayer, and touched his wound. He only healed himself for one Hit Point, just enough to stop the bleeding, saving the rest in case someone else needed to be healed later.

When he opened his eyes again, Ferrik and Denise had gone off to kill the second worg without him. They flanked it from behind on either side, approaching cautiously. Goblins screamed warnings at the worg, frantically pointing at Ferrik and Denise, but their screams only made stealth that much easier.

Ferrik held up three fingers, then two, then one. He and Denise chopped into the worg's back while its muzzle was buried in the goblin's ribcage, trying to get at its heart. They hacked and hacked like a couple of butchers trying to meet a deadline. That poor dog was most likely dead before he knew what hit him.

The goblins booed. The plan had been an effective one, but two guys hacking a dog to death while he was eating just wasn't the sort of spectacle these folks had shown up to see.

The jeers quieted down as the rattling of bones grew louder. The High Priest shook his arms and gyrated his hips until he had the undivided attention of everyone in the chamber.

He addressed his congregation in their own language while Randy collected his sword and stood up.

"What do you reckon they'll throw at us for the second trial?" asked Denise.

Ferrik stared with cold hatred at the High Priest. "Every account I've heard differs, but it's always something far more dangerous than mere worgs."

"You made an impressive display of teamwork and resourcefulness," said the High Priest. He frowned. "If not a terribly impressive display of combat. But it matters not. That little trick won't help you during the second trial." He raised his arms and shouted something in goblin.

The goblins cheered as unseen metal screeched again. Amid the noise, Randy heard something he didn't expect at all.

"Was that a fucking rooster?" asked Denise.

Ferrik's face turned a shade paler. "It's just as I feared."

"How did we go from fightin' big, scary wolves to fightin' cocks?" asked Denise. "That's almost insulting."

"They got some sharp talons on them," said Randy. "They're more dangerous than you think. My cousin Ronnie raised cocks."

"I got no doubt he raised yours."

Randy took a deep breath, then exhaled slowly. "That was a mean and hurtful thing to say, Denise. But I commend you on your clever use of word play."

"They will be chained," said Ferrik. "Stay in the center of the pit."

Denise spat on the ground. "All this fuss over some goddamn chickens." She strutted out toward one of the open gates and slapped the flat of her axe blade against her well-endowed chest. "Come on out, Cock-a-Doodle! Come see the Colonel. I got eleven herbs and spices for your ass."

Ferrik rubbed his chin. "Your friend. Does she speak in code?"

"GODDAMN!" shouted Denise, scrambling back to the center of the pit again. "What the fuck is wrong with that chicken?"

The creature that waddled out of the cage was the most fucked-up chicken Randy had ever seen. It had the face of a chicken, if that chicken was an extra on The Walking Dead. It's comb and wattles were dull red and irregularly jagged, like it was suffering from leprosy. Its whole body was grey and scaly. What few feathers it had grew in haphazard splotches. Its wings were more bat-like than bird, and its tail was like that of a lizard. And just as Ferrik had predicted, it wore a leather harness attached to a sturdy iron chain which trailed back to where it came from.

"Um…" said Randy. "Is there some kind of bird flu going around?"

Denise shook her head. "Uh-uh. That ain't no fuckin' bird flu. That's bird *AIDS*."

"Just make sure they don't touch your skin," said Ferrik.

"Oh believe me, son," said Denise. "You ain't got to fuckin' worry about that."

Randy scanned the pit. Three more of the creatures were head-bobbing their way toward them. They didn't seem hostile, exactly. Mostly curious.

"Why ain't we supposed to let them touch our skin?" Randy asked Ferrik. "Is it just 'cause they's nasty? Or do they spread disease?"

Ferrik took his eyes off the approaching creatures just long enough to give Randy a quizzical glance. "The touch of the cockatrice can turn a man to stone. This is common knowledge."

"Well excuse me. We ain't from around here."

Ferrik crept slowly and deliberately around the other side of Denise, keeping his eyes on the nearest approaching cockatrice. "If the three of us strike simultaneously," he whispered, "we can kill them one at a time, while minimizing our risk."

That was all well and good, but it was a step closer to the third trial, which Randy was not in any hurry to get underway. He needed an idea, and he needed it fast.

Until he thought of one, he'd have to go along with Ferrik's plan to team up and take these things down individually. While Ferrik circled around to the right, Randy took a few cautious baby steps to the left, keeping his sword low but ready. Denise inched forward to take it head on.

The cockatrice was still relatively non-threatening. At least as non-threatening as a diseased cock/bat/lizard monster was able to look. It jerked its head around, staring curiously at the three armed people slowly surrounding it, it's ragged wattles flapping this way and that, until Denise raised her axe.

It opened its beak wide, showing off a long, forked serpent's tongue, and emitting a crow that would have had Randy's ass well out of bed at the crack of dawn. Denise fell backwards, landing on her ass. The cockatrice spread its bat wings wide and lunged at her. She scooted away from it, and the chain jerked the creature back just before it could reach her.

"Now!" cried Ferrik, bringing his hatchet down on the cockatrice's tail.

Randy didn't need to be told twice. That was some of the scariest shit he'd ever seen. His sword was long enough such that he could strike from a safer distance than Ferrik, so he didn't bother with trying to hack at extremities. He gripped the hilt with both hands, swung the sword over his head, and brought it down on the beast's outstretched neck, slicing the head clean off.

Ferrik smiled. "Well done, sir. You are more capable than you first appeared."

Randy felt blood rush to his face. "Thank you."

"I shall not underestimate you in the third trial."

Randy frowned. "Oh. Well that's nice, I guess."

The crowd booed as the dead cockatrice was dragged back from where it had come, the gate already lowering. Randy had his idea.

"We ain't got to have no third trial!"

"I respect your resistance to violence, friend. But I intend to fight for my freedom."

"Just follow my lead," said Randy. He reached down to help Denise to her feet. She was sobbing like a fat little girl who dropped her ice cream cone. "You okay, Denise?"

Denise took Randy's hand and stood up. "I done shit my pants, Randy. I don't wanna die like this."

"You ain't got to worry. I'm gonna get us out of here."

The three of them backed up toward the closed gate of the dead cockatrice, out of the reach of the other three, which were flapping their wings in a frenzy, pulling their chains taut.

"And how do you propose we get out of here?" asked Ferrik.

"Simple," said Randy. "We release these critters into the crowd."

Ferrik scoffed. "Simple? Those chains are too thick for our blades to cut through. And you'd turn to stone well before you managed to unstrap one of their harnesses."

"That ain't what I'm suggesting. I'm saying we pull the chain. Maybe we get lucky and there's a weak link in there somewhere. Or maybe it ain't so securely fastened at the other end."

"And while we're busy playing with the chain, the cockatrice turns us all to stone."

"Don't be such a Negative Nancy. That's where I come in. You two just do as I say, and we ain't got to kill one another."

Denise wiped her forearm across her eyes. "What all you want us to do?"

"Y'all go back up toward the center of the pit, and you keep that one's attention." Randy pointed at the first cockatrice clockwise to their position. "Don't hurt it none. Just make sure it don't pay no mind to me."

Ferrik sighed. "I suppose it's worth a shot."

Randy smiled. "All right, then. That's a little more like it. Go on now."

The crowd was booing harder now. Randy couldn't blame them. This had to be a pretty dull fight to be observing. But he was about to give them some action. He kept close to the wall, despite the constant rain of goblin piss flowing down on him. He kept reminding himself that he wasn't doing what he was about to do for hatred of his enemies. He was doing it to protect his friends.

Ferrik and Denise had no trouble keeping the cockatrices distracted. All three of them were flapping and crowing and slashing at the air with their talons. Ferrik made eye contact with Randy. He looked impatient. Randy gave him what he hoped was a friendly and encouraging nod. He wanted to shout "Keep doing what you're doing!", but that would ruin his plan. Still, he thought it. *Keep at it, you two. Just a little bit longer.*

Finally, Randy made it to the chain. It was stretched out straight, jerking up and down as the cockatrice at the end of it reached for his companions. He was tempted to grab the chain and give it a good hard yank right then and there, but that wasn't the plan.

He lay his sword gently on the ground, ignoring the continuing laughter and showering of pee. *How much had these little guys had to drink?*

He held both hands near the chain, careful not to touch it, but ready to grab it at a split-second's notice, and crept toward the cockatrice from behind.

The goblins started to freak out, shouting and screaming words that Randy couldn't understand. When he'd made it halfway towards the cockatrice, the goblins started hurling things down at him. Rocks, sticks, turds, whatever. Randy ignored it all, right up until a stray rock hit the cockatrice, which turned around and locked eyes with him.

"Aw shit!" said Randy. He would have liked to have gone a little farther along the chain, but he couldn't afford any slack. Now was the time.

Grabbing the chain with both hands, he swung it around over the top of his head. The cockatrice had started to advance on him, so the first rotation wasn't so smooth, but Randy prevailed on the second turn. The cockatrice was too disorientated, and the chain straightened out. He had it securely spinning around over his head like a lasso. He couldn't keep this up forever, but he should be able to hold out long enough for Ferrik and Denise to test the strength of the chain.

"Come on, you two! Quit your gawkin' and pull that chain!"

Ferrik ducked his head as he and Denise raced past Randy and grabbed the chain. Together they pulled as hard as they could. From the corridor within, a bunch of goblins started screaming.

"I think they're holding it at the other end," said Denise. "Them little fuckers got a hell of a grip. I'll give 'em that."

"They ain't but three feet tall," cried Randy. "Pull harder. They'll let go."

Denise and Ferrik grunted and strained. Again, the goblins at the other end of the corridor screamed. One of them in particular seemed particularly distraught. He was probably the team leader, and it would be his ass on the line if they let go of that chain. His screaming was something awful. It made Randy wince.

"It's no use," said Ferrik. "They must have a whole team of them in there."

"Come on, you two!" said Randy. He was beginning to feel the fatigue in his arms. "I can't hold out much longer!"

"Your plan was a good one," said Ferrik. "But it seems we are resigned to our fates."

"Horseshit!" said Randy. "Ain't you never seen *Back to the Future III*? Your fate is whatever you make it. Denise! Use that *Bohemian Rhapsody* trick Cooper showed you."

"What the fuck are you... Do you mean Barbarian Rage?"

"Oh right. That's the one!"

"I still don't know how it works exactly."

Randy's shoulders burned and his arms quivered with fatigue. "I don't give a sow's rear end how it works. Just say the words!"

Denise's face glistened with urine and burned with anger. "I'm fuckin' pissed!"

She was already what you might call a "sturdy woman" to begin with, but when she turned on the rage, she was an absolute wrecking ball. Her muscles ballooned out so much that her neck all but disappeared. She roared like a lioness and pulled hard on the chain, which finally gave way.

The only thing louder than Denise's roar was the goblin scream from inside the corridor. It sent a chill up Randy's spine. But he couldn't think about that right now. His arms felt like wet noodles. He had a cock to set loose.

Randy scanned the crowd for a target. He decided on the group that was still urinating on Ferrik, Denise having run off somewhere else. After taking two more rotations to line up his target, he released the cockatrice into the crowd. It smacked straight into a very surprised-looking goblin, who caught it in his arms. His arms turned grey and hard. The effect spread over his whole body in only a few seconds, petrifying the shocked expression on his face.

The cockatrice struggled, but it was caught in the stone embrace of its own creation.

Randy followed the chain down and discovered why the goblin who had been holding it had had such a hard time letting go. His wrist had been manacled to it. At the end of the chain lay an entire goblin arm, all the way up to the glistening red ball of the shoulder joint.

Ferrik tugged on the chain, and leapt out of the way as the goblin statue fell off the ledge and broke apart, freeing the cockatrice.

Denise, still enraged, had moved on to the second cockatrice, covering both Randy's role of swinging the beast around her head by the chain with her right hand, and her own role of pulling on the other end of the chain with her left.

"Denise!" Randy cried. "Stop! He can't let go. You'll pull his –"

"KRRRREEEEEEE!" screamed a goblin from inside as the chain fell slack.

Denise took aim at the High Priest with her cockatrice, but released it a little too vigorously, sending it sailing over the High Priest's head. Cheers turned into panicked screams. The sounds of chaos grew louder as a manacled goblin arm bounced its way up the pit wall, painting a trail of blood with flopping tendons.

The first cockatrice shook off the white powdery remains of the goblin statue it had just created and locked eyes with Randy, no doubt still holding a grudge over having been swung round and round for so long. Without a sword, Randy's only choice was to run away from it. He and Denise were making their way clockwise along the perimeter of the pit. For once, everyone above them was too busy to piss on them.

Denise was making for the last cockatrice, but the goblin attached to the chain had wisely decided to pull it back inside and close the gate. With all of the pushing and shoving going on at the top of the pit, a few goblins had fallen in. Denise grabbed her axe.

Randy ran past her, the cockatrice still charging after him. "Denise! Behind you!"

Denise turned around just in time to swat the creature back with the flat of her axe. Unfortunately, she swatted it right into Ferrik, who had been chasing behind it, trying to catch the chain.

"NOOO—" Ferrik screamed until the stone spread through his throat.

"Well shit," said Denise. She had come out of her rage. "I ain't meant to do that."

Randy grabbed the chain and swirled the cockatrice over his head. He took aim at the High Priest and let go. With all the chaos going on, there was no room for him to dodge. He turned into stone with his arms held up defensively in front of him, and the cockatrice flew off in search of easier targets.

Randy frowned at Ferrik. "Maybe there's a way we can get him magicked back to normal."

The freshly created, top-heavy High Priest statue fell off the edge of the pit and landed on Ferrik's head, smashing them both into dust and rubble.

Denise shook her head. "Nope. I reckon probably not."

Randy, Denise, and the few goblins who had fallen into the pit with them remained close to the walls until the commotion above them died down. From what they could hear, they determined that the goblins had managed to kill or contain the two cockatrices, but not without suffering heavy losses to their own number.

When they felt it was safe to leave, Randy bartered the goblins' assistance in finding their way out in exchange for not allowing Denise to murder them.

On *Certified Organic*–

I first met Dean at a Meetup in Santa Clara for a writers group. I was sitting at one end of a long table, deciding this particular group wasn't for me. I looked across the table, sussed out he felt the same way, and that's how we started Black Hats of the Bay Area, along with Ernest Ortiz, who was sitting between us. Fate.

Over the years, I've become addicted to the unique beauty of his stories: older characters, flickering realities, and most importantly, what those characters do when everything they know about their reality flickers out of existence.

In *Certified Organic*, I thought I had it all figured out until the surprising climax, which, in retrospect, made perfect sense and was all the more satisfying for it.

—*Joan Reginaldo*

Certified Organic

Dean Fearce

—◦◦◦—

THE MORNING SUN PEEKED over the Holyoke Range catching Nora on her knees in the middle of the broccoli patch. She was dressed in her torn work pants—holy pants, she called them—and raking the soil around each bright green stalk with her fingers, looking for the inch-long cutworms that had devastated last year's broccoli crop.

The pests were implacable in their destruction. Once they shredded the broccoli, they moved to the cucumbers and then the eggplants—row after row until there was little left but compost material. She feared for the cauliflower, cabbage, and kohlrabi this summer.

Something squiggled in the dirt. A fat, well-fed grub.

"Sorry little guy. It's lights out time."

She cracked the cutworm between her fingers with a resounding snap, felt a splat of grub goo hit her cheek. She wiped her face on her shoulder, then mixed the broken carcass back into the topsoil around the emerging stem. She worked quickly down the row, squatting crab-like on her haunches. Kelsey called her the Grubinator. Kelsey had nick-names for everyone and everything. As the Grubinator, Nora ignored the spasms shooting up the back of her thighs and settling in her lower back.

If there was any money left, she would have bought more replace-ments for the plants lost to the voracious little creatures, but last year's meager harvest had disappointed her customers too keenly. She lost a slew of her cooperative shareholders. It was a devastating financial blow.

Maybe someone's trying to tell me something, but I'm not ready to let go of this place, she thought. She glanced up to survey the ridgeline of Mt.

Tom. The morning sun was bright and clear and already getting hot. It burned the haze of dawn off the rocky outcroppings with their sudden eruption of greenery. She felt sweat break out across her freckled forehead and wiped her head on her sleeve.

"Unbelievable weather," she said, talking aloud as if the broccoli had ears. "Rain, sleet, hail, snow. Now this heat and no rain. I just hope we don't see any locusts."

Kelsey and Sarah, her farm hands, were over in the U-Pick-Em strawberry patch inspecting the damage from last week's cold snap. They were wearing shorts and tank tops. Just last week they were in parkas.

Don't know how I'd manage without them, she thought, whispering a small thank you to no one in particular. They were young and strong and seriously dedicated to the farm, although Kelsey had quite a willful personality, and Sarah wasn't any pushover either.

Kelsey had dubbed Sarah Monobrow because she didn't shave or pluck any hair from her well-endowed frame. Sarah felt obliged to rename Kelsey, but hadn't yet come up with a moniker that stuck. The most recent one was Treefrog. Kelsey was tall and rangy, all limbs. When she worked the hoe, she was all angles. It reminded Sarah of a Treefrog in that way, but nothing else was frog-like about the young woman. And, Treefrog just didn't roll off the tongue quite right.

Nora wondered if the girls' commitment might waver a bit if she couldn't make the payroll next week, or any week thereafter. Losing those two would be unfathomable. And she would miss them. Their easy confidence always eased the monotony of morning chores. Their humor, though a bit morbid, was certainly entertaining. *Kids today*, she worried. They don't always have the wherewithal to stick with it when things get tough. As if in response to her thoughts, both of the girls stood up, waved in her direction, and pointed toward the house. Or was it the barn.

She looked past them and saw a car pulling into the turnaround, spraying gravel as it slid sideways in a cloud of dust. It was sleek and black. A European model that looked expensive. *Maybe a new shareholder,* Nora thought, feeling an unexpected cool breeze across her brow.

"Thank God," she said. She hoped she didn't sound as exasperated as she felt.

If they could afford a vehicle like that, then a few co-op shares wouldn't even dent their household budget. And their check wouldn't bounce. She crossed her fingers and went up to meet them with a warm smile on her sun reddened face. Walking through the cool dimness of the barn, she inhaled the musty aroma of hay and fresh manure. It was a heady perfume that calmed her. That, and the thought of a little positive cash flow.

She came out of the other side of the barn onto the driveway beside the Victorian-style farmhouse. It was shady here from a big ancient oak tree. The car had pulled through the turnaround and sat idling in the middle of the drive, neither coming nor going. Its darkly tinted windows were sealed tight against the heat. Condensation from the air conditioning dribbled onto the dusty gravel, evaporating with today's promise of a scorcher in the fields.

Remind the girls to take plenty of water breaks, she thought and went to the driver's side. Chilly conditioned air from the car's interior met her when the window rolled down. The interior of the car was a sumptu-ous grey. She heard music that she couldn't identify. It was sharp and nervous, some kind of trendy jazz.

The driver spoke deliberately into a cell phone. He was good-look-ing from the side, with a strong jaw under short, sandy hair. He was tanned and dressed in what Nora thought typical of country clubs and casual business meetings with early morning tee times.

"Just listen to yourself. You're losing it," Nora heard him say. "I said

I'd take care of it and I will. Believe me, they don't have a thing. So fehgeddaboutit. I gotta go." He tossed the phone onto the passenger seat.

"Hi. Howya doing?"

He opened the car door, stepped out. From the front, his wrap-around sunglasses gave him a slightly predatory bug-like gaze. He closed the car door and leaned back with his arms crossed in front of him, a slight smirk forming on his face. He studied Nora for a few moments then held out his hand.

"Jim Banes," he said. "Nice to meet you."

Nora hesitated, swiping her hand on the seat of her pants, adding another layer to the track of dirt and stains, before extending her hand.

"Nora Burgeson. Welcome to Ostrich Acres Farm."

"Ostrich Acres," he said. "I saw the sign. Cute. You raise ostriches?"

"No. Not anymore. The previous owners did, though. Cultivator still turns up some pretty big chicken legs out in the field." Nora chuckled at her joke. Mr. Banes didn't seem to get it or maybe he didn't think it was funny.

"Listen, I just moved into town," he said.

"Oh, great," she said. "Where are you from?"

"N-Y-C. I'm a lawyer. Our firm has decided to open a satellite office out here," he said, tilting his head back and stretching out his arms.

Nora noted the I-don't-get-it-look on his face.

"And I've been elected to run the show, at least until we're billing a positive cash flow," he said with a white, toothy smile. "Anyway, here's the bottom line. I'm very particular about my diet. I only eat organic foods. No pesticides, herbicides, or any other 'cides. I only drink bottled water. All animal products must be free range and no hormones or antibiotics."

"Well, that's great Mr. Banes. I assure you all the produce here on the farm is free of all 'cides, as you say. All of our dairy products, breads, bakery, and honey are 100% pesticide free."

"Certified organic?"

"Well, no, we're not certified organic," she said.

"Really?" he said folding his arms back across his chest.

"We actually follow a more stringent guideline than what's allowed by the USDA, which controls the certifying. Some of the practices they allow I don't agree with completely."

"Like what?"

He was making her unexpectedly uncomfortable. Nora realized that Mr. Banes was probably a very aggressive attorney and, quite likely, a successful law practitioner because of it.

"Using compost from irradiated materials, for one," she said. "The USDA allows it for certified organic farming."

"Do most organic farmers use irradiated compost?" he asked.

"Well, none that I know of," she said. He got her there. "But it's the idea of it. Any form of unnecessary radiation put into the atmosphere, and the food chain, can't be a good thing. And then there's the cost of getting certified, which I'd have to pass on to my shareholders."

"Good for marketing" he said, "being certified, don't you think?"

"To be honest with you Mr. Banes, I'm more worried about the lack of rainfall than being certified organic by the USDA."

"I see," he said, nodding his head. "Are there any other *organic* farms around here?"

"Oh, yes. There are quite a few. There's the Food Co-op on the other side of the river. They're certified. And there's the Farmer's Market in Hadleyville. They're retail, but they carry a lot of locally grown produce and organic goods from all over the country. You should definitely check them out."

"Thanks for your time, Miss…"

"Burgeson. Nora Burgeson. And it's no problem at all, Mr. Banes."

"What happened to your fingers?"

"Farming is *the* most dangerous profession," Nora said, looking at her left hand. The index and middle finger were smooth stubs at the second knuckle. "Don't worry, we keep the shareholders away from the equipment. Anyway, we still have a few shares available if you decide you want to join up. It's four…"

He was already in his car, starting it up. The car window rose up out of the door and sealed him inside with a tiny *phhhht*. He shot up the driveway spewing rocks as he pulled his sporty car out onto the blacktop, cutting off a pickup truck that had to lock its brakes.

Nora watched, stupefied. "Geez," she said and walked back through the barn into the fields and the blistering morning sun.

"Who was that?" Kelsey asked when Nora passed her weeding in the lettuces. Kelsey needed to know everything.

"New fellow in town. Interested in the farm. He might be back."

"Hope so," she said. It wasn't any secret that there were quite a few shares still available. And the first distribution day was next week.

"Got some volunteers coming tomorrow, help with the weeding," Nora said.

Kelsey smiled and nodded and went back to pulling the weeds.

"Frost nearly killed everything else, but not these darn weeds," Nora said, muttering to herself. She missed the look that passed between the girls.

"Just go with the flow, Nora," Kelsey said. "It's all compost in the end."

⌘

Three days later, NORA, Kelsey, and Sarah were bent over in the dusty pathway between seven rows of sickly looking potato plants.

Jimmy, who Kelsey called Sloppy—a perfect name that stuck to him like bubblegum in hair—was working with them. He was a new shareholder this year. He had chosen to pay off his volunteer debt today. He hadn't chosen wisely. It was kill the potato bug day.

Volunteering was a popular option Nora offered to the farm's shareholders. They could save fifteen percent on the cost of a share by trading three days of labor a month. Quite a few signed up, but not many of them actually made their way out to Ostrich Acres. That meant bookkeeping was a royal pain in the ass, because she had to go back and adjust their balances, and then collect the money. It was the one formal agreement she insisted on with the shareholders. Fostered goodwill and built community, she would tell them.

"Funny how all these folks with time on their hands suddenly have doctor's appointments," Sarah said.

"Yes," said Kelsey, "isn't that strange."

"Builds community," Nora told the girls.

"It could, I suppose, if more of them would show up," Sarah said.

Nora caught the look between the two of them, and they all laughed. Sloppy joined in, though not quite sure why he was laughing. Sloppy loved working on the farm.

Out in the field, potato bugs had hatched. The larvae were ravenous, devouring the leafy part of the nightshade tubers. Left unchecked, subsequent hatches would certainly ruin the potato crop. Each plant had to be inspected carefully for the fat pink grubs. When found, they were squished between thumb and forefinger into a smelly yellow slime. This morning's crew was already decorated with dirty swipes of bug slime across the front and back of their shorts and shirts.

The adult potato beetles were perfectly formed domes about the size of a pinky-finger tip, and adorned with alternating black and brown stripes. Their shells were harder to crush. Most were captured live and dropped into a plastic baggy to squirm and wriggle against each other in a final orgy of insect death.

Today's gruesome task was made even more grueling by the suffocating heat and humidity. Oddly enough, Sloppy seemed not to mind. He was incredibly accepting and uncomplaining.

"You having fun?" Sarah asked, standing up to drop a bug into her baggy. She was wearing a conical straw hat and had a good sweat going. Her tank top was soaked through and her large breasts splayed out from the armholes. When she raised her arms to fan herself with her hat, she displayed a shocking tuft of dark hair in her unshaven armpits.

"Oh, yeah," Sloppy said. Sloppy was ready to kill every bug in the world if Sarah commanded it.

"You're a good bug killer, Sloppy," she said.

"Ewww," Kelsey said. "This one looks like Marlon Brando, you know, before he died."

"All fat, bloated, and sloppy," Sloppy said. He snorted a laugh through his nose, launching Kelsey and Sarah into a laughing jag.

"The horror. The horror," he said. He was wearing a big floppy straw hat that kept falling off when he bent over.

Kelsey and Sarah sat back into the dirt, laughing.

"Stella," Sloppy said, on his knees in the dirt, arms outstretched. "Stella."

A car horn sounded in response, once, twice, three times, interrupting the moment and making them all self-conscious.

"Car alarm," Sloppy said.

The beeping continued with an arrhythmic staccato.

"I don't think that's an alarm," Sarah said.

At the other end of the field, Nora was already working her way around the greenhouse to investigate. The crew, energized by the cathartic belly laugh, went back to the gruesome task of crushing bug larvae with renewed vigor.

Nora stepped out of the barn into the driveway. The beeping stopped. She recognized the vehicle. It was the sleek black foreign job driven by that lawyer fellow. The name popped into her head.

Banes.

The driver's side door opened and Mr. Banes stepped out. Then, the passenger side doors, both front and back, opened. Two smaller replicates of Banes stepped out. They were obviously twins. Preadolescent. The whole tableau was vaguely unsettling and a little eerie, like an alien invasion from a sci-fi movie.

"I'm back," he said.

"I see," Nora said.

"These are my boys. Alexander and Christopher. Identical twins. Thank God they don't dress alike. Be impossible to tell them apart."

Nora smiled and waved in their direction, but they took no notice. They had walked around the car heading for the barn. Nora could hear Dexter, Jasper, and Max, Nora's old cantankerous goats, kicking the barn walls in despair. The Woolly Boys were apparently upset by the blaring car horn.

"So what can I do for you today, Mr. Banes?"

"Do you still have co-op shares available?"

"Yes, we do," she said.

"Good. That's great. Listen, I'm in a real hurry here. Do you have some literature I could take with me?"

"We have a brochure with an application form. Hang on a second and I'll track one down for you."

Nora went into the house and came back with a bright green pamphlet with a goofy looking ostrich on the front.

"Nice," he said when she handed it to him. He tossed it though the car window onto the dashboard of his sporty sedan. "Listen, sign me up for two shares, okay?"

Nora wanted to ask him about the other farms he'd seen, professional curiosity, but she didn't.

"You're signed up, Mr. Banes. Appreciate it if you'd fill out the application and return it with your check."

"Sure thing," he said. He climbed back into his car and turned on the ignition.

"This Saturday we're having our shareholder open house. Hope you can make it, Mr. Banes."

"That's great. Listen, the boys wanted to check the place out. They love animals and fresh air and all that crapola. I'll be back to get them in a bit."

Nora turned to see the twins in the barn as Mr. Banes peeled out of the driveway, spewing more gravel. She wondered why he kept tearing out like that.

In the barn, Nora found one of the twins up on the fence around the sheep pen. He was hanging over and bleating like a crazed goat. The other boy was shredding a bale of straw and tossing it at the sheep in a misguided attempt to feed them. Dexter, Jasper, and Max were kicking the barn door that led out to their enclosed sunning area. Nora hurried over to rescue them.

"Boys, please don't upset the sheep. They might bite if they're frightened."

They ignored her.

"Stop it!" Nora commanded. That froze them.

"We're going to check on the radishes, so follow me. Now, march." Nora led the two boys out into the field and away from the animals and equipment in the barn.

Five hours later, when the boys' father finally pulled in the driveway, Nora had settled up with her unrequited longing for children of her own. In the vacancy of her departed maternal desires, a new and unfamiliar feeling had moved in and occupied the space. "Murder," she said. "Another five minutes and I swear I'd have murdered those two."

Kelsey nodded in agreement: "I would have helped, but only after a dose of painful torture," she said. "Not to me. To them."

"We could have buried them under the compost pile," Sarah said. "There's plenty of room."

"In little pieces," Kelsey added. "After we ran the cultivator over them a couple times."

"They almost managed to accomplish that themselves," Nora said. "Don't ever leave the keys in the tractor again."

"Would we still be considered organic?" Sarah asked.

"Snips and snails and puppy dog tails," Kelsey said in a falsetto singsong. "That's what little demons are made of."

"We'd be pest free, that's for sure. At least Mr. Banes signed up for two shares," Nora said, holding the application form he had given her.

"Where's the check?" Kelsey said.

"Said he didn't have his checkbook."

Kelsey rolled her eyes. "No Gain Banes."

Sarah screwed up her face in mock anger and said, "No money, no groceries."

"Look, he checked off on the volunteer option," Nora said. The girls groaned deeply and without apology.

"No Gain Banes is a creep," Kelsey said. "If he brings those evil Tangle and Mangle twins again, something ugly is going to happen."

———— ❧ ————

Nora was angered when the shareholders tried to renege on their agreement. An extra squash or half-pound of arugula was fine. Everyone tried to squeeze out a little extra on pick-up day. When the harvest was unexpectedly abundant, she encouraged it, especially with the hard-working volunteers. But if you expected your fifteen percent savings, then you damn well better put in your time. About this, she was adamant.

Every summer she had at least one customer with the usual litany of overworked excuses why they couldn't make it to the farm for a few hours of honest hard work. This summer was no exception thanks to Mr. Banes.

After the third message left on his machine reminding him she would have to charge him the normal price for a share, he picked up the phone.

"Oh, hey, uh, Nora. Hi, yea, I just walked in the door," he said and then he surprised her. "Listen, how about Tuesday morning?"

"Tuesday would be great. We harvest in the morning," she said.

"What time does that start?" he asked.

"Right after chores, usually about six or six-thirty."

"Hmmm, yea, well, that'll be tough," he said.

Nora, not wanting to give him an out, said, "If you can't make it until later, say eight o'clock, that's fine. There's still plenty of work we need help with, especially on distribution days."

"Well, okay. I'll see you around eight then," he said and hung up.

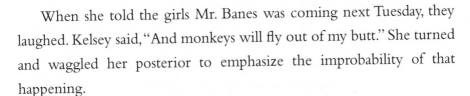

When she told the girls Mr. Banes was coming next Tuesday, they laughed. Kelsey said, "And monkeys will fly out of my butt." She turned and waggled her posterior to emphasize the improbability of that happening.

When he actually showed closer to nine o'clock on Tuesday, Sarah turned to Kelsey and said, "Let fly the monkeys!"

Kelsey held out her finger and said, "Pull this first."

126 ~ fresh cuts

Sarah rolled her eyes and tried to think of an appropriate nickname for Kelsey reflective of her toilet humor. Pottymouth and Farthead were just too infantile.

Nora walked to meet Mr. Banes at the end of the row of new pepper plant starts they were planting. He was wearing new running shoes with white socks, chinos, a St. John's Law School T-Shirt, and matching baseball hat. He smelled like a summer day at the beach, all coconut oil and sunscreen. His twin sons, Alexander and Christopher, stood at attention behind him, right and left respectively.

"Hello, Mr. Banes," Nora said. "Glad you could make it today."

He raised his hand in acknowledgment. He didn't look thrilled to be here.

"I had to bring the twins," he said. "Couldn't leave them at home without a babysitter."

"You guys want to help plant some hot peppers in the U-pick section this morning?" Nora said, addressing the two young boys.

"Yeah right," they murmured in unison.

Nora shouldered the post-hole digger and marched up the row between the raised dirt beds. She stopped and swiveled her head, sensing correctly that Banes was not following her. She assumed he would. Most anybody else would have. She waved for him to follow. He turned and said something to the boys. They dashed off back in the direction of the barn.

"Don't frighten the sheep in the barn," Nora yelled after them. "They do bite."

"They're going to play with their iPads in the car," Banes said.

Nora shrugged. "Do you like hot peppers, Mr. Banes?"

"No, actually. I don't."

"Ahh, well, we're planting mild peppers, too," she said. "We use the post hole digger to make a hole about eight inches deep."

Nora hefted the shovel off her shoulder, flipped it, buried it into the dirt, pried the handles open, pulled up and out, and deposited a canister of dirt next to the hole.

"Then Sloppy—did you meet Sloppy?" Nora nodded towards Sloppy. "He'll drop some compost in and Kelsey will drop the pepper plant in the hole. We come back and seat it by hand and cover it with that same dirt. And that's it."

Sarah was moving quickly down the next row over with her post hole digger. She left perfectly formed columns of dirt parked on the beds in her wake. Sloppy was following with a wheelbarrow full of compost. He used a plastic container to deposit a small clot of composted organic matter into each new hole. Kelsey had taken the truck back to the greenhouse to load up the flats of pepper plants.

"You want to give it a shot, Mr. Banes?" Nora asked. She held out the twin wooden handles of the digger. "Line up with Sarah's hole. Just eyeball it, okay?"

"Sarah's hole?" he said. Nora ignored him and was already on the move, leaving him with the heavy handled post hole digger and a smirk on his face.

Banes lifted the handles with a grunt and jabbed them into the soil about three inches deep. He lifted them out again, grunting even louder. A tablespoon of soil slid out from between the shovels.

"Thing is heavy," he said, but Sarah was moving quickly down the row already out of earshot.

By the fifth hole, he managed to pull out a respectable chunk of dirt about the size of a soda can. When he tried to lift the post-hole digger, something pinged in his right shoulder and he just couldn't get it up high enough to afford the leverage to bury the shovel in the earth.

Nora appeared at his side. He hadn't noticed her there. He was sweating heavily. His face was mottled pink from the heat and the exertion.

"Why don't you go back and give Sloppy a hand with the compost, Mr. Banes. I'll finish up here."

All he could do was nod. He turned the digger handles back over to her.

"There's water in the truck," she said. "You can sit on the tailgate and take a little break."

"Takes some getting used to," Kelsey said. "You still with us?"

"Little too much golf yesterday," he said. "I'll be fine."

"Next, we're going to cover the cucumbers. Helps retain the heat for these cool nights and keep the bugs off."

"I'm just going to check on the boys," Banes said, stepping through the freshly planted peppers.

"Stay on the pathways, Mr. Banes!" Nora said. "Please!" She bent over to assess the damage he'd done to the row of peppers they've just planted.

Sarah had already begun installing wire hoops over the cucumber rows while the others were planting the peppers. Kelsey and Nora unraveled a new bolt of long white row cover cloth to cover the sprouting seedlings.

Kelsey handed Sarah the shovel. "Let's do it, Monobrow," she said. "The Bane can catch up if he comes back."

Nora and Kelsey moved down the row pulling the cloth covering over the wire hoops. Sarah and Sloppy scooped a shovel of dirt and poured it over a hand span of the cloth to hold it down. They were halfway through the first row when Mr. Banes returned.

Nora explained what they were doing. "We pull the covering over the hoops and then use the dirt to hold it in place. It's not real tricky, but we want to keep it straight and tight so the wind can't get under it."

"So what do you want me to do?"

"Spread out the edge as you move down the row. Sloppy will dump a load of dirt on it."

Sarah started up again on the other side. Mr. Banes watched for a minute then he bent down and pulled the cloth covering across the hoops and opened a hand span across the soil. Sloppy promptly dumped a shovel full of dirt on it. They continued down the row with him bent over and pulling the white cloth down while Sloppy shoveled behind him. Kelsey and Sarah were moving down the other side and were almost to the end.

Kelsey stopped and looked back and said, "We're getting a little crooked. See the hem line there?"

Banes stood up.

"Uh-oh," he said.

"It's no biggy. Just pull it down tight and we'll keep going."

"No. I mean. I think I hurt my back," he said, groaning and clutching his back. "I think I'm done here for today." He turned and dragged his feet to the pickup truck, sat on the tailgate holding his lower back while they finished covering the row of cucumbers.

Nora, Kelsey, Sloppy, and Sarah converged on the truck when they were done. Mr. Banes was staring up toward the barn with an expectant look on his face.

"How are you feeling, Mr. Banes?" Nora asked him.

"Hurts like a mother…" he started to say, but was interrupted by a screaming ruckus coming from the barn.

"Uh-oh," said Nora. "Sarah, bring the truck." Nora ran toward the barn.

"Tangle and Mangle," Kelsey said, and took off after Nora.

Sloppy and Sarah put their shovels in the pickup bed and climbed in the cab. Sarah started the truck then headed toward the barn with Mr. Banes riding on the lowered tailgate.

Nora stepped into the warm gloom of the barn. One of the twin boys was perched on the sheep pen, swinging a wooden axe handle at the sheep, screaming, "You bastards, I'll get you, you bastards."

Dexter, Jasper, and Max, the three adult male sheep were crazed, foam at their mouths, running amok in the pen. They kicked and rammed the door to get out.

The other twin was standing behind his brother, sobbing and urging him on. "Motherfucker bit me. Kill him, Christopher." He was bent over clutching his hand. Nora saw blood dripping onto the hay at his feet.

"Oh God," Nora said. She grabbed Christopher by the back of the collar and yanked him off the pen. "Stop that," she commanded, and took the handle from him.

"Goddamn sheep bit my brother's finger off," he said, struggling to free himself from Nora's grip.

Nora let go of him. "Let me see your hand," she said to the bleeding boy.

"It fucking hurts," he said, tears streaming down his face.

Nora reached for his hand. "I know it does. Let me see it."

Nora held the boy's shaking arm. He seemed to relax with her touch. She inspected the damage. The index finger on his right hand was mangled and bleeding profusely. "We're going to have to clean this up," she said. "Let's go into the house. You're Alexander, right?"

Nora gently urged him toward the house as the pickup truck pulled into the barn. The other twin ran to his father.

"Dad, that goddamn sheep bit Alex's finger off. It's really nasty."

Mr. Banes followed Nora out of the barn with the other twin right behind him. "Omigod," he said. "Let me see."

"We need to clean it off," Nora said, noticing the boy's arm starting to shake again. "There's too much blood. Sarah, let the sheep out before they kill themselves."

Leaving a trail of blood, Nora led the boy across the gravel drive into the breezeway and up the stairs to the kitchen. She rinsed the boy's hand with warm water in the kitchen sink. The index finder was crushed to the first knuckle and his fingernail was nearly torn off. The ring finger also looked damaged. The boy's father was at the door. Christopher and Kelsey were behind him in the breezeway.

"We need to get this boy to the emergency room," Nora said. She pulled a clean kitchen towel off the towel rack and gently wrapped it around his hand. "The one in Hampton is closest."

"Jesus Christ," Banes said. "Get in the car, Alex."

"Let's go," Nora said, still holding the boy's arm.

"I said I'll take him," Banes reached over and pulled the boy away from Nora. "Let's go, Alex."

"I'll come with you," Nora said, following them out toward the turnaround where Mr. Banes's car was parked.

"That's not necessary," he said.

"Do you know where it is?" Nora asked him.

Banes stopped and turned abruptly and Nora almost bumped into him. "Do you have another towel?" he asked her.

"Of course. Kelsey, run and get another towel from the linen drawer in the kitchen."

"A bigger one," Banes said.

"Get a bath towel, Kelsey," Nora said.

"And yes, I know where the hospital is in Hampton. Christopher, get in the back," Banes said opening the passenger door for Alex. The boy started to climb in the front seat, but his father pulled him back.

"Wait." The pitiful look on the boy's face clutched at Nora.

Kelsey came out of the house trailing bath towels. Nora nodded for her to give them to Mr. Banes.

"Thanks." He carefully lined the seat and floor with towels before depositing the boy in the front seat. "I'll be in touch," he said. He got in the car and peeled out of the driveway in a cloud of gravel dust.

"Bastard Banes," Kelsey muttered.

———— ∞∞∞ ————

Nora called Mr. Banes that night and got his answering machine. "Let me know how Alex is doing," she said. "And, if there's anything you need, just call me."

She called the next day to check up on him. He answered the phone on the first ring.

"Mr. Banes? Hi. It's Nora, from the farm," she said.

"Hi, Nora."

"How's Alexander?"

"They had to remove his finger up to the first knuckle. It was crushed beyond repair."

"I'm really sorry to hear that. Is there anything I can do?"

"No, I can manage. Thank you. Actually, there is something you can do for me."

"What's that?"

"Today's my pick-up day. I won't have time to get out there. I have a doctor's appointment for my back. Could someone drop off my produce?"

"I guess we could do that. Give me your address. We have lettuce and greens, lots of greens. Kale, collards, mustard greens, arugula. Broccoli, radishes, turnips. Do you have any preferences?"

"Skip the turnips. Everything else is good."

After normal distribution, Nora bagged up Mr. Banes's double share, the shares he hadn't paid for yet. Nora had no reason to believe he wasn't good for the money. She put a pre-printed payment reminder in with the groceries with just a twinge of passing guilt. Whatever else happened, she reasoned, he still had to pay up.

Jim Banes lived in a small ranch-style house encased in aluminum. It sat on a lonely plot of parched and tree-less land on the other side of town. Nora turned her pickup into the dusty gravel drive. She was a bit surprised.

"Guess you can't judge a book by its cover," she muttered to herself.

The carport was empty. Nora pulled up and rapped on the side entry door. She peeked through the curtain-less window into the kitchen. The house appeared devoid of life or furniture.

She thought about checking the door to leave the vegetables inside, but finally just left the bags of produce in the carport to protect them from the heat, and to make sure Banes wouldn't miss them.

Three days later, the postman caught Nora in the kitchen during lunch break. He delivered two thick envelopes, both by registered mail. One envelope was from a legal firm with a Boston address. The other one was from the Court of Common Pleas in Suffolk County. He also delivered the regular mail, a handful of bills dumped on the mountain growing monthly in her office.

"I expected this," she said. Kelsey, Sarah, and Sloppy were sitting around the kitchen table, trading jibes. They were red-faced with laughter.

"What's that?" Sarah said, choking back a snort.

"We're being sued. That is, the farm is, and me, as the owner."

"Sued?" said Kelsey. "What happened? Ahh, Bastard Banes, I'll bet."

"Yes, it is Mr. Banes" she said, rifling through the sheaf of legal documents. "Get this, not only is he suing us for the injury, pain, and suffering of his son, Alex, which I understand, he is apparently also suing us for his back ache that turned into something more serious, preventing him from working and earning a living as an attorney. That, I don't quite understand."

Kelsey slammed her hands on the table. "What! You've got to be kidding me. I smell a big fat rat."

Nora tossed the papers on the table. "I guess I need to call a lawyer."

———— ∞∞∞ ————

After a few weeks of legal wrangling, it became obvious that Nora was going to lose Ostrich Acres to Jim Banes. Her insurance policy covered paid employees, but it didn't cover volunteer workers or visitors in the event of an injury or accident. No one had been asked to sign a waiver. It didn't fit into the spirit of goodwill and community Nora was trying to foster with her shareholders. A foolish notion, she realized now.

"Dang," Sloppy said, "If I had known that, I would have done it first."

The weather turned balmy. Steady rains soaked the fields and further irony was revealed with harvests producing a cornucopia of fruits and vegetables. Nature's bounty. The shareholders were suckled from the breast of Mother Earth. And the son of a bitch Banes still hadn't paid for his shares.

Nora hadn't expected Banes to show up on the farm demanding his shares. But he did. She politely told him he wasn't entitled to a share. He hadn't paid the membership fee. He produced a checkbook, wrote a check, and tossed it at Nora.

Banes also demanded that his shares be delivered to his house, on account of his injury. If she didn't deliver it, he would seek a court order enforcing it.

"Listen, Mr. Banes, that's just too much. I'm really sorry for what happened to your son. The sheep had to be put down. That also saddens me. I'm sorry you hurt your back planting peppers, but we're just too busy keeping this farm up…"

"I'll do it," Kelsey said. "It's no biggy."

Nora was nonplussed. "Well, you're here today, Mr. Banes, so you might as well pick up your shares."

When distribution was done for the day, and the barn was cleaned up, Nora sat on the bench watching twilight creep over the field. Sarah and Kelsey joined her.

"You girls are here late," Nora said. "Look at the bats flying over the strawberries."

"We were wondering what your plans are, Nora." Sarah said.

"Well, just keep farming until they make me stop, I guess. We made a commitment to our shareholders," she said. "I guess, well, I don't know, but they say the Lord will provide even though I'm not religious."

"The Lord provides for those who provide for themselves," Kelsey said.

—— ∞∞∞ ——

Two days later, NORA was out in field with Kelsey and Sarah transplanting new rows of broccoli. Nora was nostalgic for the not-so-far-away days when her biggest problems were cutworms and potato bugs. Banes's check had cleared, so she invested in some flats. It wasn't her shareholders' fault the farm had legal problems. They deserved what they had paid for and that included broccoli for most of the summer.

Kelsey noticed the strangers first from her perch on the tractor. She whistled with grubby fingers to get Nora's attention. The men were walking the perimeter of the field with a wheeled device surveyors use to measure land.

"Finish this row," Nora said, pointing to the broccoli yet to be planted.

They continued driving down the row until all the plants were tucked in the ground. Kelsey and Sarah rode the tractor back to the barn. Nora caught the two strangers as they headed back toward a white vehicle parked in front of the farmhouse.

"Can I help you?" Nora asked.

They could have been brothers. They were tall, lanky, and weathered like they worked outdoors all four seasons. The one with hair was wearing blue jeans and work boots. The other with the skull fringe was wearing khakis, a blue oxford shirt, and what Nora thought might be the ugliest orange and green paisley necktie she had ever seen.

"No thanks. We're all set here," the bald one said.

"May I ask what it is, exactly, you're doing here?" Nora said.

"Don Perdy, Perdy Brothers Construction," he said. He pulled a business card out of his shirt pocket and handed it to Nora. "This is my brother, Ron."

"And what are you doing here?" she asked again.

"Our client has expressed an interest in developing this property. We wanted to get a sense of the landscape," Don Perdy said.

"Who is your client, if you don't mind me asking?"

Don glanced at his brother, who shrugged.

"That would be the, uh, the new owner," he said. It sounded like more of a question than a statement.

"That's strange," she said. "Last I saw the deed, I was still the owner of this property."

"Are you Nora Burgeson?" he asked.

She nodded, her mouth set in a grimacing smile.

"I can see why you're reluctant to develop here," he said. "It's beautiful acreage, good farm land."

"I had hoped it would stay that way," she said.

"I understand," he said. "We've been hired to prepare property assessments. Just some preliminary studies while the property is being transferred."

"Well, as far as I'm concerned, you're trespassing, and if you show up here again, I intend to call the Sheriff," she said.

"There's no need for that. I apologize for the intrusion," he said and started toward the road.

"Hey," she called after them as they settled into their white sedan. "What's your client planning on developing here?"

The bald one ignored her and started the car. The other one with hair stuck his head out the window as the car rolled onto the macadam.

"Condominiums," he said, nodding. The car pulled away. Nora thought her heart might break.

——— ✑✑ ———

"This situation is untenable," Kelsey said later.

"I don't even know what that word means," Nora said. "I'm just a simple farmer. It's all I ever wanted to be."

"We're left without options is what she means," Sarah said.

"That's not quite what I meant. Our current strategy is indefensible. We're just waiting for Banes to take the farm."

"What other options do we have?" Nora asked.

"This Banes is a sketchy fellow. I think we should look him up, do some research into his past, that sort of thing."

"I don't see how that can change the outcome of what happened, Kelsey. The boy still lost half his finger. I still don't have insurance to cover it."

"Kelsey's right," Sarah said. "At least we'll be doing something. Just waiting around to watch you lose this place is demoralizing."

"Honestly girls, I'm surprised you're both still here. As far as I'm concerned, you can do whatever you need to if it helps you deal with the situation. I'm going to keep working, because it's the only thing I know how to do."

That's what she did. She cultivated, she planted, she weeded, she watered, she picked, and she distributed the bounty. Volunteers came and went. Nora waited for the end. Every day, she expected the Sheriff to come with bulldozers to push her off the property.

Kelsey and Sarah came to work every day, too. Kelsey continued to deliver Mr. Banes's shares without complaint. Nora often found Kelsey and Sarah in heated discussions in the fields, but they clammed up when she approached. She finally confronted them in the barn during a downpour that halted work.

"So, what exactly is going on here? You two have been thick as thieves."

The young ladies exchanged a telling look, one Nora had come to recognize. They seemed to communicate more in those looks than could be gleaned from *War and Peace.*

"Okay, here's the scoop," Kelsey said. "I've been digging deep into the life of Mr. Banes. The guy is way shadier than even I thought. As far as him being a lawyer, that's debatable. He might have gone to law school, but, he isn't employed by any law firm that I—"

"Where did you find all this information?" Nora asked.

"I did some sleuthing," Kelsey said. "On the internet, public record and what-not."

"She's a regular Sherlock Holmes," Sarah said. "That's a good name for you. Sherlock."

"So, what else did you find out?" Nora said, growing intrigued.

"Well, Mr. Banes has a long history of litigation. He is named in almost all of the cases as the victim."

"Victim of what?"

"Malfeasance, negligence, reckless conduct, defective products, malicious conduct, malpractice, too-hot coffee, to name just a few."

"Has he won any of these cases?"

"Enough to support himself with a comfortable lifestyle. He seems to be going after bigger scores each time. What I found most alarming, though, is that his twin boys are also named as victims in the most recent suits."

"My God!" said Nora. "You mean he's using the boys as bait? Decoys? What would you call them?"

"Well, definitely victims of an incredible form of child abuse," said Kelsey.

"What about the mother?" Sarah asked.

"Yes, where's the mother?" said Nora.

"I couldn't find any trace of a Mrs. Banes, or the mother of those children," said Kelsey. "Maybe she goes by another name…"

"You don't suppose he killed her, do you?" Nora asked.

"He's a stone cold psycho, Nora. Using his own children like that, I wouldn't put anything past him," Kelsey said.

"He has to be stopped. It's criminal," Nora said. "I'm going to call the lawyer right now."

"Good luck with that," Kelsey said. "I don't think there's anything you can do legally. He's covered all his bases."

Nora left the barn and went into the house, leaving Kelsey and Sarah to put away the tools.

"The only way to stop this guy is to operate at his level," Kelsey said.

"So, what are you thinking, Sherlock?" asked Sarah.

"What do we do when the farm is invaded by destructive pests?"

"Like potato bug larvae?" Sarah said. Kelsey nodded. "We squish them dead."

On Tuesday, Kelsey bagged vegetables for Mr. Banes's shares and put them in the back of the pickup truck. The bed was full of farm tools and a huge bolt of mud-stained row cover cloth that she, Sarah, and Sloppy had removed from the cucumbers earlier in the day. Nora and Sarah were still cleaning up in the distribution room.

"Sarah, want to ride along?" Kelsey asked.

"Go ahead, Sarah. I'll finish up here," Nora said.

"Okay," Sarah said. She got in the passenger side and Kelsey drove them through the barn and out over the driveway to the street.

"Don't you want to drop off the tools in the barn?" Sarah asked.

"We'll do it later," Kelsey said, turning on the radio.

"What're you up to?" Sarah asked. "We're not going to break any laws, are we?"

"Just go with the flow, okay?"

"I couldn't stop you anyway. You're unstoppable once you've made up your mind."

"Well, it looks like Bastard Banes is home," Kelsey said. She pulled the truck into the driveway behind his BMW.

Kelsey got out of the truck. She took a hoe from the truck bed, rested it on the doorframe, and rang the doorbell. Sarah got out of the truck, closed the door, leaned against it. Through a pane in the door, Kelsey saw Banes come from the other end of the house into the living room. He wore shorts and a tank top. He opened the door and smiled.

"You two always remind me of the lesbian version of *American Gothic*," said Banes. "All that's missing is a pitchfork. That my usual share?"

"A bit more than usual, thanks to the weather," said Kelsey. "Brought Sarah to help me bring it in."

"You know where to put it," said Banes, turning around and leading them into the kitchen.

Sarah lifted the bags of vegetables from the truck and followed

Banes into the kitchen.

Kelsey got the hoe and brought up the rear. "Where are the boys?"

"They're staying with their grandmother in Boston," said Banes, reaching for a mug from the kitchen counter.

Kelsey choked up on the hoe handle like it was a Louisville slugger and swung it in a wide arc toward Banes's head. The metal cracked his skull like the carapace of an adult potato bug. Banes fell to his knees then toppled over onto the linoleum floor. Kelsey jammed the handle across his throat and put her weight on it. Banes gurgled and bled from the head as she choked him.

"Lights out time, fucker," she said.

He jerked and twitched then gave a final spasm. His fat bluish tongue hung between his slack jaws. A long goober of spit and snot mixed with his blood on the floor.

"Holy shit," Sarah said. She still had the bags in her arms and her eyes were wide in shock.

"Let's wrap him in row cover and get him out of here," Kelsey said.

"Holy shit," Sarah said.

"Put the vegetables back in the truck," Kelsey said, not wanting them to go to waste. "We'll drop them off at the soup kitchen."

They wrapped Banes up like a mummy and hefted him into the bed of the pickup truck. Kelsey cleaned up the mess on the kitchen floor. They left and drove back to the farm.

———— ∞ ————

Two weeks passed quietly on Ostrich Acres. The sun came up white-hot one morning, catching Nora, Kelsey, and Sarah in the potato rows, searching for the latest hatch of potato bugs.

"Did I tell you that the police were at Banes's house last night when I dropped off his share," Kelsey said. She plucked a bug, fat and ripe, off a leaf. It popped between her fingers.

"I hope they arrested him," Nora said. "Look at this." Kelsey and Sarah crowded over Nora. She was crouched before a waist-high leafy potato plant. "See this dead larvae? There's a bee, well, a wasp really, that plants its eggs in the larvae. The wasp eggs hatch and they eat the potato bug. Natural born bug killers."

"That is so cool," Kelsey said.

"Kelsey," Sarah said, "now I know what your nickname is. Henceforth, you shall be known as Killer Bee. Kaybee for short."

Kelsey smiled. "I can dig that."

"What were you saying about Mr. Banes?" Nora asked, moving to the next plant.

"The police said he's been missing for two weeks," Kelsey said. "Left no trace."

"I'm sure he'll show up for the hearing next week. The lawyer thinks we'll be able to stay through the end of the season in November."

"We'll just have to wait to see what happens," Sarah said. "Right, Kaybee?"

"Go with the flow," Kelsey said. "If he doesn't show up, they'll have to dismiss the case." She bent over to pluck another bug.

———— ∞∞∞ ————

Spring came over Mt. Tom, blossoming bright shades of green in its wake. Down in the fields of Ostrich Acres, Nora, Kelsey, and Sarah marveled at the luxuriant growth of this year's crop, especially the broccoli.

"I have yet to see a cutworm anywhere," Nora said, shaking her head in amazement. "Where do you suppose they went?"

"Something in the compost must have disagreed with them," Kelsey said.

"Did you see the big leg bone I dug out of the compost heap yesterday?" Nora asked. "It sort of gave me the willies. They must have buried a dead ostrich there."

A moment passed. Nora missed the shared glance between Kelsey and Sarah.

"So what'd you do with it?" Sarah asked.

"Well, bone meal is good fertilizer. As long as that old bird was eating organic, then whatever's left qualifies as organic, I guess," Nora said. "Or at least pesticide free."

On *The Day Luke Left*–

I am a hundred percent positive that if I were a character in a story, I would be the unlikable antihero. Or the unlikable main character. In any case, unlikable. As long as I was in a Dean Fearce story, though, I'd be perfectly content. All his stories usually have an unlikable or, at the very least, unsettling main character. I think it's not an inherent or purposeful affectation of the characters but rather Dean's scalpel-like pen, which he uses, unflinchingly, to render the most natural qualities.

Rather than create characters that are unsettling with their mythically-proportioned attributes, Dean uses characters that are unsettling because they're familiar. So familiar with their flaws and vices, with their judgements and fears, that it's too easy to slip into their skin and find ourselves facing things and ideas we could not face in real life. Dean's story *The Day Luke Left*, provides the point of view of an unsettling character who could be misunderstood and hated, but at the end asks if there can be redemption if there is no crime.

—*Jack Feril*

The Day Luke Left

Dean Fearce

—⁂—

I REMEMBER EVERYTHING ABOUT that day, I tell you, except that one thing. Guess I really lost it. Must have gone over the edge so far. Too far for counseling or pharmaceuticals. Once you step over that threshold of…whatever, I don't even know what to call it. What would you call it?

It's hard to say when you fall through a portal you didn't even know existed. Hard to say whether or not you've come back through it, actually back to where you left.

Get real.

You can never come back to the point at which you left. You can never experience this exact moment, because once you try it's already the next moment.

Know what I mean?

It's like standing between two mirrors, trying to figure out the beginning and the end of something that goes on forever. It turns my brain into a pretzel, thinking about it. A big, soft, warm, golden brown pretzel crusted with salt crystals. I like to dip them into gooey cheese, or whatever that stuff is. Hydrogenated emulsified chicken fat with toxic orange coloring, probably. Anyway, I'm okay with myself now. But I'm getting hungry.

Luke's been gone six days. In real-time. I say real-time, because before he disappeared, I thought there was only time, you know, tick-tock, tick-tock? The hours of the day, the days of the week, etc. Those are the kinds of thoughts that occupy my mind since I met him. I've spent every minute, real-time, trying to figure out what really happened. I wish I could tell you I figured it all out, but I can't.

I met Luke at the bookstore over by the mall, the big one with the coffee shop. I was reading the new Daredevil graphic magazine, because they don't let you read them at the comic book stores. They never bother you at the bookstore and they have awesome, comfortable chairs. It's even quiet, like the library, except when someone turns on the PA system.

"Manager to checkout three."

It's annoying, especially after you've finished off a triple espresso latte with an eye-opener. I get as fidgety as a tin gadget wound up. Luke once said it's like having a little monster inside you trying to get out. Caffeine jitters. Used to be a cheap buzz, but that espresso cost me almost five bucks.

Anyway, Daredevil was pondering his current predicament in a thought bubble. What do you do when you have a gun held to the back of your head?

I figure you stop counting your life in days, months, or years, and start counting it in seconds. When he left—I'm talking about Luke, here—I wonder what he was thinking. It's funny that DD was thinking about it, like is that coincidence or what? Anyway, Double D goes into action and dudes get whomped, big time, even though Daredevil gets all guilty and emotional about it when things get messed up.

I was sitting in the graphic novels and comics area, by the top of the escalator. It also happens to be a good place to check out anyone coming up and going down. I get a kick out of watching people slowly appear over the horizon, up and closer and finally that little step over. Sometimes geezers get it wrong and stumble off and then look around to see if anyone saw them, and I give them a big smile. It must suck to be old.

You see girls, too, at the bookstore, and you can study them, sort of, their faces and all. They give you dirty looks before they sink down to street level or skitter off to listen to CDs in the music department. I go there and listen to tunes a lot. Or sometimes I go downstairs to read what's on the magazine racks. It's a great place to hang out and it smells better than the library, which reeks of musty old books. Full of stanky homeless people and no food or drinks. Someone's always breathing down your neck with sour denture breath if you go on the Internet. They act all uppity, like anyone who wants to go online is a dirty pervert looking for titty pictures and porn.

I never saw Luke coming up the escalator. I was reading this really good part about Elektra in the DD saga. She is so hot. Ass-kicking assassin in a red loincloth with those forks she uses for weapons. Daredevil wears a skin-tight costume, but she always manages to prong him to the wall by his sleeve or something and nary a scratch on his bulging bicep. Elektra's kicking shit out of some ninja dorks, and I'm slunk down in my chair, when this guy sort of invades my little comfy space and squats down and starts thumbing through the books. Some people have no consideration. Finally, I got so annoyed I put down my book and asked him, "What are you looking for?"

He didn't turn around; he just said, "Swamp thing."

He had long scraggly hair. He was wearing a faded flannel shirt and grubby jeans. His construction boots, the yellow kind, weren't laced. They looked pretty beat up. I was wondering if he could afford anything in this store. Definitely not the coffee. I wondered if he really knew anything about *Swamp Thing* or if he was just some kind of comic collector wannabe.

"Which one?" I asked.

I thought he was about my size, but he was taller when he stood up. Wide across the shoulders. Girls probably thought he was a hunk or something. That's what I was thinking, a hunk of something you accidentally step in and have to scrape off your shoe.

"The ones by Alan Moore," he said.

I decided to postpone judgement on this guy on account of he appeared to have some knowledge of Alan Moore's work.

"What about Sandman?" I asked him.

"Sandman? I haven't read those," he said.

Chump. How could you know Swamp Thing and not know Sandman? It's like peanut butter and jelly. Okay, so I was going to write this guy off, but this is where things turned weird. The only way I can describe it is with pizza.

You order from the local franchise, and it's fun to haggle with the delivery person to give you the pie for free because it didn't arrive in thirty minutes. Either way, you feel righteous when you stiff them on the tip. If it's a hot chick, she always says she hates pizza when you offer some, which stands to reason, I guess. I might let her keep the change. If she's a Bow-Wow, forget it. I'll wait her out until she coughs up my seventy-five cents, even if she has to go back to her heap mobile to get it.

I can recognize Losers and Alkies and Bimbos, and the rest of the human nature categories. I visualize people caught in big Venn Diagrams. Your Bow-Wow pizza delivery girl could be stuck in the intersection of three circles, Loser, Bow-Wow, and Dumbshit, which explains why she's jockeying pizza for chump change. What I mean is there are sometimes crossovers, people who are multi-categorical. Like Luke.

So, you're eating the pizza, and it's okay. Spicy pepperoni, cheese with that chewy brownness, too much crust, grease and sauce dripping on your clothes, but if you consider Valentino's authentic Italian grandma-style pizza with the old lady's face right on the box? No comparison. Valentino's is the real thing, not some factory pie. And that's what Luke was like, authentic. And, he was looking for Alan Moore's books.

So, I said to Luke, "Oh yeah, *The Sandman*. It's cool. If you like *Swamp Thing*, specifically, Alan Moore's Swampy, you should be checking out *The Sandman*."

"Thanks, I will. I'm glad I ran into you. My name's Luke," he said and he stuck out his hand.

I hate touching people's hands. You never know where they've been. Like guys who don't wash up in the bathroom after taking a dump. Stuff like that makes me so mad. I always use a paper towel to open the door when I leave.

Luke's hand seemed clean enough. It was dry and calloused. From doing manual labor, I suppose.

We shook hands and I remembered high school commencement for some reason, walking down the stairs and flinging the tassel to the other side of the mortarboard with a goofy look on my face and getting blinded by flashbulbs.

"I'm Jason," I said.

An announcement came over the PA system, interrupting us.

"Wednesday Night Writers Group is meeting on the second level with Erma and Dave. Anyone interested in the meeting is welcome."

I wonder how things would have turned out if that announcement hadn't come on right then.

Luke smiled again. He had a mouth full of big white teeth.

"I'm going to check out the writers group," he said. "Come with me."

Now I'm thinking: Is this guy nuts? I don't even know him from Adam and he's already getting too friendly.

"No," I said. "I'm no good at that stuff."

"Come on, give it a try," he said. He put his hand on my shoulder and flicked his noggin sideways. I could smell shampoo and something like paint thinner, which must have been on his shirt. It stung my sinuses. "You might learn something about yourself."

I followed him to the other side of the store. He was jabbering the whole way. Motivational stuff like, "You never know your potential unless you test it."

"Oh, right, Mr. Human Infomercial. Like I need that. I work morning shift at the candle factory."

"Is that what I smell?" he asked.

"Yea, well it's an okay job except for that."

"It's like your own personal global positioning system. I bet I could track you down in this store with my nose."

"Whatever," I said.

We found where they had a couple of tables set up end-to-end in front of a big window overlooking the busy street. Standing around the table like a gaggle of hungry grackles were a pimply-faced kid with puffy eyes, fat lips, wearing a Green Mountain T-shirt two sizes too large; a pint-sized dumpy lady with cropped steely hair and bifocals on a chain around her neck. Definitely a dyke. A short one. She was talking to an obese black woman in a garish kimono that would safely canopy a large wedding party in a heavy downpour. Sitting down next to her was a living angel, I kid you not. She wore her blond hair tied back in a scrunchy thing, a younger Sharon Stone with a young Meg Ryan's perky cuteness. Sophisticated, but approachable. The rest of the crowd was a mass of faceless white hairs probably on furlough from the nearest nursing home, this being the only entertainment they could muster.

The angel-face sweetie was wearing a pink polo shirt, which I thought highlighted her warm-looking tan quite nicely. The shirt was unbuttoned and stretched tight across her chest. Maybe Mr. Human Infomercial wasn't as dumb as he looked. She turned and watched us weaving between the cozy reading chairs. Her gaze flickered across my face and I gave her my best I-am-so-cool-that-you-really-want-to-get-to-know-me look. She looked at Luke, Mr. Inspirational Hunkadocious, smiled, and looked away just a little too abruptly, I thought. I figured he hadn't scored any points.

I stepped past Luke and sat down across from her. She was doodling flowery doily designs and I was trying to think of something smart to say when Luke sat down next to me and said, "Hi, I'm Luke."

Brilliant, you Doofus, I thought, that should get her attention.

She smiled. "I'm Justine," she said. She had a little gap between her teeth. Nothing a couple of years of braces couldn't have fixed. I figured her idiot parents didn't spring for the orthodontia when she was a gawky teenager with nubby boobs and now she wasn't quite perfect after all.

"Have you been here before?" Luke asked her.

"My first time," she said. "How about you?"

"First time for me too," Luke said. "This is my friend, uh, what's your name again?"

Justine laughed, or I should say, she guffawed and snorted like a horse. "You don't know your friend's name?"

"We just met. I'm terrible with names."

"I'm Jason," I said, "but everyone calls me Killer."

I casually reached over and snatched a pad of paper from the stack in the middle of the table and one of the cheap pens. I could tell I had their attention.

"Okay, Killer," Justine said. I saw her eyes rolling like greasy blue eggs. You'd think I had a booger dangling from my nose by the goofy look on her face.

"Okay, Jason, why does everyone call you Killer?" Luke asked me.

"You know, Jason Voorhees, Friday the 13th movies. Hockey mask serial killer. I dressed up like him on Halloween once. People started calling me Killer."

Justine snorted again, but Luke apparently didn't get the connection.

"They must have made like twenty films. Didn't you ever see one?"

This conversation was getting boring.

"I never watched those movies. I was into Star Wars. Luke, I am your father," he said in a deep, sort of cheap Darth Vader voice.

"Well, you sure didn't miss anything," Justine said, "I mean, with those movies."

I ignored them both because the gray-haired dyke, who was Erma, started talking to the group. Luke and Justine were getting on my nerves. I wanted to leave, but it was too late to get out, so I stayed and listened to Dorky Dyke and her faithful assistant, Pimple Puss, talk about sappy shit that happened to them since last week's meeting. They asked us to write about a similar experience of our own. Something that moved us.

What a joke. I was thinking about moving a huge watery turd and the tremendous vacated feeling it left and thinking how I might start the story so no one would catch on until I revealed the piece de resistance, so to speak, but everyone stopped writing and they went around the table and read about their moving experiences.

It was all totally lame, full of butterflies and rainbows. The fat black lady talked about how she saw God in the way the golden rays of the sun speckled her lover's back through the window while he was sleeping and that got me thinking about her naked. Thankfully, Justine's turn came and dispelled the image.

"I wrote a poem," she said.

I felt my stomach lurch. I hate poetry. It reminds me of sixth grade English class with Mrs. Argrist. I hated that class and smelly old Mrs. Assgrass reading her poems about lovely woods dark and deep and asking what it meant. Pretty self-evident, don't you think?

So I try to retain my lunch, and I also tried not to put another strike against Justine, but it's inevitable since I already had the thought. Once the thought is thought, you can't un-think it. Strike two.

"Oh, a poet," Erma said. "How marvelous."

Everyone was smiling at Justine and she turned red, but she straightened up and cleared her throat and read her poem. I probably don't have it all exactly right, but it went something like this:

Softly swaying

Muscles resting

Floating, river tongues lapping

She caught my attention there even though I didn't have a clue what she was talking about. I looked up and the sun was behind her casting a glow around her head and blinding me for a second. She kept reading.

Against thin veneer

Quiet murmuring

Inward readiness

Bang!

I might have missed a couple lines here because Justine started reading much faster.

Sinews snap

Paddles sparking

Water churns

Heaving hammer coxswain barking

What the heck is she talking about? I was waggling my tongue at her. I checked to see if anyone was looking first, but they weren't.

A perfect tango

Dancing the surface

Only the moment

The exertion

The exhaustion

The exhilaration

Her poem sounded like a freaking orgy: tongues, cock swingings, churning to exhaustion. I thought, yea baby, you want it. But everybody just smiled and Luke said, "That's awesome."

I had a boner.

Then Luke read his paper about some quasi-religious rapture experience. Hypnotic psycho-babble would be my best description. I didn't catch it all. I was trying to make eye contact with Justine and give her the eyebrow wiggle. I didn't notice when Luke finished, but he did, and everyone was looking at me.

I nearly choked.

I looked down at the pad of paper in front of me and there wasn't anything there, so I made a story up right on the spot about a dog I once sort of had and how she was hit by a car and I watched as she rolled underneath the vehicle and out the back only to get nailed by the next car, which splashed her bloody guts all over the asphalt.

Everyone was moaning and groaning all sad and weepy by my story, but I was laughing my ass off inside because it was all bullshit. I never had a dog, but I did hit one once on my bicycle when I was a kid. It was a mess, but I didn't kill it. I would have if I'd had a gun back then. I would have put it out of its misery. Damn dog bit me and ran off limping. My front tire was bent to hell.

The group started to break up after Erma and Dave gave us a commercial trying to sell us some books on how to write fiction. Luke asked Justine if she was still crewing, and I laughed because it sounded like he said, still screwing. She said no, not since she left school. He asked her if she wanted to go for a coffee downstairs, which was what I was going to do.

"We're going for coffee, Jason. Want to come?"

"Sure," I said, and anyway, that's how we met. Luke and I. And Justine, too, though she and I haven't really hooked up. Her and Luke, they were a couple of Goody Two Shoes. They were both blind to the wilder sides of life. I was like a dark knight. Luke, he was like Daredevil.

He would track me down in the bookstore on Wednesday nights—probably sniffed me out with his nose—and drag me to the writers group. I didn't mind so much. I kept making up stories. They weren't all bullshit, either. We would hang out other times too, which was cool, because it was definitely easier to hit on girls with two of us than just myself.

The thing of it is, though, sometimes I got the feeling he was a little funny. One time, I can't remember where, I called someone a fag, sort of under my breath, but Luke heard me. "Do you know where that word comes from?" he asked me.

I said something smart like freaking ass grubbers and he got bent out of shape and gave me a lecture about the Dark Ages and burning perverts at the stake.

"Seems like a good solution," I said.

"That's harsh, Jason." he said

"Why do you care," I said. He was making me sick and I was afraid he was going to get all touchy-feely, but he changed the subject.

"Justine and I are going to the movies. Want to come along?" he asked me.

"What movie?"

"Don't know yet," he said. "It's her pick."

"What's up with you and her?" I asked him. I thought this conversation might shed a little light on the mystery of Luke's funniness.

"Good friends," he said.

"Did you get her in the sack yet?" I asked him.

He just snorted and shook his head, which I took for a no, so I beat feet out of there. Mystery unsolved until another day.

When I saw him Wednesday, I asked him what movie they had seen, though I already knew since I saw them at the theater, but they didn't see me.

"Spiderman," he said.

"MJ in a wet T-shirt," I said and whistled.

He nodded, which gave me hope.

I don't remember the story I told at the writers group that night, but I still have it if you don't believe any of this. I have a couple of Luke's too, which he gave me to take home because I didn't always understand them when he read them at the meets. His stories were like episodes of Twilight Zone, only without any plot structure. Mindless meanderings of a twisted mind. The topic that night was a journey we had experienced.

"You mean like a trip or a vacation?" I asked Erma, our dyke—I mean, writers group leader.

"That would qualify," she said. "But it could also be about a personal journey of some sort, like a quest."

"Across inter-dimensional portals of the mind," Luke said. I thought he was being sarcastic, but now when I think about it, maybe he wasn't.

Luke told a story about growing up and getting drunk for the first time when he was twelve or something and how he became a Doper for years until he had this moment of pure bliss, he called it, which changed his life forever.

What a dork, I thought.

"Why would you tell people stuff like that about yourself?" I asked him later.

"Why would I not?" he said.

"Because it's embarrassing."

"I discovered a truth about life," he said. "And I think it's worth sharing with everyone I meet."

"So what's the truth?" I asked him.

"The truth is reality may not be what you perceive it to be."

"What does that mean?"

"Well," he said, "there is the past, which no longer exists, and there is a future, which is unknowable, so all we really know is this moment."

I was getting mad. Luke was acting like he was smarter than me, and knew secrets that I didn't.

"You trying to get clearance to take off on the astral plane?" I said. "Maybe I can help."

Anyway, that's the last time I saw Luke, because he left, disappeared. Poof, like spontaneous combustion.

I'm telling you, I've tried to remember what happened that night. It's been six days, and I feel like I fell into one of his stories and I can't find my way out. I keep dropping deeper and deeper into it and I'm not sure what to do. Every moment tugs at me like sand in an hourglass and when I hit bottom, there won't be anything left.

On *When Joe's Memory Failed Him—*

Owlster issued the challenge: Hey, Dean, my Joe Memory poem was actually what I settled for instead of writing a short story titled *The Gadget.* The gadget in the story was to be a box with wires that people attached to their scalps when they went to bed. The gadget would record their dreams and put them on a disc that could be played when the sleeper woke up. They would be able to watch all their dreams on a screen exactly how they saw them when asleep. People waited in lines at stores for days to get this thing, and for some it would be a positive or at least entertaining experience, but scores of them would be driven to suicide.

—Dean Fearce

When Joe's Memory Failed Him

Dan Tompsett

Joe sat down for breakfast
with last night's dream of flying
clearly recollected and then the dream
of climbing a rock of knowledge reoccurred
and the dream of walking naked down
a city street came along then the short dreams
started rolling by. The fraction-of-a-second
dreams flickered across his eyes mind between
the completely out of character and morally
outrageous dreams that caused him to wonder
and worry. The fear dreams
of heights and crimes
came through and the earth
turned a little bit more
so that the sun
shined through the kitchen window
and onto Joe's blood and brains
sprayed all over the walls
and his bowl of Shredded Wheat.

On *For Immediate Release*–

I met Dean when I was in a dark place with my writing. Which, I guess, was an appropriate location to meet someone like him. As clichéd as it seems, he encouraged me to be myself in plot and character development. Even when he'd spent some time in my tenebrous mind-playground and discovered all the stygian humor within. Or maybe he encouraged me because of all that. Maybe I reminded him of himself.

One of the things I've come to appreciate in Dean's stories is the tightness of design. The stories are poignant, concentrated little balls of emotion and wonder aimed at the reader's gut. *For Immediate Release* is one of those stories, cleverly providing a dystopian view of a possible near future.

—*Joan Reginaldo*

P.S.: *For Immediate Release* is Dean's response to Owlster's (Dan Tompsett) challenge.

—*Dean Fearce*

For Immediate Release

Dean Fearce

———⟨ల⟩———

THE JOURNAL NEWS AGENCY…[blah, blah, blah]…The success of the Udream technology has caused an explosion of elective surgeries for the forebrain implant…[blah, blah, blah]… The popularity of Udream gave rise to a whole new medical practice overnight: wet implants.

The underground market for this procedure also exploded. Unscrupulous unqualified brain surgeons hacked their way to countless cases of irreversible brain damage…[blah, blah, blah]…

Cut to chase…*Bl-ack, ack, ack…*

When they went wireless—no tapping the wet outlet directly into the dream lobe—they couldn't make Udreams fast enough. People waited in line for days; they turned malls into campgrounds.

First month's sales outpaced all other handheld communication and entertainment devices, combined. That's right, combined.

We're talking Ubox, Ucall, Ubook, Ueverything. Trillions of dollars of every denomination. Cha-cha-cha-ching-chang-chung! Everyone had to have one! The Rapture had arrived, for Utruly.

That's a fact, Jack, because I got a clip from the journal. Burned it offline, which isn't easy to do, you know? No way I'm falling for roll-overs, get trapped in another Iraqi Corn-Fed Trans-Fat debacle.

Even went back in time. Got clips on those first wet devices you can't find anywhere now, the clips or the devices. Rich folks shelling out big bucks for a lobotomy. That was a genius scam if there ever was one.

They already had the wireless tech in the hopper. I can't prove it now. Those clips are gone like they never were. But stands to reason shareholders are wringing out the "exclusive" money before going downtown.

Clips above are corporate highlights. They're rare, been disappeared from the news factories, even the indies. You might find something scraped together on underground nets.

Be diligent.

Good news turns into bad news, and bad news doesn't last. You don't see wet plugs cruising the tunnels neither. They're all sent to the wet plug home in the sky. Didn't notice that until later, either.

When the knock-offs poured into the market. I picked up a Dreamgadget. Had the same features, and didn't brick when you cracked the operating system. Hacking into your own dreams. Sweet syrupy trans-fat goodness!

Dreamgadget wasn't sexy like Udream. Didn't have little white taps magically stuck on your noggin all night. Dreamgadget taps, held on with a clunky band of rubber, squeezed you into headache realms. That's what I thought when things went ugly.

By now, Ueveryone is having nightmares, so maybe it wasn't the hardware.

The interface? If it got hacked, for sure, but maybe it's our dreams... wouldn't that be a kick in the maximus?

The weird thing was the Upoems. Been ripping the core, flighting the output, gleaming the surreal reality of my subconscious mind's eye. Kept a notebook, filed, classified, and cross-referenced like a Freudian Apostle. All anal with organizing, like with the clips.

The flying dreams were, well, hell, they're favorites.

And the sex dreams—the more outrageous, the better! *Cr-ack, ack, ack.*

Certain sexual perversions could get you "permanently" banned. I'm not talking about the ubiquitous "I forgot my homework and I'm in my tighty-whiteys".

Just a rumor. I don't know. Never went there, and got no clips on it. None. Undercurrent whisper on the nets. Wackadoo madness anyway; how can they ban you for your dreams?

I don't remember. *Fl-ack, ack, ack.*

But the darker dreams, the murder, the torture, the serial killings, soul-rending nightmares, ugh, you got to be a hardcore freak to get off there. Takes all kinds.

When the visions started coming, I was all: What the heck? Where's this coming from? At first I thought it was poetry, but it's not, it's just terrible.

Hellish light
Flickering
Boiling
Death essence soup
Who are these people?
Dream world victims
Rendered into pieces parts
Demon spawn
Gnawing
Bloodied limbs
The Other One
Turning
unblinking eyes
shimmering
golden granite
Watching
Always
Watching
Fangs and horns

Upon a throne
Of our
Denial
Ten-hundred-thousand
Dead and dying
Maybe more
not a squeak.
Life a pitiful
Prologue
To death's
dark dreaming

It is what it is, whatever it is…you tell me. *H-ack, ack, ack.*

Dreamed about a gun. Fat shiny hand cannon. Playing with it, spinning the cylinder, pushing the miniature torpedoes perfectly into their smooth round chutes.

And dreamed of suicide, the cool barrel against my head. The explosion, the discharge ruining my skull, the wall spackled with blood and brain, falling face first into a bowl of soggy Uflakes, my breakfast.

Peace, at last.

Son of a bitch sold me the gun. He knew I was coming for it. It'll all disappear in the clips like the others.

Sm-ack, ack, ack.

On *KryogenX*–

Dean is the wise writer you should be friends with. Since I met him in 2011, I've always noticed his brilliant use of first person perspective in delivering his character's story with wit and humor even in serious situations. His example has led me to write a sci-fi thriller using that same perspective with skill. His story, *KryogenX*, is an excellent example of his work. The main character is someone you would have coffee with despite his unapologetic flaw.

—*Ernest Ortiz*

KryogenX

Dean Fearce

—◦◦◦—

WHEN I WAS A LITTLE kid, I did something really bad. It wasn't like breaking a window bad, more like burning down the house bad. The broken window got me paddled and sent to bed without supper, common punishment for breaking a window. But, burning down the house? The enormity of it defied punishment. My parents didn't know what to do. So, they did nothing. I grew into adulthood with the idea that, past a certain point, people can't understand, can't cope, can't fathom teaching *consequence* to someone operating beyond the pale.

That's why I need to tell you this, not to give you excuses like *oh, I was raised that way*, but to tell you I've grown. I understand consequences now, the difference between punishment and absolution, and my sweet, there is no absolution for what I've done. Without a doubt, I will burn in hell for eternity. It was my fault. I know it's messed up, but losing your love will give me some relief for what I've loosed into the world.

Just to set the record straight, I did get punished a lot when I was a kid, you know, for the broken window offenses. It wasn't that I was a bad kid, some kind of evil seed. I was a prodigy, a genius, and like all geniuses, immensely curious. But no common sense. Couldn't foresee the consequences of my actions, being so caught up as I was in juvenile scientific discoveries. I'm sure they have some acronym for that now, like FCDS—Future Consequences Deficit Syndrome.

Anyway, the FCDS plagued me throughout my early career, but it was also the engine that drove my success. They called me fearless, but it wasn't that at all. It was arrogance. I fear greatly for myself and what I've done, and most especially for what I'm about to do to you.

Hold on, hold on. The things you've accused me of are just stories spread by jealous peers. Mostly. Let's set things straight between us. We both deserve that much.

I never held a high school teacher's dog hostage for a good college recommendation letter. Nor did I kill said dog and use it for experiments. I was dog sitting. That damn wiener dog tried to eat an entire rotisserie chicken. After some mouth-to-mouth, things turned out fine.

Any who, despite all my shortcomings, I got into MIT when I was sixteen. My parents were glad to get me out of the house, our new house, before anything bad could happen to it. And my high school, my home town? They practically threw a parade to escort me out of the state; I already had some notoriety in that part of the Midwest. The experiment that almost went nuclear comes to mind.

But, minor mishaps is all they were. Nobody was hurt. Much. Some property damage. You know, biology was my thing, especially biophysics. The physics in biophysics could get wonky, but the biology, the living organism was completely unpredictable. You see, I'd discovered Erwin Schrodinger's, *What is Life?* It turned me into a sort of Dr. Frankenstein. To break it down, I became obsessed with the physical aspects of life: the what, the why, the who, the when, the where, and most certainly, the how. By the time I arrived at Cambridge that September of my sixteenth year on this planet, I was fully prepared to cure the disease of death.

What MIT gave me was access to information. In-depth, proprietary, and how-to information that couldn't be found even in the deepest pits of the Darknet. I was surrounded by the brightest minds across a wide spectrum of scientific endeavors, though I didn't come to appreciate that until later, being the arrogant little bastard I was. But, I knew I had to focus and let go of all the little side projects to channel all my incredible intellect and energy to a single-minded purpose: reanimation of human tissue. To bring the dead back to life.

Excuse me a moment, I have to take this call.

Yes, Daniel, it's me. You got my order? Yes, commodities. No, not shares in commodities, actual commodities. I want the compound filled with every morsel of food you can get your greedy little hands on. Weapons and water would serve us well, too. Just do it.

So, yes, anyway. Where was I?

Ah, MIT. Those surely were the most formative years. And lucrative years, too, I must say. This facility we're in now—and it's fabulous, isn't it?—was built by wealthy investors looking for a way out, you know, a way to cheat Death. Of course, we all know better now. Death is far too clever to be cheated by us mere mortals. The best we can do is make a deal.

This company, KryogenX, is the first company I started, by the way. The concept of people giving you money, then basically dying, it's brilliant, isn't it? I mean, really. No matter what the outcome, you'll always get to keep the cash. But honestly, I've never been concerned about the money. Any idiot can get rich. For me, money is the fuel that drives the rocket of scientific progress.

Were we making progress? Hell yes! Our experiments were showing quantifiable and reproducible data indicating cryogenically frozen tissue could be thawed and returned to a living state. *Living*! That was a huge hurdle. To be able to freeze and defrost living tissue and not end up with a cut of steak? Investors thought I was a god. Dollars poured into our coffers.

The thawing process was a solid win because we could put our clients into a cryogenic state before they were actually dead. Brilliant, right? So, we went to step two.

See, I had a strategy, a step-by-step plan to achieve our goal. People were saying I was crazy, a maniac, a tyrant, but I got results, and that's what counts. The few people who knew the end game thought I was nutty as peanut brittle, but I didn't care. I told them I had that baseball player's head, old what's-his-name?

Right, right, him.

So, I said we were going to field a Red Sox team of .400 hitters from our freezer full of peoplesicles. They loved that shit. Hell, it didn't matter what I said. Once I started carting out results, everyone wanted a piece of KryogenX.

Anyway, what nobody knew was we had set up a shell company, and built a family planning clinic. Right here in this building as a matter of fact.

Yep, that's right. That's how we met, Doctor. And you never knew we owned Dynasty Progressives, lock, stock, and stem cells, did you?

Fortunately for us, abortion can be a lucrative process, because step two in our program took way longer than anticipated. We burned through so much cash, KryogenX nearly went bankrupt. After some mighty lean and meatless years, we started to see results with the reverse aging treatments. We commercialized those treatments immediately and, once again, we were darlings of the One-half Percent.

Our value proposition was this. KryogenX would freeze you and keep you in cold-storage until a future came when we could defrost you and restore you to some semblance of youthful vigor by reversing the aging process. We made more money than God's loan shark with those treatments.

Of course, our marketing strategy was brilliant: Can't take it with you? Then don't go! Stay, defrost, and spend, spend, spend! This threatened havoc with legacies who were heretofore patiently waiting for kickbacks when Grandpa kicked the bucket. So KryogenX spun off investment firms and estate management services. Since you're technically not dead, there's no pesky tax bite either. More brilliance!

Things were going so well. The stem cell experiments looked promising, based on our reverse-aging treatments. But those were temporary, merely cosmetic fixes. We needed to turn the corner on the whole rejuvenation process by plugging into the code of life. We wanted to manipulate the DNA of disease and put an end to the pesky bite of death as well. And when I say we, I mean me, which was true at that time.

Anyway, we needed subjects for experiments, live people riddled with terminal disease that would allow us to freeze, thaw, and try to cure them. By any means necessary. It could get messy doing tests like that on live subjects, so we tried packaging it in something socially acceptable and socially imperative. Give us what's left of your poor sad self and you could help find a cure for the rest of the world.

It should be noted that only after we added "and you get One Million Dollars" to that promotion did the applications start pouring in. We had to build a brand new facility. Fast.

I can see by your face that you've realized your mistake in listening to the wrong people, Sweetums. Let me give you a little satisfaction by telling you how some of those...fictions grew around a grain of truth.

Think about this. If a person is put into a cryogenic state while still alive—we *stop the presses*, so to speak—what happens to that person's soul?

Okay, so you don't believe we have souls. I didn't either.

But, Tommy Javorsky—he had a nasty brain tumor and about 3 minutes to live—was the first guy we froze. Then we defrosted him, and now I'm convinced we have souls because the moment Tommy popped his head out of the amniotic regeneration tank, he tried to eat me alive.

Hang on, I'm getting to the punchline now. Mind you, this is still just a hypothesis, but I think you'll agree with my theory.

So, if the physical body is put into a deathlike cryogenic state, where does the soul go?

Well, let's say the person's soul severs the connection, because, really, why would it stay? You follow this? Good.

Okay, we have a frozen specimen and a severed connection to the soul, right? Then, we revive the body. And the body is essentially alive, but without a soul. An abandoned house on some prime real estate. So, what will inhabit it?

Well, guess what? A zombie will.

These aren't the mindless rotting soul-less foot draggers from the movies. They're literally demons-from-hell type zombies. And they need human flesh; raw, living, and marinated in the natural juices invoked by extreme terror. Apparently, it's what's for dinner for the zombies from hell. It keeps them alive.

The bad news is I made a deal with Tommy. In exchange for getting to stay alive and pursuing the endless mysteries of our expanding universe, I have to keep making more demons-from-hell zombies. And that sucks for you, my Darling, because Mr. Klem is about to pop his head out of that amniotic tank, and he's looking for dinner.

So, so sorry my love, but I have to go now. Let the screaming begin.

On *Take Your Daughter to Work Day*—

Joan has been my guide along the Caverns & Creatures road since the very first draft of *Critical Failures*, which she made me rewrite from the ground up. I wouldn't have achieved the success I have so far without her valuable input. I've done my best to offer my input on her work, which varies wildly in genre and style. Sometimes goofy, sometimes frightening, always keeping me on my toes.

I'm thrilled to be a part of her publishing debut. *Take Your Daughter to Work Day* is a good example of how she makes the reader feel nice and comfortable in her fictional world, then pulls the rug right out from under them.

—*Robert Bevan*

Take Your Daughter to Work Day

Joan Reginaldo

IT'S THE LAST WEEK of summer vacation before my senior year of college and I can't wait to get the hell out of my parents' place and back to school. It's not that I don't like being at home with the folks and my little brother. It's just that I miss my friends and this place is gouge-my-eyes-out boring.

It's suburban purgatory. Worst thing on the police blotter in this week's paper is a delivery drone crashed through someone's skylight.

Sometimes it feels like we're all drones doing our droney things until we die, and the only thing that gets our blood pumping is news from PanGen that they've anchored another planet we can harvest. There's a rush of volunteers to go study and colonize it. That would kick ass, and maybe I'll do it some day.

Mom works at PanGen but she's in the Earthside science and tech division. Absolutely no desire to go off-planet. Mom's so...Mom. She wears the same type of business-casual collared shirts, slacks, and sensible flats every day. All in abandoned-asylum shades of gray.

Her routine: wake up at six, coffee and reconstituted frozen organic fruit bowl, out the door by seven. Then she goes to the gym, comes back around five, cooks dinner while helping Ben with his homework, we all sit down and talk about our day at six, then bed by nine. Rinse and repeat, ad nauseam.

On the weekends, maybe we catch a flick, maybe go for our thousandth hike around the simulated lake, maybe buy some clothes over at Sundry. Even when she and dad are doing things like that with us though, she's not a hundred percent there. Like a bit of her is some-where else, re-reading a passage in her memory, solving an equation, making plans and contingency plans.

She wasn't like that when I was a kid. As embarrassed as I was about her being a room parent or school dance chaperone, I now realize how much I took that for granted. I lost her by imperceptible increments, like water evaporating out of a glass, here and then gone. Her disappear-ance wasn't sudden but suddenly she wasn't there anymore.

So I'm glad I'm leaving for senior year and after that, right after that diploma hits my palm, I'm jetting the fuck out of the country. Maybe... maybe even off-planet like some of my friends are planning to do. I mean, yeah, I'll miss my folks and I'll miss Ben something awful, but they're improving space-communication all the time. We'd probably be able to communicate in real time if I stay Inner-System.

It just feels like there's more to life than the same old coffee going cold in front of me, the same damn eggs, the same damn view of Mrs. Mahajan's roses across the street.

"Bonny Anne."

That's Mom's nickname for me. She must want something big.

"Yeah?" I say.

"Do you have any plans for today?" she says, putting her coffee cup down slowly. It makes no noise when it touches the tile countertop.

Both wary and excited, I say, "No. Not really."

She looks relieved and disappointed. Maybe it's the answer she hoped for but not the one she wanted. "It's Take Your Daughter to Work Day. I'd like to bring you."

I push my eggs around my plate, making an egg angel, as I pick apart what she's just said. She's never asked me to PanGen's yearly brain-washing day before; the company has a strange but effective method of maintaining employee loyalty—get them while they're young, then get their children. And she'd *like* to bring me? Why not ask if I want to go. It's nice to hear she wants to bring me. Why? Why does she *want* to bring me? Maybe it's, like, a last-ditch effort for some mom-daughter bonding. Ugh, too little too late, Mom.

"Aren't I a little too old for that kind of stuff?" I say to give us both an out.

Mom picks up her coffee mug and holds it between us. A defensive maneuver. Question is: is she afraid of something, or is she afraid of *me*?

"I'd really like you to come," she says. "It's up to you, of course, but there won't be time for us to hang out like this when you've graduated."

She says this like she's read my mind and I feel a little guilty, like I'm abandoning them or something. But she's never pulled guilt trips on me and Ben. This guilt I feel is real enough to make me agree to the damn Take Your Daughter to Work Day thing.

"Is what I'm wearing okay?" I hadn't planned on doing anything with other people, so I'd just put on some jeans that didn't smell and my UCML dance team tank top.

"Grab a sweater and I'll meet you in the car."

PanGen is a shark-blue building at the edge of a cliff at the end of a very long private road north-west. Every mile or so, there's a security gate. At subtle gunpoint even though all the guards greet her with an informal "Hey, Jess," Mom has to do a retinal scan and she and I have to get our fingers scraped for DNA confirmation.

I'm used to it. We come a couple times a year, my family and I, for the annual Christmas and Founders' Day parties, but we've always parked in the tree-bordered visitors' lot next to their multi-use amphi-theater/cafeteria/conference hall building.

Today, we veer left and continue on a patrolled road that goes right by the Pacific Ocean. I sit up, interested in the view of choppy water, dark, reflecting the ubiquitous gray of the sea of delivery drones in the sky. We spiral down under the building, deeper, deeper, for silent minutes. The car gets scanned at each level. The air grows warm. The spiral down takes us through several levels of underground parking. Five, six, seven. As we descend, there are fewer and fewer cars in the levels. We even pass two that look completely empty.

"Mom, where are we—"

"We're here," she says, pulling out of the spiral and into a parking level that has three other cars in it. She positions her car closest to the elevator door, which I'm glad about. I hate being lost, especially in parking garages because the only person I can blame for getting lost in a garage is myself.

We enter the elevator and I marvel at all the buttons by the door. PanGen doesn't advertise what it does and only a few people in the city work in the building. Many others commute via private subway lines from San Francisco, LA, and Vegas. I'd always thought of PanGen's building as a throwback to pre-21st century architecture, employing maybe two hundred people at the most, but there are over a hundred buttons on the elevator.

Mom presses number negative sixty-three.

The ride is quick. I don't feel us move. Then the doors slide open on a level brightly lit and smelling of that acrid scent of air-purifiers.

"My office is the last door on the left," says Mom. "But the bathroom is here on the right. Do you need it now?"

"No."

"Let's go to my office then."

It's awkward between us, like she doesn't know how to talk to me when we're not at home.

We pass by many white doors, more than half of them closed and their identification panels blink red. Locked. Some doors are open.

"Hey, Bill," says Mom, pausing at one of the doors. "Hey, Leslie."

This office is shared by a man and woman, both desks against the wall closest to the door, to us. On the far wall is a star chart pricked by red and green pins. More green than red.

At the two desks are Bill and Leslie, and both have attentive, shiny-cheeked, bright-eyed preteen girls with them. Good future-PanGen drones. I assume daughters of Take Your Daughter to Work Day who've probably been coming to every Take Your Daughter to Work Day since they could sit still, and I'm self-conscious of my double-digit age.

They're too young to have hung out with me at the company holiday parties so we do the round of introductions.

"This is Helen," says Bill.

"This is Emma," says Leslie.

"This is Anne," says Mom.

"Ah, the one named after the pirate," says Leslie.

Mom chuckles. "I'll see you later Bill, Leslie. Pleasure to meet your kids."

In the hallway, I say to her, "You never told me you named me after a pirate."

"I thought you knew!" she says.

I ponder this and other things we've assumed about each other as we go to her office at the end of the hall. It's small, which is understandable; she's not sharing it. Only a gray desk with a large gray computer screen on it, which is an oddly out-of-date thing to find in PanGen. On the wall behind the desk is an old bookcase with shelves dipping under the weight of astronomy and hole-to-hole physics books and, oddly, a thick, leather-bound tome.

From the closet, which is empty except for a dusty umbrella and nappy cardigan, Mom takes out a rolling chair. She puts it next to her own chair and gestures for me to sit. The large, nearly obsolete computer screen completely hides my mom from the doorway.

She turns on the ancient machine and says, "Are you keeping up with what's going on with genetics law?"

I'm surprised by such a specific question. "Yeah, I guess."

She turns toward me and looks me in the eye. I realize I haven't been this physically close to my mom, with this much eye contact, in a long time. Longer than I can remember. I feel uncomfortable but there's nowhere for my chair to roll.

"'Just because we can, doesn't mean we should,'" I say, paraphrasing an entire semester's worth of AstroBioGen 101.

Her eyes are deep and brown but with a pale blue outer ring, like an island of rich, fertile soil. Her gaze is not impatient, but there's an expectant feeling. I'm being tested. I don't know what else to say.

Her dark brows knit. "And Literature?"

"Boring. Dropped it. Not required for my major."

She turns back to the computer, which is on now, murmuring something about it being too late.

"What do you actually do here?" I say.

She glides fingers over the trackpad embedded in the fibers of her desk. "This department is Route-Analysis. We check the ebb and flow of gravity around the stabilized black holes, find patterns in it, figure out ways to maximize distance while minimizing energy. It's all very boring stuff." Under her breath, she adds "Monkeys could do it."

Another reason why I want to get away from all this boring shit. I'm annoyed she keeps doing something monkeys could do, when at home, she's always all about being better, improving, optimizing the *you* you've been born with.

"You can read that book while I do some housekeeping," she says, pointing at the leather-bound tome.

I trudge to the shelf, take it down, trudge back, plop it on the desk which doesn't bother her at all. Leafing through it, I'm surprised by the vivid pictures of people in fancy period outfits. And the book seems to be completely hand-written in fine, right-leaning cursive. Looks kind of like dad's handwriting.

While mom goes over star chart fragments, tweaking lines here and there, I skim a few of the titles. I recognize a few of them of course—the Arthurian Canticles, Odysseus, Paul Bunyan, Chupacabra, the mysterious death of Edgar Allan Poe, the moving stones of Death Valley. But outnumbering them ten-to-one are myths and stories and legends I've never heard of—Anasazi, the Devil's Graveyard, Kapre, Pangu. There's a list of dozens of "monsters," hundreds of dragons, maybe a thousand heroes, warriors, princesses, and notable witches and shamans.

The pages are thin, almost transparent. They crinkle like onion skin but they don't tear or bend easily. I come to a page marked by a green ribbon of irregular fibers. Maybe natural fibers. But that would be impossible, or the cloth is centuries old, which would be improbable given the vibrant hue. It's the green of grass grown in deep shade.

The story it marks is about someone named Princess Urduja.

I skim: Urduja was a warrior princess from a place called Tawalisi.

Racking my brain for where that might be proves futile. Then in the margin, "Pang., PHL".

Portugal? No H in Portugal.

Philippines?

I continue reading: Urduja commanded armies of mixed sexes; men and women fought side by side. She was famous for challenging anyone who wanted to marry her to a duel. She would only marry a victor.

An original self-rescuing princess. Cool gal! Why haven't I heard of her?

According to legend, she co-ruled with her father prior to the invasion and occupation by Spain.

That would be…around the 1500s. Prior to Spanish occupation… If that was like a typical colonization, local culture and politics would be decimated so the invaders could establish their own religion and culture in the power vacuum.

I skim on, looking for date of death, reason for death, descendants, or legacies but the impossible "history" continues with a long list of Urduja's accomplishments, including *ousting Magellan* and subsequent Spanish incursions, establishing strong trade with China, India, Australia—

An incessant beeping pulls me out of Urduja's story. I look up to see Mom's chair empty. The display on her computer doesn't show a star-map anymore, but a land-transport map of red, green, blue, and yellow lines that's supposed to show Pan-Pacific shuttles, California-to-New York tubes, and New York-to-Europe Faster-Than-Sound pond-hopper routes.

Instead of the usual spray of dozens of transport lines between California and the entire Russian-Asian coastlines, there are perhaps five. Eight at most.

I leap out of my seat, frightened there's been a natural disaster that's destroyed transportation centers and route markers. A closer inspection of the map shows those routes never existed! Even some of the cities are not where they should be, and some are labeled with names I'm not familiar with.

The muted but incessant beeping matches a blinking route, which I trace. The PanGen building, *this* building, across the Pacific Ocean, to the archipelago I know as the Philippines. But on this map, it's labeled Udaya.

"Anne." Mom's voice. At the doorway. I have to stand to see over her screen. She's changed her outfit from…well, I didn't pay attention to what she was wearing, but now she's wearing something weird but colorful. A purple pantsuit with a pink blouse underneath. She waves a similar outfit on a hanger at me. Mine is green and yellow.

"Change," she says, tossing it. "Quickly."

The snap in her voice brooks no questions. I drop my jeans and shimmy into the clothes that seem to be made of the same material I'd found in the book. They're soft and scratchy, heavy and light at the same time.

"Linen," Mom says, going to her closet.

There's a false bottom. She lifts it and drags out two bags big enough to carry babies. Both are blue canvas but one is grimy with strange gray and brown stains. The other looks brand new. She tosses me the new one.

"Clashes with your outfit," I say, trying to break her tense mood.

"Check your supplies. Quickly now, Anne."

I mirror her as we open our bags. We both hold up, to confirm their presence, foil-film packets of spaghetti-flavored ProCarb rations, some fruit leathers, five water-purification sticks, a couple small spray cans of SynthSkin, and things I'd only ever seen in museums: matchbook, compass, flashlight, thermal blanket, and a weird folding knifey thing.

"Are we going camping in these outfits?" I joke.

"There'll be water where we're going," says Mom, "So don't use your sticks unless you think you won't be able to get to potable water in a reasonable amount of time. Stay with me. Don't talk to anyone unless I say it's okay."

That kind of pisses me off. Since when do I need her permission to talk to anyone?

"You probably won't be able to understand anyone anyway," she says.

"What's going on? What are you talking about?"

Mom slings her bag across her chest so I do the same. She goes to the door, sticks her head out and looks both ways.

I feel like I'm a little kid again, worried of being left behind, of being lost, of losing my mother in the crowd. At the same time, I'm mad she'd make me feel like that with all this strangeness. She's treating me like a child right when I need to strike out on my own, and I tell her so.

She only waves at me to be quiet and slips out of the room.

I could stay, maybe even go home, pack up, and leave home. This is ridiculous.

But my mom is doing something out of the ordinary. She is alive in a way I've never seen before. It's like she's no longer my mother, but a stranger going off on an adventure. And she's invited me along.

I leave the room and jog down the hall of closed doors, scenting her like a bloodhound. Then I catch a glimpse of her purple clothes at the end of the hall, on the right. She's waving at me to hurry. I run to reach her.

Together, we stride down a shorter hallway of closed doors and I think we're heading for the stairs at the end, but Mom opens a door on the right, slips in, pulls me through, locks the door.

The room is small with a tile floor and a little sink, a wire rolling rack with napkins and toilet paper rolls, a musty-smelling wet-vac in the corner.

"Help me," she says.

Together, we pull the wire rolling rack away from the wall. Behind it is a mirror-door on a thin metal frame. Unlike the usual transport dock, however, this mirror-door is black. My reflection is in negative so my dark skin appears pale, my bright clothes look black.

"Stay back a sec, sweetie," says Mom.

I back up. She brushes the edge of the metal frame, activating it with DNA from sloughed skin cells. The metal frame beeps a familiar sound.

The same sound her computer had been making.

"Where is this taking us," I whisper, suspecting but not believing the impossible.

The black mirror shimmers. My reflection breaks up into millions of tiny brilliant particles until I'm looking at a field of stars.

"What the fu-udge?" I say. It's supposed to be the other side of the transport-dock, a busy terminal in Japan, New York, or Paris. There should be people on the other side, customs officers beckoning me through. There is only a black void. I feel a deep cold emanating from the door and I'm frightened that I'll freeze or I'll suffocate so I try to move farther back only to meet the cold resistance of the metal rolling rack.

"It's safe," says Mom. "Do you want to hold my hand?"

I do. Her hand is cool, and it's smaller than I remember, but then again I haven't held it since I was ten, twelve maybe.

"Don't be afraid," she says. "I'm with you."

She steps through the doorway. Space envelopes her body like black sludge filled with diamonds.

"Mom!" I whisper.

I don't know if she can hear me but her hand tightens around mine and pulls surely but gently. I watch space envelope our clasped hands and it *is* cold. As cold as holding an ice cube. It prickles, starts to hurt. The pain spreads through my body as I let her pull me through. I take a deep breath and tell myself *relax, relax* but when Space hits my face, I am suffocated. It's a cold hand pressed against my nose and mouth. I cannot draw breath, cannot see, cannot feel anything but the prickling cold taking over my entire body, and the warmth at my back shrinking, shrinking, gone.

It's cold. I can't move. Can't breathe.

Then I'm released into brightness. Heat. Humidity.

The air smells so fresh and...and salty.

"Anne. Anne, can you hear me, sweetie?"

That's Mom's voice cutting through the roar of static. And then Mom's touch on my face.

"Yeah, Mom. But I can't see. I can't see!"

"Shhh... It'll come. Don't breathe so hard, just try to breathe normally. Yes, like that."

The first thing I perceive is blue. Brilliant blues. Sapphire on the bottom, followed by powder blue, then a gradient into darker lapis lazuli. Then I see the ocean and chuckle. It wasn't static I was hearing, but the soft crash of waves on a beach of pristine white sand.

I'm having trouble getting over how clear and blue the sky is. Is this what it looks like beyond the drone sea? And because the sky is so blue and so clear, the water is turquoise, emerald, every hue between blue and green, clear enough for me to see schools of red and yellow fish dithering to and fro between strands of dark, undulating kelp.

"This is Udaya," says my mom.

"Part of the Philippines?" I say.

She laughs. "It *is* the Philippines. On *this* Earth, Udaya is the name of the country because Magellan never settled here, never claimed it for Spain, never named it for Phillip. Come this way."

I look behind me. Where the terminal end of the one-way transport would be, where I should be able to see back into that utility closet we came from, is just air. I look down. There is a small bar of rough white metal, about the size and shape of a transport terminal threshold, half-buried in the sand. Mom covers it with more sand.

"How do we get back?" I say.

"There's an out-going transport dock in the PanGen building in the city," she says. "That's one thing you need to know when you start porting from Earth to Earth. Only use PanGen docks because they'll only take you to alternate Earths that already have an outgoing transport dock, far enough away to have a stable anchor, near enough to reach within a week's worth of walking."

"What do you mean Earth to Earth? There's only... I don't understand what's happening."

"Do you know what the name of my company means?"

"PanGen? Pan-Genetics, right? You guys just study DNA on all the planets and stuff. For built-to-spec babies, new organs, curing diseases. Right?"

"Pan-Gen means all genetics. *All*. Not just from *our* universe. I didn't fully understand what that *all* meant until my team was picked to test this secret Earth-to-Earth transport and map the destinations, which was, incidentally, developed on Earth 87."

Eighty-seven earths. "So these are all like, what? Alternate realities? Like, Hitler didn't exist in one of these Earths? Or, like, the north didn't win the Civil War?"

"I'm going to skip a lot of things and get to why we're here now, Anne. You're close about these alternate realities. They are truly alternate realities, some with physics that are beyond our ken, physics *we* would call magic, just as there are Earths with civilizations who would call *our* technology magic. We are, fortunately, on the upper end of a vast technological spectrum." She furrows her brow. "That's not right either." She's led us to the edge of a forest of palm trees. We follow a worn footpath away from the beach. When I can no longer hear the ocean or see the sandy beach, we stop at a stone bench and sit.

"Stop me if it gets too technical for you," says Mom. "A spectrum is linear when, in reality, the reality you and I comprehend and perceive, the technology spanning across the hundreds of Earths is more like a fluid network of three-dimensional, four-dimensional properties—"

"Why here, now?" I say to lead her back to the answers I need.

She takes a deep breath and there's a look on her face that, despite the heat and humidity, makes me shiver.

"There is a group within PanGen that wants to go to all the Earths and harvest a specific type of DNA to use for nefarious purposes."

"Like pathogen DNA?"

"Among others. I mentioned that there are some Earths with superior technology. There are Earths with superior people too. Greater strength, greater resistance to disease, greater intuition. Think of anything that could make a human unique, magnify it a hundred-fold, and there would probably be an Earth with such a person, if not an entire country or planet of such people. The Stitchers, the people in PanGen looking to take advantage of such advantages, have already harvested DNA from Kibuka, Hercules, Robin Hood, an Imoogi, a cecaelian—"

"A cecaelian?"

"Half human, half octopus."

"I know what a cecaelian is, but that's...that's a myth. If they're somehow using the DNA of heroes and monsters, how can we possibly stop them. Is that what you want us to do? Are we here to stop them? The...Stitcher people?"

"We can't," she says. "For now. Eventually, we'll figure something out. But for your safety, don't ever let them see you. That can be both tough and easy. Tough because you might stand out in the world you're in. Easy because you might blend in, but they will too. Best thing to do is get in, get the DNA sample, and leave."

"We're...doing the same thing? How does that not make us a...a Stitcher?"

"Because we're not going to do anything with our samples," says Mom. "We're just going to build up a bank of our own...*qualities* in case the Stitchers do something our own world's defenses can't handle."

It sounds a lot like making nuclear bombs in case we get attacked by nuclear bombs. But she doesn't look like she's in the mood to discuss morals and ethics.

"What are we here to get?" I say.

"Hopefully, skin cells from the hilt of Princess Urduja's *kampilan*."

Mom opens her bag and takes out a glossy museum leaflet but I can't read the writing. The Philippines back home had adopted Roman numerals and English as one of its main languages, owing to Spanish, then American occupation, so almost everything touristy is produced in English. What my mom is holding looks like it was written in Sanskrit with Chinese and Japanese influences. She unfolds it to a central page.

"Luckily, it's a permanent display," she says, pointing at a slender sword with a long pale hilt. The blade is an almost-fluid silver. The business end is broader than the base, like a scimitar, with a fine barbed tip.

And over the whole thing is a glass case. Probably with several alarms.

"How are we even getting close to that sword?" I say.

"I've managed to secure a private viewing," she says. "We need to be there in..." She scrounges in her bag, takes out half a dozen watches in her grip. After consulting the largest one with a pink leather band, she says, "Two hours. We can make it five miles on foot in less than that, yeah?"

"Sure, Mom. Lead the way."

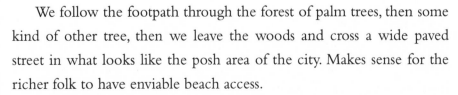

We follow the footpath through the forest of palm trees, then some kind of other tree, then we leave the woods and cross a wide paved street in what looks like the posh area of the city. Makes sense for the richer folk to have enviable beach access.

It's completely unlike any city in the Philippines that I'm familiar with. The sky continues to be blue and clear; there is no pollution from under-serviced cars or under-regulated factories. The buildings are brightly colored, dome-shaped, and rise ten to twenty feet off the floor on stout bamboo columns.

"Typhoon- and earthquake-resistant architecture," Mom says.

The streets are so clean, I would literally eat something I dropped on the sidewalk. Following the five-second rule, of course. There's no stench of urine, no black grimy residue usually creeping up the buildings in large cities like San Francisco, Boston, Manilla. And the torpedo-shaped cars are all in lanes! No one is honking, no one is straddling the lane demarcation lines, no one is running red lights strung on thick black cables between the dome-topped buildings.

I marvel at this as we walk towards where many cars are headed. Though no one obviously stares at us, I'm very aware of how dark I am compared to everyone else, probably as a result of them wearing broad-rimmed hats to keep the tropic sun off their faces. I'd questioned mom's fashion choices with these colorful outfits, but our pant suits are helping us blend in with the colorful crowd getting denser as we approach a large white dome, maybe four or five stories high not counting the foundation made of thick wooden pillars. Across the dome are broad green and purple stripes interrupted by two large windows and three sets of arched double doors.

At the bottom of the stairs to the building entrances, there's a small crowd around a person standing on one of the steps. I can't make out what's being said, but it seems like the person might be some kind of bouncer, turning people away. The crowd looks irate. Someone in a dark green uniform, the same color as that ribbon I'd found, comes out with a sign on a footed pole. The writing on the sign is translated into five languages, this much I can tell, but none of them are English. Whatever the sign reads, it placates the crowd, which disperses.

We stop in the plaza a bit away from the crowds.

Mom glances at the big pink watch again. She has a worried look on her face.

"Are you hungry?" she says to me. "Thirsty? You should eat before you go Earth-hopping. While many are very similar to ours, you never know what kind of pathogens they have that we haven't built immunity against, and it'd be bad to get the squirts while sneaking around a museum."

"Squirts? God, mom!" I say. "I'm not hungry, thirsty, or five years old. Thanks."

She shrugs and eats a Spaghetti-flavored ProCarb bar in three bites. She folds the wrapper and tucks it into her pocket. "Also, try not to leave anything from our world behind. Where is that guy? He said— Ah, here he comes. Don't say anything."

Coming towards us is a man who looks incredibly familiar, but I can't place his face. He looks like a foreigner here, though, with his light brown hair and his thin, lanky frame. Then I realize, if he were just a bit more filled out, he would look exactly like Uncle Tim from Dad's side of the family. The man gets waylaid by a group of tourists who ask him to take their photo in front of the building entrance. I tug on Mom's elbow.

"Is there a Dad here?" I say. "I mean, is there one of each of us in all these alternate realities? Shouldn't we be avoiding them or something happens with the space-time folding mechanism-thing?"

Mom chuckles. "There probably is a copy of us in some of these alternate universes. But think of that more like a happy coincidence, and not an absolute. A lot of things had to happen for you to be born as *you*. Remember that." She chases the Spaghetti bar with a mint just as the Uncle Tim doppelgänger gets to us. He smiles. The likeness is uncanny. The lack of recognition and warmth is disturbing.

He thrusts a hand out and in a too-loud voice, slowly says, "Hello. Welcome to the Metropolitan Natural Museum. We are very pleased to have you."

Mom takes his hand and shakes it. "Thank you. We've met before, Mr. Donelm." She speaks in a sane manner.

"Oh yes, of course," says the fake Uncle Tim, Mr. Donelm, in a normal volume and speed. "I'm sorry, Professor Laling. It's been a very strange morning. And this must be the guest you mentioned in your correspondence. Evelyn Donelm, Assistant to Professor Imaya. Pleasure to meet you."

I look at Mom, realizing why she'd wanted me to ask her for permission to speak. She is not a professor. So, should I use my real name?

"This is Anne," she answers for me. "She's also interested in fifteenth century dynasties."

Donelm's hazel eyes light up. His hand is clammy and practically trembling when I shake it.

"Always a pleasure to meet a fellow archeologist," he says. "Now, Professor Laling, I'm afraid there's been some, how can I put it, annoyance in the museum today. There was..."

He talks to my mom and ignores me. I can't place his strange accent. Might be the same as the language in which the museum pamphlet and signs are written.

"Was anything taken?" Mom says. She's close enough that I can feel the tension running through her body.

"Fortunately, no," says Donelm. "The guards were able to apprehend the kids before they caused too much trouble."

Mom chuffs out a breath. "Just a prank?"

"That's what we're thinking. The issue is, Professor, they caused quite a commotion and did some damage to priceless artifacts. It's quite noisy and chaotic at the moment. Are you sure you wouldn't rather postpone the visit for another time?"

"We've traveled a long way," says Mom. "We'd like to see the exhibition today."

Donelm is unreadable. He bows a little, practically clicks his heels together, and motions us toward the stairs. He and mom climb abreast in front of me, murmuring about the provenance of the sword. At the landing before the door, he fumbles with a ring of plastic badges. I glance around us and regret it. Heights taller than a few feet make me dizzy with vertigo. When Donelm opens the door, I practically push Mom out of the way in my haste to get inside.

It's blessedly cool and dry within. It's museum-dark. I take a few breaths of crisp, air-conditioned air as my eyes adjust to the dimness.

We're in a spacious atrium with cream-colored tile floors. There are beautiful wooden benches all around that look like they're polished mangrove roots bent into seat-shapes. There's a wall made of large glass panels separating the atrium and ticket booths from the museum proper. The two glass panels flanking the main entrance to the museum proper are shattered. A man in gray coveralls is sweeping the scintillating shards into the wide mouth of a vacuum at the bottom of a trashcan on wheels.

"This way, please," says Donelm. We take an elevator to the third floor.

The door opens and the hallway beyond is lit by glowing panels along the entire ceiling. The floor is a grate and I almost faint at the sight of some kind of fan several floors below us. I grab the handrail along the wall and try to rush to the solid ground of the white room at the end, but Donelm blocks my way.

"A moment, please," he says.

There's a gust of hot wind, smelling like heated metal and burning hair. It blows all over us, so hard on my face, I feel like I'm drowning. Then it's gone, and I hear the clank of metal on metal coming from far below us.

"Sterilizing wind," says Donelm. "I'm sorry, I should've warned you, Ms. Laling."

"It's fine," I say.

"Mr. Donelm," says Mom. "Could we continue our conversation about ancient methods of preservation used on the sword?"

"Of course, Professor."

They outpace me. I'm going as fast as I can, trying not to look at the huge drop below, paranoid that should I step on an unsecured panel of grating, the only thing keeping me from certain, painful death is the handrail.

Don't look down. If you fall, you'll be applesauce. You'll be grape jelly. You'll be marinara. Don't look down.

A sharp pain on my left forefinger interrupts my food-based death fantasies. I look at it. There's a piece of fine wire or something wedged in a bloody gash on the meaty pad of my finger. A drop of blood falls on the handrail I was holding, slides down its concave curve, doesn't drop immediately. I lean down, curious. The blood dangles like a pendant on a spray of wires gnarled and out-of-place in the glass and marble museum. Tracing the wires towards where Mr. Donelm and Mom are standing, I find it makes a sloppy loop around the handrail near them, slacks to the grate, and ends at a small strobing, glowing irregular shape like a wad of gum.

In the back of my mind, I see myself walking with my cut finger, walking towards and matching the strobing pace of that glowing wad.

"Mom! Look—"

The explosion blinds me, deafens me with a rocket's roar, knocks me on my ass. Debris scratches my face. I shut my eyes tight, roll over, put my hands behind my head, letting years of school "natural and man-made disasters" drills take over.

In the silence of being deafened by the blast, with terror flinging wide the adrenaline gates, my senses are painfully acute. My eyes water from the heat of the blast. All my exposed skin feels scoured with debris. My mouth waters from the bitterness of fear.

Then the heat fades and the air stills. Deafness gives way to a high-pitched ringing. I open my eyes, blink to moisten them. Blurriness shrinks to definite shapes, revealing the absence of a large chunk of hallway. The heat hadn't been just from the blast, but from air conditioning escaping through the blast zone that forms an almost perfect gap between the hallway and the room beyond.

"Mom?" I say. "Mom!" My voice sounds breathy, like music from a dirty flute.

"A-a-a-anne!" It's Mom's voice. Sounds weird.

Rising to find her, I nearly topple over from dizziness. Must've hit my head on something. I lean hard on the right hand rail and straighten.

"Mom, where are you?"

"You're facing me, Anne. Beyond the beach."

Beach? What beach? Oh, breach. I squint against the sunlight streaming in but I can't see beyond it.

"Are you hurt bad?" she says.

"No."

"Keep coming then. We haven't much time."

My body aches, but I've danced through worse. One foot in front of the other gets me to the breach.

"Don't look down," says Mom.

Of course I do, and throw up a trickle of breakfast on Mr. Donelm's headless, legless torso below. It looks like an over-microwaved burrito that's blown its ends out.

"You'll have to jump," Mom says. Her voice is closer now. And I can hear a grating alarm coming from the room she's in.

"It's too far," I say, unable to gauge its length due to the fact that it's a very, very long way to the ground and boy, if the fall doesn't kill me, it'll hurt spades.

"I know you can do it," says Mom. "I've seen you do longer *grand jetes* while hungover."

Her voice soothes me while the fact that she's seen my *jetes* means she's been to my shows or competitions.

"Okay," I say. "I'm gonna... Stand back, Mom."

I eye the pitiful clearance of the hallway ceiling and how much of the original hallway length is left. Both come up short.

"Hurry," says Mom. "We really have to go."

Putting all my trust in a higher power, I ignore all the pain and dizziness and run back down the hall. Then I sprint toward the breach and leap.

And clear the ceiling.

And realize midair that I'm not going to make it, dear God I'm not—

"Gotcha!"

I flail and somehow, somehow Mom keeps hold of my hand even though half her face looks like it's melting off.

"Come on, sweetheart," she says, grimacing. "You gotta give me a little help. Grab hold of that piece of floor. Got it? Okay, easy now. Pull yourself up. That's it. You can do it."

I'm not aware of any pain, not aware if I'm even breathing. I just stare at the floor grating curled down like a flower petal. That's probably my left hand crawling up that grate.

Then Mom yanks me up by my pant waist. On all fours, I pant a moment, get everything back in focus.

I can feel Mom rummaging around in my bag.

"Only two cans of SynthSkin left," she mutters, putting them both back in my bag.

She looks like she needs more than two. Her entire left side, the side that had been facing the blast, looks scorched off. She must've applied her own two cans of SynthSkin; her face, arm, and some of her torso look wrinkled and plasticky.

"Use it," I say.

"You might need it."

"We should be home soon, right? If you don't use it to cover your exposed muscles and stop that bleeding, you'll go into shock. I'll be... alone here."

Mom takes the cans out, sprays the SynthSkin on her. White foam flocks her wounds then melts, turning into a pinker, lighter shade of her own skin tone.

"You see that alcove to the left?" she says while spraying her leg.

The room we're in is bathed in natural light from floor-to-ceiling windows and sunlight reflecting off the pale marble floor. Reminds me of the Getty Museum in Los Angeles. I see the opening into the alcove but can't see within.

"Yeah," I say.

"Princess Urduja's sword should be in there. We need to get it."

"Won't that set off the alarms?"

She gives me a look. "The alarms are already on."

"Oh. Okay, we get the sword. Then?"

"The transport dock is three miles south of here. A building called Gichee Entertainment. Last time I was here, I programmed the dock destination to—"

There's a clamor from the other side of the breach. Sounds like it's coming from the elevator. Then a ping. Then a hiss. A hole the size of a marble smokes on the wall by Mom's head.

"Run!" she whispers.

I stumble towards the alcove she'd pointed at. Her footfalls are uneven behind me. We reach the alcove. It's empty! There's a white pedestal where the sword must've been. Shattered glass glitters on the gray marble.

"No!" says Mom. She quickly goes behind the pedestal, checks the ground, then sweeps her hand along its top, like she thinks the sword might've turned invisible. "There's nothing left."

There's another ping, another hiss, and a hole appears on the pedestal in front of my mom.

"People are shooting at us," I say.

Mom says nothing, only balls her hands into a fists on top of the pedestal.

"We were too late," she mutters. "How could that be?"

"Mom! People are shooting at us."

From the room behind us comes a dense blue fog. My throat starts to itch, and my eyes water. But I see what looks like a door in one corner of the alcove.

"Come on, Mom!" I say, pulling her from behind the pedestal. Then I see the hole in her chest. A perfect hole, leaking bright red blood down her pink and purple outfit. Oh God, it clashes. "It'll wash out, Mom. Mommy, it'll wash out."

"Oh sweetheart," she says, collapsing to the ground, pulling me down into the burning blue fog.

I can't see her, only feel her hand, her arm, her messed up face. I try to staunch the flow but it must be coming out the other side too. Hot blood soaks through my linen pants, making my knees squelch against tile.

Throat hurts. Eyes are watering bad. Everything burns inside me.

"Mommy," I try to say.

She's too heavy for me to drag. Either I leave her or we'll both go down. It's such a clear choice but I'm finding dozens of stupid reasons to stay. Most of them wordless. Most of them locked in my heavy, thudding heart.

Go! I yell to myself. *Go, you moron!* I cough in the fog. A ping, then a hiss on what might be the pedestal beside me. So I get down prone on the ground and use my forearms to drag myself toward the alcove door, trying to make as little noise as possible but the urge to cough is making me chuff through my nose. Is it enough sound?

Ping! Hiss!

My forearm gets scalded on a marble-sized hole in the floor.

Everything gets darker because I'm holding my breath, trying not to breathe the harsh blue fog. The darkness creeps in. There's a buzzing in my ears that drowns out the alarm. The door is yards away. Too far. Can't find it. Won't reach it.

Ping! Hiss!

Black.

It sounds like a vacuum running very close to my head. And it's bright, so bright. Car headlights on high beams. A cold, stinging gel gets jammed up my nostrils. Hurts bad! Try to yell but a moist hand clamps over my mouth.

"Breathe through your nose," says Mom.

Mom?

Looking down on me.

Everything must've been a dream. Or I took a bad fall during dance practice. Concussion. Must be. My eyes water again, this time with tears of relief.

"Can you walk?" she says, taking her hand away.

I open my mouth to speak, she covers it again.

"Just nod or shake your head."

I nod. She stands up. Weakly, I get up too, wanting to hold her hand or use her shoulder for support but she seems weird. Aloof.

It wasn't a dream. We're on the street. At a different plaza. People aren't looking at us; they're too busy taking photos of the gutted museum. It hadn't been one explosion, but many. The white dome looks like swiss cheese, with black smoke billowing out of the irregular holes.

"How'd we get out?" I try to say. Big mistake. I taste blood. Feels like I deep-throated a sandpaper dildo. I turn to ask Mom if she has something for the pain, but she's gone. Threading through the gaping crowd. Would've lost her if she hadn't been the only person in the area moving *away* from the museum.

I run to catch up with her, noting a long cylinder she has strapped to her back, and that she has somehow managed to change out of her bloody purple and pink linen outfit into something somber gray and slick, something more like what I'd wear back on our Earth. There's no way I'm gonna yell for her to wait; I'm spitting mouthfuls of blood on the pristine sidewalk. Only thing I can do is run, weave around bystanders, dodge medical personnel running in the opposite direction. Thinking of it as a ballroom dancing competition makes it easier to twist, jump, and sidestep. There's also the added advantage of moving in the space she clears for me. I reach her, grab her elbow, motion for her to stop.

She looks at me with surprise in her eyes. And a bit of...fear?

"What are you doing?" she says.

I gesture to my throat and spit out some blood, screw my face up to show her my pain.

She shakes her head. "Fine. Come with me. I'll give you something for the pain when we get to my supply chest, but after that, we part ways."

Part ways? Supply chest? She's also going in the opposite direction of where she'd said the transport dock was. We've headed north, not south. And the way she looks at me...like I'm a stranger.

This isn't Mom. My mom is dead. We left her. I left her. On the floor of that strange place in this strange country that shouldn't even exist. The grief is cruel, doubly so, catching me off guard at the happiest moment of my life.

There's a flicker of something on her stoic expression, gone before I can understand it.

"Come with me now, or we part ways," she says.

I nod, gesturing for her to continue, wondering if she knows who I am. She doesn't seem to.

She walks a brisk pace like a woman trying not to be late to an appointment. We go down alleys and narrow side streets but there are a lot of people going to and from the little boutiques. I duck my head to hide my dirty face and bloody mouth and front. Now and then, I glance up to make sure I'm still following the woman.

We seem to be leaving the city and entering a park-like housing complex of lush green lawns, hibiscus trees, tall shrubs with fragrant white flowers, pink and turquoise dome homes. It's almost magical, how suffused with life it is. There are dragonflies and birds at every bush and tree, dogs in every yard. The woman turns the corner up ahead. I'm behind a few yards. By the time I get to the corner, she's gone. I can't see her down any street at the intersection.

Then I hear her angrily yelling in a language I don't understand. There! That van. There are two men and a dark-haired woman trying to shove her through the side door, but the woman's all legs and arms, like a star-shaped peg being forced into a square hole. Strong, too, to take on three people, but not strong enough to overcome them.

I hesitate a moment. This woman's not my mother. She's shown me a bit of kindness but I don't owe her anything. And who am I to go up against three kidnappers. Three fit, muscular kidnappers.

"Hey!" I yell to prevent more cowardly excuses.

The three kidnappers look around.

"Hey, you shitheads!" Don't know if they understood that but they home in on my voice. Some people are coming to their doors and windows. "Help us! Please, help!" I implore, pointing at the kidnappers who are trying to push the woman in with renewed vigor. My panic and yelling and the commotion are riling up the neighborhood dogs who, whimpering, pace their yards and claw at the fences.

Their owners hover in the darkness of their domes.

"Help! *Ayuda!* Um... *J'ai besoin d'aide!*" I yell, making the dogs bark and bay. That's all I remember, and it doesn't help.

The neighbors shrink away from the windows, drawing their curtains, calling in their dogs.

Their dogs!

I open the gate of the fence nearest me. A white dog shoots out the yard and darts across the street to the van. He immediately goes after the female kidnapper who wards him back with the cylinder the woman had had strapped on her back.

I open the next gate, and the next, freeing a retriever and a collie. The retriever runs off, but the collie dances around me, both dogs not as smart or helpful as the white dog. Opening more gates draws more people out of their homes who are yelling at me, threatening me with sticks, holding up their phones to signal they've called the police or something. I don't care. There are three dogs going after the kidnappers now, and five barking and jumping and dancing around me. I run across the street, taking the five dogs with me.

"Attack!" I yell, pointing at the kidnappers. Two dogs bark and lunge. Three dogs start humping whatever leg they can get. One of the legs is mine. I grab the corgi, try to hurl it at the female kidnapper. Fucking dog weighs a hundred pounds. Best I manage is lobbing it at her. The weight pushes her back against the woman, who pivots, letting the kidnapper roll off her and into the van.

The woman grabs the kidnapper's legs and throws them up, rolling the female kidnapper completely into the van.

"Attack!" I scream at the dogs, tasting blood misting from my raw throat. They probably don't understand but like most dogs, they're responding to the frenzy and fear-sweat in the air and the tension in my voice. The smaller ones are getting trampled so I toe them out of the way. The two male kidnappers aren't too bloody but they're pinned against the van side, smearing red streaks on the glass and doors.

The woman, breathing hard, wades into the crowd of dogs. She wrests a gun off one of the kidnappers.

Ping-hiss! Ping-hiss!

The two men slide down to slump against the van tires. Because their heads are bowed, I can't see the holes, but wispy steam comes off their hair. The dogs are as shocked as I am. We are silent. The woman slides the van door open, aims into the gloom.

"Don't," I say. "You don't have to kill everyone."

Ping-hiss!

If I'd known the kidnappers had had guns, I might not have let the dogs loose for fear they'd be shot. Why didn't the kidnappers just shoot the—

The woman then turns that terrible weapon on the dogs that had just helped us. She stares down the muzzle of the gun at the white dog who'd been first to her aid. I put myself between them.

"Move aside," she says. "We have to go."

"Then go!" I say, throat aching, heart aching. "If you're this fine with killing, I don't even want to know you. Just go already."

Her dark brows furrow. "You don't belong here. You'd be so quick to sacrifice your way home for these mutts?"

"I don't think you belong here either. But if you're here and I'm here, there are others around that can help me. You're not my only option."

She smirks. It's an expression I've never seen on my mom's face and serves only to make this woman more of a stranger.

"Little girl," she says. "You have no idea what you've fallen into."

"I agree. This is my mom's thing. *Was* my mom's...This isn't...It's all I've got right now. I just want to go home and tell my dad and my brother...and tell them..." I sniffle. Tears course down my cheeks, snot runs down my nose, but I'm a hot mess anyway. And who am I trying to impress right now.

"Your dad and brother?" says the woman, staring a million miles away.

"They'll need me." I'd had no purpose, and the very idea of having kids and starting a family had been in the far distant future, but now I realize how much my family means to me, especially my little brother. Being his older sister is one purpose out of many that I'm suddenly seeing. "If you can help me get home, cool. But not at the expense of other peoples' lives."

The woman tucks the gun into her waistband then holds out her hand. "Jess."

That had been my mother's name.

"Anne," I say.

"After the pirate?" says the woman, Jess, softly.

"Yeah," I say. I'm curious how she would know. Did she...could she possibly have an Anne in...wherever she came from? She'd shown interest when I mentioned Dad and Ben, too.

But now's not the time, and I don't feel warm enough towards her to talk about my family or my recent loss. Make her work for it.

The sound of sirens is familiar but also alarming. People have come up to their fences, armed with those thick wooden sticks and even, strangely, narrow swords that look like scimitars. But no one has approached us. They call to their dogs, who mostly heed or wander away.

"We should go," I say.

"The locals won't bother us," says Jess. She's dragging the female kidnapper out of the van. "They won't do harm unless we're on their property. Streets are neutral zones. This..." She gestures at the bodies. "This is really rare. This country only has maybe one, two homicides a year. Man, this'll be a good news day."

"I doubt it's good news for anyone," I say.

Jess chuckles. "You coming or what?" She nods at the passenger side door.

She'd dumped the woman's body next to one of the male kidnappers. Too far to jump, forcing me to step on the man's chest in order to get in. I'm dizzy with the horror of it.

The weird white dog whines and paces to come with me, but I see its mistress at the gate of her fence.

"*Kaya!*" says the owner. "*Ibit! Ibit!*"

"Go home," I say to the dog.

It just paces and whines even more.

"What's the problem," says Jess.

"That dog won't go away."

Jess knocks me away from the open window, pins me against the chair with her right forearm, and shoots at the dog.

I can't breathe.

Then I hear the sound of claws on pavement. Jess releases me. I look down. There's a smoking hole near where the dog had been.

As we drive off and turn a corner, I see the owner opening her gate and the dog prancing through.

"I didn't kill it," says Jess.

"I know."

"This time."

———— ✺ ————

The sirens are getting closer but Jess drives like a grandma, caressing the wheel and softly singing, "I got a va-an. I got one of your va-ans. Hopefully with gu-uns."

If we get caught, I literally can't talk my way out of this situation unless I throw her under the bus and claim she's kidnapped me. My legs start to shake. Nervous habit. Jess glances at them, looks at me an uncomfortably and unsafe long moment for someone who's driving, then goes back to staring at the narrow road without saying anything.

"Where are we going?" I say.

She doesn't respond. I literally hear crickets. We're driving through a large, wooded park. She slows the van, checks the mirrors, looks all around.

"See anyone?" she says.

I check. "Nope." I wince at the pain in my throat.

She flicks the windshield wiper bar on the steering wheel down five notches. Panels on the center console roll up and back, away from a screen about the size of a cereal box coming out. Magic!

Jess touches the screen. It flares to life, showing a star map with a blinking solar system. She pinches the display until the solar system shrinks to a tiny glowing star. Then she chooses another star, expands that into a solar system, expands that to show a planet. Looks like Earth with its water, dark lands, streaky swirling clouds.

I say, "Is that—"

She touches the planet. Everything flashes white. The crickets are silenced like there's a predator in our midst.

— ∞ —

Almost immediately the flash subsides. As my vision returns, I can tell we're not in Kansas anymore. Are we even still on Earth? Well, the Earth my mom had taken me? It's impossible that Jess and I went through a transport dock at the same time. Even more impossible for something as large as a van to go through one. And yet here we are, no longer in a jungle on a bright afternoon.

The van shudders then stills with a sigh and the star map darkens. Jess presses the start button. Nothing. She tries the star map pad. Nothing.

"Goddamnit," she says, slamming a fist on the steering wheel. "Anti-theft device. Strands an unidentified user off world. Sacrificed my supply trunk for this. That means I don't have anything for your throat. Can you tough it out?"

I nod.

She peers at the black-clouded sky beyond the windshield. "At least this is the destination I wanted."

Hell. For all intents and purposes, this is what I imagine Hell to be. Dark and hot and suffocating with the smell of sulfur and brimstone. Whatever brimstone is. The stench and heat seeps into the van. Through the windshield, I can discern what might be a street flanked by the feet of skyscrapers, but I can't see their tops which are shrouded in a black mist. The skyscrapers seem to be freakish living things with reddish orange lights in the windows flickering like a hundred eyes blinking.

"Where are we," I whisper, wincing again.

Jess takes a deep breath. "Earth Five-Eight-Three."

Five hundred and eighty-three earths. I don't remember what number earth we were just on. Worse, I can't recall if Mom ever told me what number our home-Earth is. And Mom said I'd be okay as long as I only used PanGen transport docks because there would always be a way home. Jess and I didn't use a transport dock. Mom said... Mom... My calm erodes. I hyperventilate and gulp bigger and bigger breaths. Panic and grief set me atremble.

I seize the grief, stuff it into a mental box, and duct tape it shut. Then I put that box in another box, and another. The grief abates but I'm still wheezing.

Jess leans over and rummages in the van's glove compartment, nothing but bits of paper and gum wrappers. Then she looks in the back, gaze darting quickly.

"Damnit!" she says. "No masks. But...I hope that's what I think it is." She crawls into the back.

I wasn't imagining it. It *is* getting harder to breathe but Jess seems fine. I peer into the gloaming outside. There's one heavily shrouded person walking towards a building to our left. Another crossing the street. Both don't appear to have any issues breathing.

Jess comes back with a black cloth lunch box. She unzips it, flips open the flap. There are compartments and labels, but it's mostly empty except for maybe a dozen silver squares the size and shape of condom packets.

After rifling through them, Jess holds one out to me. There's small writing on it. Looks like the same information in ten different languages. Luckily there's an English version, and a Spanish one.

"327MB1892" seems to be the most important information in bold.

"If I'm right, that should help you breathe in locations with lower oxygen content," says Jess.

"And...if you're...wrong?" I say.

She gives me a half-smirk. Feels condescending. Mom never smiled that way. "Then you're dead, and that's that." She finds a square for herself. Before I can see its number, she's opened the pack. Within is something that looks like a nicotine patch but bright red. She rubs it quickly between her hands. It starts pulsing red like a small heart.

I do the same with mine as I watch her roll her shirt up, revealing a lean, flat stomach covered in those patches. Some are bright red and beating fast. Others are dark purpley red and beating sluggishly. Three are black and not beating at all. She peels those off and sticks them in a pants pocket, then sticks the new patch on some bare skin.

Then she gives me a *hurry up* look. Clumsily, I shove my hand under my shirt and stick the patch on my stomach. Breathing immediately gets easier. The raw pain in my throat fades to a dull ache.

"Tell me when you start to feel the downside," says Jess, stuffing the other packets into a myriad of pockets on her slick gray jacket.

"Downside?"

She returns to the back of the van, puts the cylinder strap over her head, quickly rummages through compartments in the seats and panels. "Medications have side effects, Assets have Downsides." With one hand, she lifts up her shirt, flashes the patches at me. "These are Assets." Without even looking, she points at specific ones. "Strength, Agility, Intuition, etc. The Downside is—"

"The opposite effect?"

She pauses, gives me that condescending half-smirk again. "No. Each Asset is derived from the DNA of a…a…easiest thing to call them would be heroes. No one, at least no one in any Earth involved, has been able to isolate the specific sequences to incorporate the desired qualities into a person, hence, the infusion patches."

"Yeah, but what do you mean about the Downsides?"

She seems to be done going through the van and she's strapping and pocketing a bunch of weird tube things that look like shorter versions of her cylinder and puffy black envelopes.

"Coming with me?" she says, opening the van door.

A blast of hot air saps my eyes dry. This dead van is like a sarcophagus.
"Yeah," I say.

We leave the van and I follow her closely to avoid losing her gray form in the dark street.

"The Downsides?" I say when she's slowed enough for conversation.

"Everyone has flaws," she says. "With heroes, they can be tragic flaws. Achilles had immense strength but using it caused decalcification of the bone. Used judiciously, and with other Assets balancing it out, it can be beneficial. But in our initial experiments, when we didn't fully understand..."

I picture a human quickly losing bone density, and the worse picture of if said human were lifting a car or elephant at the time. Then I can't help but imagine the legends and myths I'd only known as stories and fables, imagine the heroes in them and their tragic flaws. Hercules and his madness, Sepnenmar's insatiable lust, Wen-shi's suffocating agoraphobia.

My heart beats so hard I can almost hear it in the eerie silence. I'd been afraid of external forces and now I fear a betrayal from my own body.

"What did you give me?" I say.

Jess glances back with that despicable half-smirk. "Let me know if you suddenly crave raw flesh."

Her saying it puts a picture in my head. A thick slab of marbleized steak ready for the grill. My mouth waters. I choose to think of it as anticipation of the sizzling and the smell of barbecue char. Yeah, that's it.

We leave the skyscrapers behind and enter an area that reminds me of San Francisco's old industrial district except there aren't any cars on the streets or alleys, there's no colorful graffiti, and all the windows are boarded up but there's weak white light shining between slats. Jess goes to one of the bigger four-story buildings and unlocks the door.

"Come on, come on," she says, beckoning frantically.

I squeeze in between the door and doorframe, helped by a hard shove from Jess. Behind the door is a broken vending machine full of cinderblocks, cemented to the floor, preventing the door from opening more than the width needed to let people, slipping in sideways, enter one at a time.

It's a small, dull green reception area with doors to bathrooms on either side and an open elevator shaft at the far end. We take the stairs behind the door to the right. It's a gloomy stairwell of linoleum steps and pipe railing, cool but moist, and it smells like old pee. Reminds me of the never-quite-clean smell of doggie day care facilities back home. On my Earth. Mom's earth.

God, there won't be a grave for me to visit.

I wipe away a tear and stifle a sniffle. Unnecessary in the clamor of Jess tripping on a step and crashing against the metal banister. Her cylinder sends a clang echoing up and down the stairwell.

"You okay?" I say.

"Can hardly see," she says.

"Yeah, it's kind of gloomy."

"It's nearly pitch black," she says. "You can see fine?"

"I can see okay." I could see better than okay.

"Huh. Must be a bonus to that Asset."

Movement above catches my attention. Something slides over the edge of a landing two stories above.

"You woke something up," I whisper.

Jess flattens against the wall, pulling me away from the stair edge. She lets out a perfect imitation of a rat squeak. From above, an answering *scritch* of coin on cement. Jess squeaks twice. A bright white light beams down the center of the stairwell, blinding me.

"Took you long enough," comes a male voice.

"Complications," says Jess.

I feel the air move, a blank space where she used to be.

"I can't see," I blurt out.

"The light?" says the voice above. "Interesting."

The light shrinks to a pencil-thin beam, which seems to be enough for Jess without completely blinding me.

We reach the landing of the fourth floor. There's a man in a gray suit-thing similar to Jess's waiting for us. Maybe a few years older than me but his shaggy dark brown hair, wire-rimmed glasses, and the bags under his large blue eyes make him look older. He turns the pen-sized flashlight off and slips it into one of his many pockets.

"You the complication?" he says to me.

Jess grunts.

The man makes a strange face at Jess but she's already entering the room. "Hey Jess, your complication looks an awful like—"

"What the fuck, Kyle," says Jess. "What the fuck."

"Uhhh..."

I enter the room after them. It's vast, maybe takes up the entire level, with sixty percent of the space used by a raised rectangular indoor garden in the center. Large grow lights, the source of the light shining between the window slats, are suspended above rows of lettuce, tomatoes, kale. Closest to the door are two lab tables and a perimeter counter with small refrigerators, test tube racks, microscopes, replicators, and dozens of tubes and cubes I can't identify. In a corner, there's a photo of four dark-haired people in dark clothing taped to the wall. I want to take a closer look but Jess and glasses-guy, Kyle, are having an argument of increasing intensity.

"There's no way we can grow enough food to feed this many people!" Jess says, pointing at the dimness beyond the bright glow lights.

I'd thought the humps were piles of old clothes or garbage bags but now I can see pale faces as they turn towards us. A dozen, maybe twenty adults, not counting about a dozen children from toddler to teen.

"They're homeless because of us!" says Kyle. "Our last skirmish with the Stitchers blew up half a block of living quarters. These are the survivors. Survivors! Besides, you're one to talk." He tilts his head towards me.

Jess wipes an arm across one of the lab benches, clearing it of papers and beakers and cubes that flutter and shatter on the floor.

"I had to," she says through gritted teeth. She slams down the cylinder she's been carrying since the museum. "Your theory worked. We just didn't take into account all the variables."

Kyle looks affronted. "I did so!"

Jess's gaze flicks to me, then back to the cylinder. "I used the stolen transport pad you modified to go to an area we thought was too backwater to draw anyone's attention. We were wrong. I set the traps for the Stitchers you said would come. And they did. But in between, that trap was activated by..." She rubs a hand over her face.

"By me," I say. "You killed my mom."

Jess takes her hand away, revealing a face so much like my mother's it's like a punch in the gut.

Kyle clears his throat. "So you brought her here. Well..."

I lunge for the cylinder. Something rattles within, rolling against the leather container. With a sinking feeling, I twist off the top half and pull the two ends apart, laying a slender saber or scimitar or whatever on the table. The blade is shiny silver. The hilt looks like it's made of bamboo.

Jess reaches for it. "Don't touch the—"

I grab the hilt.

"...hilt. Ok, that's fine. Just put it back down, Anne."

I wave the sword, testing its heft. It's lighter than a tennis racket.

"This is mine now," I say. "I'm claiming it for my mom." Doing so feels like I'm putting my boxed grief into another box, steel-lined, with handles. Makes it manageable and easier to bear. At least for a little while. My thoughts are a little clearer and I'm calm enough to accept that I could eventually find my own way home, but Jess and this Kyle guy could help me, and it'd be stupid if I don't use whatever help I can get. And it would've disappointed Mom if I don't offer help if I can.

Jess leans into my space. "Now see here—"

"Let her have it," says Kyle.

"Whatta ya mean—"

"You never wanted it in the first place!" says Kyle. "That was supposed to be just a reconnaissance mission. Test out the mobile transport platform. We never agreed to those traps. I never—"

"This isn't a...a democracy," Jess says. "I took you along. You work for me, or you get gone."

Between their jabs, I hear an incessant, achingly familiar beeping I think will haunt me forever. I put the sword back in its container and strap it across my chest. They're talking about the survivors now, the people huddling against the dark sides of the long loft. The beeping continues. It's coming from a stack of papers near a DNA replicator. When I get near, it's not a stack of papers but a stack of paper-thin plastic sheets. A dark blue one is flashing a bright red dot in the corner. I take it out.

It's a star map but more sophisticated than any I've ever seen. For one thing, it's on material that weighs and feels like one of those cheap plastic cutting boards I used in my dorm room freshman year.

"Hey guys," I say, turning around to face Kyle and Jess.

As I turn, the image of the star map moves too. I move it around some more. It looks like it's showing me the stars and travel routes of whichever direction I'm pointing at.

"Guys, this thing is beeping," I say. "And uh, something's coming this way. Fast."

"Yeah, we know," snaps Jess.

"I've been tracking that thing since *it* started tracking us," says Kyle. "Don't worry. Won't be here for another three days, a week on the outside. We'll have moved camp by then."

"How long does it take you to move camp?" I say. "Cuz guy, this thing's coming in fast and hot."

Kyle takes it from my hand, orients it so we can see the large white blip moving at a bit of an angle instead of right for us. "We'll be fine," he says.

"My mom works—used to work—the star-nav at home," I say. "I know acceleration when I see it. And I've seen her calculate the arrival of a shipment to the hour. You can't just account for the gravity, the atmosphere, the big things. You have to keep in mind the little tidbits— what time of day it is, what season, the amount of pollution or radioactive activity."

"I *did* that," Kyle says. Two red squares flare bright under his gray shirt and pulse quickly. I wonder what Assets he's using to be triggered by anger or fear.

"Did you check it again since *I* got here?" I say. "We used a freaking van to get here. That's a huge power draw."

Kyle shakes his head and he gets a little pale. "We've transported bigger things than that. But the fact that you brought a van here. *Their* van. Damnit, Jess, you've led them right to us. They have our location. They're coming at full speed."

"How many days do we have," says Jess.

"Hours, not days," says Kyle.

"Oh, quit being so melodramatic," I say. "Twenty or thirty hours."

"That's enough time to relocate everyone if we go to mid-tech," says Kyle.

Jess takes a long look at the people huddling in the dark. Then she looks at me and Kyle, and it feels like she's judging our worth so I stand a little taller and feel like I'm betraying my mom at the same time, wanting to go with this woman who killed her. But *this* Jess is my ticket home. She can send me back to Dad and Ben.

But all those people...

"Pack our things," says Jess. "Pack two of each plant. That should be enough to feed three people."

"But what about everyone else," says Kyle.

"We're not going *backwater* for them," says Jess. "We're not going backwards."

With one last cold look at me, she leaves out the door we came in. Kyle slumps and leans over one of the lab tables.

"What does she mean by not going backwater?" I say.

Kyle gives me a half-smirk. On Jess, it's caustic. On Kyle, it looks like he's letting you in on a joke.

"That's Jess-speak for mid-tech. And that question reveals you're from mid-tech or," he clutches his chest in mock alarm, "good God, low-tech."

"Be serious."

He taps a rhythm on the star map sheet we were looking at. The display darkens to black. He draws a white circle in the center.

"This is Earth in a low-tech universe," he says. "Maybe nuclear wars wiped out the centers of developmental tech. Maybe a comet killed half the population. What have you. Point is, they're really easy to get on because they take very little energy to get to. Tradeoff is, there won't be a lot of useful tech once we get there. We'd be trying to build a PCR with popsicle sticks and wood resin."

"Seems like everything's got a *downside*," I say.

Kyle looks at me, gets my drift, does that half-smirk. He draws three concentric circles around the white circle on the plastic sheet. With another rhythmic touch, the circles come to life, emanating from the planet like tidal waves.

"This is a basic mid-tech Earth," says Kyle. "We're talking maybe the start of inter-stellar travel. Maybe some folks playing around with black holes or starting genetic splicing. These rings here would be things like lines of defense, higher levels of radiation, depending on their modes of transport or sources of energy, etc. On our end, it takes a greater expenditure of energy to get through all those defenses and variables."

Then he draws more and more concentric rings, sometimes overlapping. Once animated, it looks nearly impenetrable.

"This is a high-tech Earth," he says. "There *will* be defenses because they *have* done interstellar travel, and they've found neighbors. You know what they say about good fences making good neighbors. Interstellar transportation usually uses incredible amounts of radioactive fuel, some of which your earth probably hasn't discovered yet. Maybe won't ever discover. Moving between high-tech Earths requires energy we don't currently have. The thing is, the farther you move backwards on the tech levels, the harder it is to go forward again."

I take all this in to help me figure out how to get home. "How do the Stitchers get around all that?"

Kyle shakes his head and shuffles the pile of plastic sheets into a blue backpack. "We haven't figured that out yet."

Wanting some time to think and process everything, I leave him to pack.

Though the loft is spacious, it feels small with all the plants and the timid people in the shadows. I still can't make out their faces because the light is so bright above the lab station. There's another light source, though. A dim blue light outlines the shape of a door on the right side of room, between the lab space and where the timid people are sleeping.

I head there quickly.

The door handle turns easily but the door is heavy. The area beyond is a sheltered fire escape balcony about five feet out, ten feet wide. There are two wooden boxes, and between them is a big wooden spool, the kind used to hold large cables. I sit on one of the boxes and stare out at the twilit street.

The sky gives no indication of night or morning, but there's a faint orange circle through the low, thick black smog. I look down at the street again. There are no trees, no shrubs growing against buildings, no grass or weeds pushing through sidewalk cracks. This whole world is such a stark contrast to the one I'd just been in with its lush streets, bright blue sky, and abundance of colorfully-clad people.

And then home, a world that seems to be between the two, creeping towards a world like this with its silvery sky full of delivery drones. I can't remember the last time I saw an unblemished sky in my home earth. Though it's dark and ugly, I miss it. I miss Mrs. Mahajan's stupid roses. And I miss my little brother.

I miss him more than I miss my mom. And I'm sorry for that. I don't know why I don't miss her as much as I think I should.

I miss Ben. I miss the chubby toddler Ben, and the annoying ten-year-old Ben, and the begging-for-rides Ben, and the Ben I might not see anymore now that he's finally old enough to actually have a cool conversation with.

"Knock, knock," whispers Kyle, pushing his head through the gap.

Hastily, I wipe my tears away. "Yeah?"

"I'm sorry to bother, but I thought you'd want to change into something cleaner." He holds a pile of folded clothes at me.

"Thanks," I say, taking it.

"If it's not... Do you think I could take a look at that sword?"

I hesitate.

"I won't let Jess take it," he says. "Won't even let her touch it."

I slip the strap over my head and give him the cylinder. It clangs against the door as he leaves.

My pastel outfit is stiff and crusty with blood. It scratches my face as I lift it over my head. The Asset patch Jess had given me pulses evenly and glows bright red. I slip on the gray outfit quickly, nervous the glowing will draw unwanted attention.

The gray outfit is snug but breathes. It's like wearing a full-body leotard. There are hidden pockets and clasps all over it. In a pocket over my left breast, there are five condom-sized Asset packets. I squint to read some.

1260BCHGI002

2500BCGS007

1500SW324

I take them to Kyle. He has the sword out of its cylinder, and he's feeding a swab into a DNA replicator.

"What does this I mean?" I say, showing him one of the packets.

"Well, that's called writing," he says.

"I'm about to impale you with this sword."

"Sorry. I wasn't trying to be funny. You can never tell about people you meet in other universes. It *is* writing, but tell me which ones you can understand."

"Just the English and the Spanish."

He looks inside the replicator. "That's a good sign."

"A good sign in the replicator, or a good sign that I can read English and Spanish?"

He gives me a big, excited grin. "Both. A good sign that we have a main language in common. Easier to work together if communication is unhindered. You see, from my travels with Jess, I've surmised my world is unique in that the um...what's that term. Ah, *Americans*, didn't win the um...their Battle for Independence."

"You mean, the American Revolution?"

"If you say so. Back home, the British Empire owned half the world."

"Do we get to go back to our homes?" I say.

His excitement dims. "Well, about that...You could go back to yours. I'm sure Jess would allow—"

"I'm not really the type to wait to be *allowed*."

"—but I don't have one anymore." He turns away from me.

"I'm sorry. What?"

"A...casualty in the war against the Stitchers. There were more of us, you see. More of me, I mean. We'd found out what PanGen was doing, and we staged a coup. Which escalated into a war. Which...destroyed my planet. Jess happened to be there on one of her missions. She got me out, but it cost her..." He nods at the picture that had gotten my attention earlier.

I take it off the wall. It could be me and Dad and Ben and Mom on a hike in the woods, but in Jess's reality, we're all very serious, and very well-armed.

"I've never even held a gun," I say.

Kyle puts it back on the wall. "Jess's Anne and Ben were in the castle when it blew up. Her husband was on the grounds. There was a slim chance she could've saved him. Slim, but she could've. Instead, she saved me."

"Why would she sacrifice us—I mean, *them*—for you?"

"Because I knew where Excalibur was."

"You're shitting me."

He pulls the replicator away from the wall. Doing so also moves the microscope and a box of test tubes. Duct taped to the back of the replicator and microscope is a strange blackish sword. It's hard to see the blade's edge because it shimmers like I'm seeing it through heated air.

"It's smaller than I thought it'd be," I say.

"It's not the size of the sword but the skill of the swordsman," Kyle says, blushing and scowling, as he pushes the replicator back. "It's also the only time Jess has taken something from a reality other than a blood sample. Until now."

He nods at Princess Urduja's sword, which looks so plain after seeing the real fucking Excalibur. Still, its value lies in what it represents, not in how it appears.

"You done with it?" I say.

"Yes. I'm excited to see what Asset it holds." He takes a tray of pink pulsing glop from a slot in the DNA replicator, which I'm starting to suspect is more than just a replicator.

The saucer-sized glop looks like dried jelly. Kyle looks around for something. His gaze rests on the Urduja sword.

"May I?" he says.

"Uh. Sure?"

He picks it up, swings it with the grace and ease of someone who's used to swords, and cuts the saucer into four quarters. He peels the quarters off and flattens them inside foil bags, which he labels with c1550UT53.

"Circa 1550," he says. "Urduja Tawalisi, Earth fifty-three."

"So that's what all those codes are?"

"The approximate time the artifact was most used, the name of its owner, and the Earth the sample came from. Would you like to do the honors?" He points at the last quadrant.

"Stick that on me?"

"Well, I would ask one of them, but I haven't figured out their language yet."

Them is a small crowd of the timid people who have bravely approached our rectangle of light. They're extremely pale but not albino or leucistic; they look as if they haven't ever been exposed to sunlight. Even their irises are so pale they almost blend in with the whites. Though they're silent, they look on with interest which betrays intelligence.

I change my stance to include them in what we're doing, unzip my gray top, and adhere the last jelly glop on my chest. Unlike with the square from the silver packet, I don't feel any change at all.

"Well?" says Kyle, staring at me intently. "Your pupils have dilated a tiny bit. Can you see into the absolute dark over there?"

He points, but it had never been absolute dark for me. I see the blanket lumps of the timid people. Some of them are occupying the children with a complex game played with fingers and strings.

"Nothing's changed," I say.

"Still might. Our extractor isn't as good as it could be, which could explain the delayed reaction. Do let me know if you develop a higher perception with one of your senses. Or if you can suddenly lift something you shouldn't be able to."

"And what about the whats-it-called. The...Downside."

"Yes. Craving for blood or flesh, sudden paranoia, heightened lust. The usual. Do let me know if you feel any of those."

"Sure. Funny."

He winks and there's a titter of breathy laughter from the timid people. I lean over Urduja's sword to examine it, trying to figure out what would make it so special that Mom died to get to it. But it's plain except that the hilt is made of bamboo. Uncommon. Such a resilient material.

Kyle assembles a bunch of the plastic computer sheets together to form a square about eight feet by eight feet. Then he ties hair-thin silver filaments to the borders and secures the filaments down with a chunk of duct tape.

"Is that the transport pad?" I say.

He nods as he programs things into another computer sheet on the table.

Jess comes in, places a crate of clanking weapons in the center of the transport pad.

"Almost ready?" she says, looking at me and Kyle.

"What about them?" I nod at the timid people. There are more of them watching us now.

Jess leaves, saying, "Be ready," on her way out.

Kyle stacks more boxes and equipment on the transport pad. As he does, the computer sheet on the table beeps and a few lights on the star map dim to dark gray.

"The more we bring," says Kyle, "the fewer high-tech worlds we can go to."

"I understand," I say.

He leaves a worn-out sack on the bench and takes more of his equipment to the transport pad. I look in the sack. There's a bunch of condom-sized Asset packets on them, but there's a black X going through the labels so they're difficult, but not impossible, to read.

"Are these Assets expired or something?" I say.

"Oh those. Loot from dead Stitchers. Jess told me to throw them away, but I can't bring myself to. The Stitchers made them for a reason. If I could figure out why, I think they'd be useful to us."

Based on how he'd parsed out the Urduja label, I try to crack these codes.

1431JDA752

Judas? No, that would be far earlier. What was significant in the 1400s? J-D-A. Joan D'Arc! Holy Christ on a platter. Hoping I'm right, I tear it open and put it on my chest, because my mom is dead and I'm stuck with a crazy woman and her lab monkey so why the fuck not? I could do worse than temporarily have one of Joan of Arc's qualities.

I grab two more, one which might be Katrina Von Tassel, who disguised herself as a headless horseman to scare off suitors and bandits to protect her family's wealth. The other might be Slue-Foot Sue. Both American women were legends for their cleverness and riding. There wasn't much opportunity to ride here, but maybe their Assets would manifest as different qualities.

"These are the ones Jess likes," says Kyle, handing me a box that looks like a sunglasses case.

Within are four cloth pockets attached to the two sides. Each pocket has eight of the same four Assets.

"Hercules, Gilgamesh, Li Kui, and Atlas," Kyle says, pointing at the pockets. "Those are—"

"Heroes of legendary strength," I say. But at great cost.

A glance at Kyle's face reveals he knows this too. He puts the case in his blue backpack.

"That's Jess's obsession," he says. "To find the blood of the strongest heroes. The stronger, the better. And from all their blood, create a set of Assets that can help her, and maybe a few chosen and tested allies, to defeat the Stitchers."

"Who seem to be going after the same thing. Only with better tech, and a thousand disposable lackeys. She's going about it all wrong. Like a chicken with its gun half-cocked. No wonder she got her family killed."

Kyle freezes, looking over my shoulder. I sense Jess's anger before turning. Her face is pale, lips twisted in a grimace, eyes dry and sparkling with wrath.

I feel a strange and foreign courage rise in me like a gushing spring. Joan of Arc's Asset!

"You're weakened by your obsession with strength!" I say. "It doesn't mean only *physical* strength. It means... It means..." I pound the table in frustration. Urduja's sword rattles.

I grasp the hilt to still the blade and my thoughts crystalize, spreading, spreading in my mind like the crystalline coating within a geode. The conviction and intuition of Princess Urduja!

"Strength isn't killing your enemies," I say. "It's not being cruel or demeaning. Anyone can do that. It isn't about one thing like physically overpowering people or being the smartest person in the room. Strength is as multifaceted as a diamond; it's having integrity, seeking truth, doing the best with what you've got. But at its point, the thing that makes someone a strong person is using all the qualities you've got to change life for the better. *That* is true strength."

Color has returned to Jess's face but she still looks unconvinced.

"You know what they call a hero who doesn't have people to lead or protect?" I ask her.

Kyle says, "What?"

"A villain."

Even *I* am stunned by my audacity. I'd never have spoken like this to my mom. Then again, she'd never leave people in harm's way. But the confidence in me doesn't fade. A small part of me feels warm with righteousness. Actually, the warmth is coming from my hand that's wrapped around the hilt of Urduja's sword.

"Why is that glowing?" says Kyle, pointing at the hilt.

I drop the sword. It falls a few inches, stops short of hitting the table. I back away but it follows my hand. On a hunch, I spread my fingers wide. The hilt slaps against my palm and on reflex, my fingers curve around it. I try to drop it and it falls away, hovers, then slaps back into my hand like a yo-yo. Which pricks the memory of something I learned long ago: the yo-yo was a weapon that originated in the Philippines.

"Do it again," says Kyle. "That's bril—"

A series of loud pops surrounds the building, as if someone's stepping on a sheet of giant bubble wrap. The boards on the windows tumble in all at once, pushed in by gales that knock me against the wall.

"They're here!" says Jess. "I thought you said they'd be—"

"I know, I know!" Kyle gets a crate out from under the counter and starts sweeping things into it. "I don't know how they got here so fast."

"How much more time do you need," says Jess.

"Ten minutes. Fifteen. I don't know."

"Hurry!"

Kyle tosses her the case full of her Assets. She unzips her top all the way. Her chest is covered in a dizzily blinking patchwork of Asset squares. Without looking, she scrapes four specific ones off with her thumb. Then she grabs four out of the case, tears off all four edges with a single bite, and sticks them on her chest.

As she does all this, I'm edging towards the transport mat almost full of their equipment. There's barely enough room for the three of us to stand. I pick a box that doesn't look important and kick it off the mat. I'm about to chuck one away when large dark things fly in the windows and land in the midst of the timid people.

The creatures that have come in force a double-take. They're lean men in suit jackets above the waist, octopuses below. Their tentacles look shiny and rubbery like wet bike tires but they've got fantastic, terrifying grip. The two creatures closest to the timid people each have a timid person stretched between their tentacles. With a sickening squish and series of pops, their victims have been twisted and pulled in half at the waist. The air immediately fills with the thick scent of blood.

That took seconds but it feels slower to me. My sword hand is scalding hot. There's power flowing in me not unlike the heat built up from a hard dance routine.

"Cecaelians!" Kyle yells to me. "Stay away from their tentacles."

No duh. I'm far enough away that there's plenty of other targets for the cecaelians to go after.

"If you can fight, fight!" I say to the timid people. My voice rings in the room. There's an unrecognizable timbre to it. The charisma of Joan of Arc! "Defend yourselves with anything in reach."

I grab the crate of weapons, spill its contents on the floor in front of the timid people. Surprisingly, only a few pick them up. As the timid people shuck their blankets, I see that they are wiry like acrobats. They have their own weapons: knives strapped to their arms or ankles or backs or waists.

In this hot, dark planet, the timid people fight what they can see, and they can see only what's near enough to see. They fight like knife-wielding wrestlers, hacking, slicing, stabbing at tentacles until they're close enough to sever a jugular. Those who picked up guns from the weapon pile are using them, quite effectively, as cudgels.

We could be evenly matched against the cecaelians, but there are more coming in through the windows.

"*Creeeeeeeeaaaaargh!*" yells one of the timid people as he's squeezed to death between the tentacles of two cecaelians.

Our numbers are dwindling.

"Help me get the last...stuff," Kyle yells at me as Jess stands between him and the cecaelians, shooting keenly but only hitting tentacles.

Kyle is trying to get the bulkiest of the lab equipment, the DNA replicator/Asset extractor. As he pulls on it though, he's dragging a bank of microscopes and other things are falling to the floor. He changes angle. Excalibur is still duct-taped to the back of the equipment.

"Get your sword!" I say to Kyle. "We can rebuild that damn machine."

"No we can't," says Jess. "We need it."

"Your family died for that sword," I say.

She grimaces, doesn't say anything, fighting a battle within even as she fights the cecaelians.

"Get your sword, Kyle. And help me get these people on the pad. You and you," I point Urduja's blade at two large timid people who have just finished killing a pair of cecaelians. I should stop calling them timid people. "Get this equipment off the pad."

"Not all of it!" says Kyle.

"Can we take people if we keep the important stuff?" I say.

"Yes...I think so."

To the uh...pale people, I say, "Leave anything that looks important."

I'm not sure how much they understand, but they had seemed to follow my conversations with Kyle. They get to work, flinging boxes and equipment as if they weigh nothing, aiming for some cecaelian heads. One catches the back of a cecaelian that Jess is fighting. It goes down. Jess is red, panting, veiny, and frothing at the mouth. Crazed with bloodlust.

"The madness..." Kyle grits out as he slices through two thick tentacles, "of Hercules. She'll...kill us too."

"Just like he killed his wife!" I say, ducking a blow only to be knocked down by another tentacle. A third tentacle comes out of nowhere and wraps around my neck. It squeezes hard, quickly. I hack at it clumsily with Urduja's blade until another tentacle grabs my wrist.

"Anne!" Kyle yells.

He launches towards me, gets swatted away by a tentacle.

Suddenly, the tentacle around my neck falls slack. A pale woman comes into view, slices through the tentacle that had been around my wrist. I somersault out of the way just as another tentacle comes slamming down. The pale woman hugs the tentacle, wrestles it away from me.

"Anne?" Kyle yells.

We can't see each other.

"I'm fine," I yell back.

"Jess!" yells Kyle. "Take off the Hercules Asset. Jess!"

I catch glimpses of her as I fight and shove and hack tentacles away from the pair of pale people trying to clear the transport pad. Jess can't seem to hear over the fighting or the chaos in her own mind. With sinewy arms, she scalps the nearest cecaelian, laps at the scalp as it weakly throttles her. And her tongue, lapping at the dark cecaelian blood, makes my mouth water, and a hunger I've never known overwhelms me.

Everything turns black.

A flash of light and sound.

Another flash of light and a scream.

Something hot and slick and mineraly is in my mouth. The world expands from that morsel until I see my own little patch of hell and dismembered bodies.

"Oh no," I say, voice raspy but still eating that delicious morsel that's becoming chewier and not so delicious. I spit it out. It's a nose. Oh God, Kyle. Jess. The sight of Jess licking that scalp must've triggered a Downside from the original Asset patch.

I look around for them. They're both alive. Both still fighting. Jess looks more normal but now Kyle is the crazed one, a sneering blur as he wields Excalibur in a bloody whirlwind across the room, injuring cecaelians and pale people indiscriminately.

"Kyle!" I say, but my voice is lost in the fray.

And there's a half-dead cecaelian on the floor in front of me. He's missing his nose and four of his tentacles have been gnawed to shreds, but he's clawing his way toward me.

I raise Urduja's blade to deliver a fatal blow, but I still can't bring myself to do it.

Ping! Hiss!

Jess does it, not to save me, but to kill.

"Box-es," someone says near me. One of the timid—I mean, *pale* people. She points at the transport mat. It's clear except for the backpack of Jess's discarded Assets, a box of those plastic computer sheets, and a large crate of artifact cylinders, old broken guns, two small pitted shields. I catch my reflection in one of the shields. The lower half of my face and my teeth are bloody.

"Perfect," I say to them. "Get everyone onto the mat. Children first. They can stand on things. Then, moving backwards, constrict on the mat."

"They...to be...surround us," she says. Can't tell if it's present or future tense. We are definitely outnumbered now. Many of the pale people I'd been trying to save have given their lives for their children. This hones my purpose.

"It's fine. Trust me."

I turn to go help Kyle with Jess, but the pale woman holds my shoulder.

"That...warrior," she says pointing at Jess and making a Jess-like frown.

"I'm getting us out of here," I say. "With or without her."

Would I sacrifice the woman who looks like my mom? Yes. If she would turn her back on people who need her, I could turn my back on her.

With a pair of pale people fighting beside me, Urduja's blade and intuition, Joan of Arc's courage, and whatever is coming out of the first patch Jess had given me, and maybe more than a little luck, I make it across the floor, slippery with blood and guts, to where Kyle and Jess are trapped.

We breach the cecaelians surrounding them. "Come on!"

Kyle comes to me. Jess, eyes dead, fighting mechanically, doesn't.

"With or without you!" I yell. Then I think how that must sound, coming from someone who could've been her daughter in another life. "I'd rather you come with us, Jess. Don't waste another family."

She looks at Kyle. Then at me. Then finally she comes and we're fighting our way back to the very full transport mat.

Kyle kneels and gets hold of the filaments he'd secured under the edges of the transport mat. While we cover him, he rests the ends of the filaments on a computer sheet he dug out of one of the boxes. The filaments fuse to the sheet, which flares yellow then shows a star map with more than half the destinations grayed out. Kyle puts his finger over one, hesitates.

"You might never get home!" he yells to me above the noise of fighting. "But I'll help you with everything I've got!"

I swallow a sob for Ben and Dad and glance at what he's "got." Ex-fucking-calibur, the skills to get it, and the compassion to make such a deal. "I trust you. Do it."

It's a gut-wrenching feel, like riding a very fast elevator descent. Everything is dark and so cold it hurts to breathe. I reach out with my left hand and find someone's right hand. We grasp each other tight.

Then we land with a thud, boxes crashing, glass breaking, and children screaming in terror. There's a rain of tentacle tips that had been too close, severed by the bubble of energy from our transport pad.

"Shut them up!" Jess whispers. "We can't draw attention."

But the screaming gets louder as more and more children join in. They hadn't been this frightened during the chaotic fighting in the near-dark. The dark.

They're afraid of the light. It's not even that bright. Actually kind of hazy early morning.

"Cover their eyes," I say to the adults. "It's going to get brighter. It's daytime. Day. Sun." I point at the rising sun throwing out gold shafts on the wide pasture we're in.

Feels good to see it and feel its radiant warmth, different from that sulfurous heat of the last Earth.

A bell sound, small but deep, carries over the plain. Then a few more. Cows come up from a little valley to the west and, ignoring us, start grazing just a few feet away. And in that valley, I see a large farm by a large white house. Stables and, oh no, horses. Horses for transportation would mean we're in a very low-tech world.

"Goddamn it," says Jess, aiming her bloody gun at the nearest cow. Must've figured it out too.

"Don't!" I say. "What the fuck is wrong with you? Killing things because you're frustrated doesn't make you strong or badass. It makes you weak and pathetic."

"I've just about had it with you," she says.

I laugh coldly. "Oh please. You're not my mom."

It hits me as soon as I say it. Jess roars at the sky. So much for not drawing attention to ourselves. She hurls her gun at the cows before I can stop her.

The gun goes through the nearest one. The cow flickers, then solidifies, without pausing its grazing.

"Holograms!" I say.

"Good sign," says Kyle.

"I can work with it," we both say at the same time, then laugh.

Jess breaks away from us to retrieve her gun. She limps right through the cows, which earns giggles from the kids. Instead of returning, she scans the horizon. I go to her slowly, feeling like a rock that's been tumbled in a rock tumbler. My joints and appendages feel bruised.

"We can't keep doing this," I say. "We've all lost people. This...thing my mom dragged me into. Take Your Daughter to Work Day. It was just supposed to be a stupid boring bonding thing. And...I don't know what else to say." The eloquence and confidence I'd felt before are abating. I glance under my shirt, at my chest. One of the squares is dark. I add, "I'm sorry I said you got your family killed."

In the awkward silence that follows, I prod the nested boxes of my grief. Not yet time to unpack it. Soon.

Then Jess says, "I'm sorry too. I keep seeing my Anne when I look at you, but when you talk, you don't sound like her at all. It makes me... angry. With myself. And I'm taking it out on you and Kyle. I'll try to do better."

I go to help Kyle, who's making bandana sun-shades for the kids. Then I remember to ask Jess, "What was that Asset you gave me. To help me breathe on that last Earth. I think...it made me eat people or something. Oh crap!" I unzip my shirt and scratch it off, drawing blood. The air is wetter in the next breath, heavier in my lungs.

"That was Mercy Brown from New England, around the turn of the nineteenth century. I forget which Earth. Most histories have her as a vampire. Actually, she was a ghoul. Had the biology to maintain functioning at low levels of oxygen."

"The Downside was, that biology required consumption of human flesh?"

Jess shrugs. "I've found it doesn't have to be human, most certainly not alive, but has to be very freshly dead."

I don't ask how she's learned those specifics.

There's a small smile on her face as she stares at the horizon. I trace her gaze to glinting spires in the distance. Definitely not low tech. From there, hopefully we can find the nearest PanGen, infiltrate it, and use their transport dock. If that's not possible, we can get our hands on some tech to put together a stronger transport mat.

And while we're here, if we have time before the Stitchers tracking

Kyle and Jess figure out where we are, might as well figure out how this Earth is different, and who were the heroes that shaped it.

On *Chasing Skins*–

Ernie has a straight in your face writing style and he doesn't skimp on the hard-boiled. In Ernie's debut story, Dean detects the influence of classic noir-detective fiction writers before *Chasing Skins* swerves off that road into the unexpected. After reading it, Dean recalled the Dinosaur Jr. song *Start Choppin'*. Read the story, it will all make sense when you finish.

—*Dean Fearce*

Chasing Skins

Ernest Ortiz

ANDY'S FACE SCRATCHED ALONG the damp asphalt as he finally woke up. Moonlight and shadows danced their eternal struggles. Brick walls, dumpsters, and trash bags were the first things he saw. The stench finally registered in his nostrils. The wail of sirens and yowls of cats in heat sounded in the distance. He sat up and leaned against the wall. Every muscle in his body burned and his joints were stiff.

He searched the pockets of his black jacket and blue jeans and found a keycard and a slip of paper. The keycard pictured a local pizza joint and a phone number. The slip of paper was a map of a hotel. The number 223 was circled in black and the name Motel Sierra displayed at the edge of the paper with a line between it and the building.

Andy stood and brushed off the dust. He exited the alleyway and wandered around. The streets were void of any human presence. All the little knick-knack stores and run-down beauty parlors were closed. A stray black cat ran across the street then fed from a spilled garbage can. Cars parked tight along the curb. At least it was cool enough that the stench from the garbage cans, dirty diapers, and decaying meat wasn't too bad. He put his hands in his pockets and scrolled down the commercial area.

Main Street. *Such a generic street name*, Andy thought. As he walked further down the street, the business names were getting vaguely familiar. Bank of Americano. Kentucky Fried Ducks. The Peach Store. He'd been in those places before but couldn't remember when he last visited them. His stomach growled and he checked his pockets again. No money. Andy kept walking until he spotted a Devron gas station across the cross. He stepped off the curb.

Zoom! Honk!

"Watch where you're going, asshole!" said the passing driver.

"Fuck you!" Where did that come from?

Andy entered the gas station's convenience store. An elderly man in a turban glared at him as he stepped closer to the counter.

"Excuse me, do you know where I can find Motel Sierra?"

The man mumbled.

Andy leaned closer. "What?"

"A few blocks that way! Now leave!" He pulled a baseball bat from underneath the counter.

"Jerk off," Andy mumbled. He tried slamming the door shut on the way out, but it closed too slowly.

The bright lights from the gas station faded behind him. He looked over his shoulders every few steps and listened carefully for nearby noises. He didn't have any money but that didn't stop scumbags from trying. Speaking of scumbags, Andy wondered if he had been beaten and robbed. That would explain the lack of money. But if that was the case, why leave the keycard and paper slip in his pocket? Why not take them and loot his hotel room?

The pain faded slowly. That was good. Motel Sierra's neon sign appeared in the distance. Andy climbed rickety steps to get to Room 223. The curtains were drawn and no light came from within. He listened through the door and there was silence. He swiped the keycard but the light remained red. Another swipe and a jiggle. Still locked. He twisted, yanked, and pushed the door. The lights inside came on. A burly man opened the door.

"What the fuck you doing?" the man roared.

Andy quickly scanned him. Long brown hair, thick beard, and tattoos on both arms. For some reason he knew the man was a biker.

Acting on instinct, Andy weaved and tried to slur his speech. "Oh fuck, sorry man. Shit, I got to stop drinking." Andy stumbled away from the door and hoped the biker didn't grab him by the shirt and drag him in the room for a beating. The door shut as he turned the corner. Andy couldn't understand why the keycard didn't work. Maybe it expired. He went to the night window but it was unoccupied. He thought about pushing the call button but he didn't like the idea of waking someone up.

Then on the glass of the night window, he saw the reflection of a neon sign for a motel on the next lot. Motel 69. He climbed the fence separating the two lots and went to the other motel and searched for 223. The curtains were closed but there was light. He put his ear to the door and the TV was on but he couldn't hear any voices.

Andy inserted the keycard and the door unlocked. He slowly opened the door and the first thing he saw was a woman sitting on the bed. The woman turned sharply. Her face showed confusion, then lit up with recognition and she rushed towards him.

"Andy!" The woman hugged him.

All he could do was hug back. Maybe that would trigger a memory. Nothing. He looked at the woman. She had short brown hair in a pageboy style framing a round face. She wore a blue t-shirt and black jeans on her thin but athletic body.

"Hello?"

The woman slapped him. "That's it? That's all you can say? What the fuck is wrong with you? And where have you been?"

"I don't know. I don't know who I am or who you are."

"What? Don't be stupid. What do you mean you don't know who I am? What, do you have amnesia?"

Andy shrugged. "I don't know. All I know is that I don't remember who I am, who you are, or why we're here."

"I'm Sarah, your wife. We've been married for three years. Dated two years prior."

Andy looked at his ring finger. No ring, but there was a tan line. Where was his ring?

Sarah took a step back. "Oh my God, you really don't remember, do you?"

He shook his head. It seemed to hit Sarah as she walked back to the bed and curled up. "I guess it's gone now."

"My memory?"

She looked at him. "Yeah, I guess."

Andy walked over and grabbed her hand. "All I know is that I woke up in this alleyway, only had this keycard and this piece of paper on me, and they led me here. I can show you where I came from and maybe I might remember something."

She caressed his face. "I hope you do."

There was a loud bang at the door. It wasn't a knock. Someone was trying to break it down.

"Oh shit, it's Thomas." Sarah gave Andy a pocketknife.

"Who?"

Bam! A large muscled man burst through the doorway and charged towards Andy. He kept his knife hand out of sight, about to open it, when Sarah tried to distract Thomas. He backhanded Sarah and she crumpled to the floor. He then struck Andy and threw him against the wall.

"Where's the fucking money?" Thomas roared.

"I don't know what you're talking about."

Thomas shoved Andy on the floor and started to choke him. "Where's my fucking money?"

Thomas's face blurred in Andy's eyes. Andy tried to loosen Thomas's grip with one hand while quietly opened the knife in the other.

Thrust! Right in Thomas's side, just underneath the ribcage.

That only made Thomas madder and he squeezed harder. Now it was a game of who died first. Andy kept stabbing without resistance and Thomas's face drooped. His eyes went blank and his grip finally loosened before he collapsed on top of Andy. Andy pushed off Thomas's dead body and stared at the blood on his hands and clothes.

Sarah grabbed his arm. "We have to go."

"But I just killed a man."

"We have to go now, dammit! Where'd you park the car?"

"I don't know."

"Fuck."

They ran down the stairs and zoomed through the parking lot to look for the car but couldn't find it. At the fence, Andy gave Sarah a boost over, then he climbed over to Motel Sierra. An image of him inside a car at an unknown street filled his mind. There were no street signs nearby. Brick-walled businesses lined the street. He left the car keys in the ignition and got out of the car. As he closed the driver door, he noticed the exterior was green and there was a silver horse on the front grille. His mind went back to the present.

"I must have parked the car somewhere along the street but I don't know where, exactly. I also left the car keys inside just in case."

"That was stupid."

They ran across the property before scaling over another wall that led to a 24-hour diner. Andy looked at Sarah as she scanned the alley behind the restaurant. She stared a moment at a fixed camera pointing at a back door and dumpster, but luckily it wasn't pointing at them and there weren't any other cameras nearby. She then looked at a drain and water hose next to them.

Sarah said, "Take off your shirt and stuff it in there. Then rinse off."

Andy complied. The water was freezing, but he looked cleaner than he did a few minutes ago.

"You'll have to change once we're safe," said Sarah.

Sirens were now wailing in the neighborhood. Police cars drove past the restaurant and out of view towards Motel 69.

"We have to keep moving," said Sarah.

Andy and Sarah did their best staying away from the sidewalks, streets, cameras, and lighting as much as possible. Questions popped up in his head. One minute he woke up in an alleyway not knowing who he was and where he came from. The next he was on the run with a woman who claimed to be his wife. For some reason the thrill of the chase and the idea of being married to a beautiful woman excited him. Then it hit him, were they criminals? And what about the money Thomas was willing to kill him over. If Andy did have the money, maybe he hid it somewhere safe. Maybe it was in that green sedan with the silver horse. They entered a nearby park. Andy grabbed Sarah by the arm and dragged her to a line of trees.

"Who am I?" said Andy.

Sarah stuttered, "You're my husband."

Andy shoved her against the tree. She didn't resist. "Who is Thomas and why did he try to kill me?"

She opened her mouth, but the words didn't come out.

"Look, if you don't tell me right now, then we're going back to the motel and we tell the cops what happened."

She sighed and said, "Okay, okay. First, let me go."

He complied.

She sat on the ground. "First off, we are married and we're bank robbers. Thomas is, *was*, our next door neighbor, along with Danielle, his wife."

Andy lost his footing and stumbled onto the ground. *Bank robbers? It couldn't be!* "The money. We robbed a bank?"

"The four of us, yeah. And not *a* bank, *many* banks. You, Thomas, and Danielle would do the robbing while I would be the getaway driver. The last hit we did was the big one. But we ditched them so we could keep all the money."

"And that was why Thomas tried to kill me."

Sarah nodded.

"And what about Danielle?"

"I don't know. Haven't seen her since the hit."

"And what about the money?"

"I was hoping you'd tell me."

"Why did I end up in an alleyway a couple of miles away?"

"I don't know. Before you left, Thomas called your cell and wanted to meet to get his share from the heist. You took the money to find a place to hide it in case Thomas knew where we were."

Bright lights came from behind them. Andy immediately recognized the green sedan with the silver horse on the front grille. There was another flash, smaller and less bright, and a sharp crack that launched wood splinters from a nearby tree.

He grabbed Sarah's hand. "Quick, over that hill."

"It's Danielle."

"How do you know?"

"That's her car."

Andy and Sarah ran over the hill, hoping that Danielle would have to drive around to catch up with them. However, the bright lights remained on target. The car went over the sidewalk and grass and was halfway up the slope by the time Andy and Sarah tumbled down to the other side. They ran to the street but then maneuvered back into the park and ran through the playground and back the same way they came.

Danielle had to drive around the playground to catch up with them. When she finally did, Andy realized that they ran past the same Devron gas station with the asshole turban guy and they'd reached the end of the same alleyway he'd woken up in.

"Why are we stopping?" Sarah yelled.

Crack!

Andy felt the bullet pierced through his thigh. He fell to the ground. The car was getting closer. He turned to Sarah and said, "Get out of here!"

"Not without you."

"Go! I'll try to catch up."

Sarah hesitated but eventually ran down the alleyway. Andy got up, pressed his hand against his thigh, and started to run. The pain overwhelmed him. He lost balance and slammed against the wall. The bright lights flooded the alley. Using the wall, he got up and hobbled as fast as he could.

Slam!

Metal struck Andy's back, lifting him onto the car. The car stopped and he rolled onto the concrete. He heard the car door open, close, then footsteps. Black leather pumps were the first things he saw coming out of the overwhelming light. Then someone grabbed a chunk of Andy's hair and lifted his head enough to see the butt end of a pistol before he blacked out.

Andy felt a jolt in the ribs. Another one. Again. He finally woke up and tried to move.

Clang!

His right hand was handcuffed to a steel pipe. He tried to pull but the pipe was too thick to move. He looked at his thigh and found his belt wrapped around the wound. He then looked at Danielle. She was thicker than Sarah, but not heavyset or obese. She had long red hair and she was wearing a black pantsuit.

Andy looked around and said, "Where's Sarah?"

"She's safe for now. As long as you tell me what I need to know, I'll let you see her."

"I don't know where the money is."

Danielle dug her two-inch heel onto his bullet wound and Andy screamed.

"Where's the money?" she yelled at him.

"I don't know!"

She kicked him in the crotch. "Where's the fucking money?"

After a couple of heavy breaths, "I don't know."

"Fine. You want to play that game?" Danielle walked around to her trunk and pulled out an axe.

Andy tried to slide the handcuff off his hand but it was tight. He focused on the axe as it got closer.

"Wait, you can have the money. All of it. I just don't know where I put it."

Danielle scoffed, "You trying to tell me you have amnesia?"

"I really do. I'm trying to remember, just give me time."

"I don't have time. This wouldn't have happened if you and your precious wife hadn't double-crossed us. You tell me where the money is now, or I start chopping."

Andy remembered that adrenaline helped revealed portions of his memory. He squeezed at his wound as hard as he could but his mind refused to reveal more.

"Maybe I can help." She swung down.

Left arm. Chop!

Andy screamed but his cries faded in the night. His mind flashed to Sarah in a wedding dress about to kiss him, then flashed to him sitting in the dining room with a pile of unpaid bills.

Right arm. Chop!

Andy was now free from his restraint, but with no arms, he couldn't push himself up. His mind flashed to him loading a chamber in his AK-47 before entering the bank. He fired a couple of rounds in the air and everybody inside screamed. He ordered them to the floor.

Back to reality. Andy tried to shuffle away from Danielle even though it was futile.

Left leg. Chop!

In his mind, he saw himself and Sarah running to the green '67 Mustang sedan. They drove off with Danielle and Thomas shooting at them. Once they got away, Andy showed Sarah the thousands of dollars in the duffle bag. They kissed.

Right leg. Chop!

Andy remembered being in the same alleyway he found himself in. He placed the duffle bag in a dumpster before he met with Thomas on the rooftop. Thomas wanted all the money and Andy refused. Thomas grabbed Andy's shirt collar but he fought back. With one powerful shove, Andy was pushed off the rooftop. Thomas's face was all he could see before he blacked out.

Andy's eyes widened as he stared at the dumpster and the money it hid. Everything came back. All the pieces of the jigsaw puzzle finally came together. The memories and adrenaline overloaded his system before he passed out.

He finally woke up and looked around. He couldn't move. Everything came crashing back to him. His limbs. They were still gone. He now had stumps with pieces of cloth tied around them in tourniquets. His limbs were stacked in a pile nearby. He was still in the alleyway.

"Awake now, are we?" said Danielle.

He looked up at her. She smiled and turned her head away towards someone else. "Got it?"

Andy looked towards the dumpster. Sarah was dirty and sweaty, but she was smiling as she held up the same duffle bag he remembered putting in. Danielle grabbed it, opened it, flipped through a stack of bills, then put it back in the bag. She grabbed the back of Sarah's head and pulled her in for a kiss. Afterwards, she looked at Andy and said, "I guess I'm sorry that I didn't believe you had amnesia. Anyway, thanks for killing my husband. And now that we don't need you anymore—"

"Fuck you!" he yelled.

Sarah took the axe from Danielle and raised her arms for that final blow. All Andy could do was close his eyes. When he opened them the last thing he saw was them blowing kisses at him and his now detached body.

Gone to Hell: A Love Story

Dean Fearce and Jack Feril

THE DAY HAD BEEN one long hairball, and it was about to cough up a cold bolus of nocturnal bullshit when I was visited by a religious figure. I like to think it was divine intervention sending salvation in my hour of need. Maybe it was, but it was the cloak that drew me, having vowed not to freeze another night under nothing more than a blanket of cold starlight. And, there was the bright gilt cross hanging around his neck, glinting like grocery tins in the moonlight. Its flashing beauty was mesmerizing. I almost let the cloaked figure pass across the alley's entrance where I'd been camped out in this city of fallen angels.

Almost.

I wrangled him into my alley and we grappled. He was stronger than expected and, like me, had fighting skills. It wasn't my intention to kill him, but when he stomped my foot with his heavy boot (I wanted those boots) and crushed my toes, I reacted with fury. I grabbed the gold chain of the cross with one hand and crushed his trachea with a stabbing blow. Then I broke his neck without being cruel. Cruelty is a plague in the end-of-world days (EOW) and totally unnecessary.

Simple life rule: Don't be cruel.

I dragged the body behind a dumpster where I'd been sleeping, removed the worn leather satchel he carried, and shucked the cloak off his lanky frame. It was scratchy, smelly, still warm from his body heat, and fit me okay. With the cross in hand and the satchel over my shoulder, it all felt good, especially when I cracked open the tarnished clasps of the satchel. The old leather released a whisper of salvation with a twinkle of precious jeweled trinkets. I wanted to grab a handful, feel their diamond-hard deliverance, but more cloaked figures had arrived at the alley's entrance.

Damn interruptions!

Closing the satchel, I prepared for fight or flight from the three who had gathered at the alley's mouth…Oh, wait, and oh, no. Identical cloaks. These were Brothers of The Brethren. Shit on a shingle, this was bad. I was doomed.

One of them carried a lantern. "Brother John?" he said. The voice was stern, a righteous God-like narrator from when the airwaves were full of such pre-EOW things.

"Come," God-voice said. "The situation is dire."

"Most dire," said another, beckoning me to follow.

In the dark alley with the hooded cloak covering my face, they mistook me for Brother John, who now lay cooling behind the dumpster. This had all the makings of a personal catastrophe, but the wisest course of action was to follow until I could make an escape. I took my place at the end of the single-file procession still clutching the golden cross under the cloak as we moved away from the alley.

The citizens on the street, mostly Asset Migration Specialists like me, and scavenging savages—known colloquially as Scavages, lovable scamps that they were—shrank away into shadowy corners to avoid us Brothers as we marched through the unfortunate landscape.

My regret in the moment was if I managed to get out of this alive, someone else would have already found those boots on the dead Brother John. Beyond that, I wished only for a speedy, merciful death, because the Church's reputation was well known for delivering harsh retribution against sinners. The streets of the uncivilized EOW were teeming with The Brethren's tortured, maimed, and disfigured.

They led me to an empty strip mall, the storefronts on the block all gutted like everything else in the EOW. Placards in a few unbroken windows screamed:

SALE!

MARKDOWNS!

PRICES SLASHED!

EVERYTHING MUST GO!

This neighborhood used to be a 24/7 beehive of pre-EOW debauchery before things clenched up tight like a buggered bitch. I missed those days. Life was easier in ways I didn't appreciate. Seemed everything's tighter than a buggered bitch in EOW days.

The leader with the God-like voice stopped in front of a door appearing to lead to a second floor above the storefronts. "Brother John," he said.

There was a time the authority of his voice and manner would have pushed me to anger. I would have struck out against it on principle. But this was not the time for that response. The others stepped aside and I bowed my head, tensed for whatever came next.

"The client is upstairs," he said. "We have it on good authority the case is rather severe. Please attend to the client with due haste while we scout the area."

His elegiac tone made me want to kick him in the church bells, but again, I brushed it off as suicidal. Simple life rule: Do not crap thyself. It's a rule that should need no further explanation.

"And we shall pray," the leader said. "God speed, and deliver us from evil."

"God speed, and deliver us from evil," the other two chanted.

I was only too happy to get away from this circle jerk cult, and went through the door into the lobby and up the stairs in no particular hurry, thinking it would be easy enough now to make my escape from those cloaked idiots. I figured The Brethren had been called out to give last rites to the "client," some unfortunate believer who had likely passed away at a young age like so many do in the EOW. Brother John was here to get them moving on their journey to the other side with his satchel full of sacred relics, a.k.a., my retirement plan. Might even find a few more assets to migrate into my possession while assisting the client through their dire dying situation.

This place had the look and feel of a posh apartment complex, like it had been a nice crib once. Now it was barely on the sunny side of squalor. The carpet was threadbare and mangy, and the walls were a violent entropy of graffiti in the meager light. Not too much litter, but the rotten stench made me want to puke. Breathing through my mouth helped, but not much. The smell was aggressive, coating my tongue, getting inside my head. I moved faster, anxious now to vacate the premises.

The stairs ended at a dark hallway that stretched, deserted, in both directions. I tried a few doorknobs on the closed doors but they remained locked tight. The hall had turned cold as a dead whore and my ears buzzed. It felt eerie, like I'd stepped into the bad part of Weird Town. Murky shapes appeared in the murky hall playing a game of peek-a-boo that made my stomach spasm. I had to get out of here. Now.

A light blinked on farther down the hall. Working electricity was rare these days, so it felt like it was meant for me, some sort of sign. Maybe even a miracle.

When I grabbed the doorknob, the overhead bulb fizzled and popped, showering me with sparks and glass shards. The door swung open. I felt compelled across the threshold into a black hole. Literally. No light, no sound, no up or down. Fathomless black, and a disgusting smell like a thousand rotting rats. A primeval fear came on me fast and strong. I retched, but my stomach was empty. Nothing but bile came up.

It's not bragging to say there isn't much scares me but damn if my sphincter wasn't loosening. The worst part was not being able to see into the bottomless depth of darkness. I knew with absolute certainty if I stepped off the spot where my feet were planted, I would be falling, falling, falling into an eternal black hole.

Falling.

Forever.

A hellish forever.

Could have been seconds later, or millennia—it was hard to judge—when a thin strip of light flashed below me on what I hoped was the floor. The light burned an after image on my retinas and gave me bearings. I moved toward it, found a doorknob and went through a door into what had to be the client's chamber based on the god-awful stink of death in the place. It smelled like rotten forgotten eggs and burning hair.

The room was lit with a smiling kitten nightlight and decorated fiendishly cheerful with the same smiling kittens on the wallpaper, the silly kid furniture, and a bedraggled assortment of pillows everywhere. The irony was palpable. I just hoped the lump in the bed wasn't a kid. That's all I ask, don't let it be a kid.

And thank you God, it wasn't a kid, but this client didn't look close to death. Just ugly as hell. Her face was contorted into a hideous mask. There was something evil about it. I felt relief supposing she was near dead, and no one but me was around to give a shit how ugly she was.

"Sorry, Sister. Looks like we missed your send off, but journey well and tip the boatmen generously." I moved toward the window to escape when the nightlight flashed off. It rooted me to the spot, again with the certainty there was nothing but the big black empty in every direction.

No floor, no walls, no light. Nothing. I had never experienced anything like this horrifying void.

I stood there wondering why the light had even flashed on before, leading me to this room, when it came on again and I screamed like a little kid because the bitch's teeth were chattering in my face, the rancid stench of her breath stinging my eyes.

I freaked, swung the satchel, smacked her head. She took it like a champion cage-fighter and cackled like a demented jackal. I scrabbled away, disoriented by her hideous screeching. She was on me, clawing with talon-like nails, yellow rodent teeth gnashing as she tried to sink them into my sweet, sweet flesh. The dead-alive bitch wanted to eat me.

Hell, she hadn't been dying at all. This was worse. She was possessed. This client wasn't meant to get her last rites. She needed a freaking exorcism. And Brother John was supposed to do the wet work.

Holy shit on a shingle, I was toast.

The window and the door meant two possible escape routes, and I had to get out before exiting through Door Number 3, her digestive tract. Avoid being eaten is a simple life rule I hadn't considered before.

I was on the floor and backed into a corner, landing a few kicks to her head with my sore foot when she grabbed it and chomped. I yelped with the pain, felt her rip a toe through the cheap ass shoes—if only I'd gotten Brother John's boots, everything would have been different—I'd stolen from God knows where. She lapped at the blood, gave me a bloody demented grin like she was going back for seconds.

I still had the gold cross in hand, so I lunged and buried the long end into her eyeball. It popped like a little tomato, leaking fluid down her face. I pushed it harder and she pulled back, yowling, the cross stuck in her eye orbit, blood hissing as it bubbled up. What was that shit?

She tried to pull the cross out of her skull and it burned her hands, the acrid smell of singed flesh adding another layer of horror to this horror show. So, maybe there was something to that blessed holy cross after all?

The banshee was really howling now, her head twisting and turning like an insanely sprung bobble-head, arms flailing as she crashed through the useless smiling kitten furniture and pin-balled off the walls.

I opened the satchel and dug through the beautiful jeweled trinkets—necklaces, bracelets, watches, earrings, a fine assortment of goods one could retire upon—to find another weapon. There was a worn bible, a canteen, a wicked looking dagger crusted with jewels, a chalice. I hefted the knife, was heading for the door thinking I might escape, felt claws tear into my shoulder, pain ripping through my arm. I lost the blade and got spun around into her acid-spitting face.

On reflex, I punched the cross deeper into her bubbling eye socket. She loosed a piercing wail but didn't back off. Her other unblinking eye bulged and fixed an unholy gaze on me and I was falling backward into the bottomless hellhole of blackness from which, I knew, there would be no return.

Desperate, I reached into the bag and came up with the canteen, which felt full, hopefully with holy frigging holy water. I thumbed off the stopper, swung the canteen hard and smashed her rabid mouth. Water splashed over her face and her skin erupted like boiling lava. It *was* holy frigging holy water, and she did not like this consecrated stuff. I splashed the rest on her while she screamed and clawed at me, getting only air because I ducked, grabbed the knife, came up and buried it to the hilt in her chest.

She shrieked and her body twisted into a wicked disarticulated spasm, her good eye going milky and churning like a cement mixer. The window exploded inward, showering us in glass, and the door blew wide with a hot, sulfurous wind further scattering the chaos of this happy kitten sepulcher. Weird evil shit.

It got weirder when she said, "Thank you, merciful one," in a dying whisper.

Me? Merciful? How weird and ironic is that?

She deflated, literally, with a last breath, slid free of the knife, and crumpled to the floor. Her face softened, peaceful, even pretty you might have said, except for the blisters, the nasty eye damage, etc., etc. Her body twitched savagely, like her struggle with death wasn't over, then stilled.

I fell against the wall, slid to floor, tried to wrap my head around this whole shit storm. Felt like I was going to lose my mind here. Needed something to hold onto, something like a simple life rule.

For example: Unless you had personal experience of being possessed by a devil, how would you know when someone else was possessed by a devil? Sure, you could look at this creature who tried to kill me. She had looked possessed. She had acted possessed. Yet, could I remain skeptical?

It's true, belief in science had fallen out of favor in the EOW, but there could be any number of legitimate reasons for her behavior, including psychological, toxicological, even hormonal; or, all of the above. Honestly, this wouldn't be the first time I had been trapped in the bedroom of a crazed bitch from hell.

So, simple life rule here is: be skeptical. But keep an open mind. And don't be stupid. Remain calm, gather your jewel-encrusted goodies, and get the hell out of there.

The cross came out of her goopy eye orbit with a soft hissing sound. I wiped it and the knife with the bedclothes, tossed everything into the bag, departed quickly from the premises of the newly departed. Or, as fast as possible with a toe hanging by a smidgeon of toe flesh. It was starting to hurt as the adrenaline began to subside. My shoulder, too, where she'd dug into it. Probably a few other things if I had a chance to feel them.

And this had all happened because I wanted a scratchy, smelly-as-hell cloak to curl up in and keep me warm at night.

But, I was alive and had successfully migrated a shitload of valuable assets into my possession. Courtesy of The Church of The Brethren.

They were fanatical murderous zealots, so there was that. Running into The Brethren would likely lead to an unpleasant situation, and I try to avoid unpleasant situations whenever possible, as a rule. It's not so easy in the End of World times since the civilized world was consumed— or cleansed, depending on your perspective—by simultaneous disasters, natural, biblical, and man-made. The surviving hordes, including me, soldiered on quite naturally into our current uncivilized lifestyles as if we were born to it.

Now I had a serious foot injury and intended to seek qualified medical help appropriate to the situation. If I found a licensed medical practitioner, preferably a surgeon who graduated from a good pre-EOW institution, a specialist in the re-attachment of a phalange, who possessed a generous notion of anesthesia with a well-stocked medical cabinet to support it, all while waiving his fee as a thank you for the public service I'd performed of ridding the world of a demon bitch from hell, then that was the Doc for me.

If he'd lost his license for abusing cadavers,—certainly a victim-less crime—didn't know a phalange from a hemorrhoid, was already well-intoxicated from whatever anesthesia he could pilfer, believed all surgery could be performed successfully with a meat cleaver, and would accept this cursed horse-hair cloak for payment, well, that certainly qualified as appropriate in this situation.

Fortunately, I knew just the doctor and his practice was within hobbling distance.

The novel, *Gone To Hell: A Love Story*, by Dean Fearce and Jack Feril, will be available soon from Chophouse Books.

About the Authors

Robert Bevan

Robert Bevan has been living and teaching English in South Korea for the past fourteen years. He is the unashamedly self-published author of the bestselling Caverns and Creatures series of comedy/fantasy novels and short stories. He and his family live in Gimpo, up near The Wall, protecting the realms of men from Norks and wildlings.

Dean Fearce

As one fan writes about Dean Fearce:

You are twisted, demented and it has never been proven you are not an alien. I don't want to join kickasser...fartstarter...whatever, but I do want these incessant threats to stop, so PLEASE!!!! tell me where to send my money!

Jack Feril

I don't consider myself an introvert. It's just that I prefer the company of animals and small children over the company of other adults. Mostly because animals and small children don't talk too much. And there's always fun to be had when you combine animals and small children.

There's this thing that people say about other people they think they like and it's that the other person seems to always see "beauty" in the world. I think I'm the opposite. Not that I see or seek out ugliness, but that, to me is the most beautiful because it's genuine. It's like that thing, you know. Truth and beauty being the same thing.

In writing, that's what I strive for: to dig out the truth-beauty, filet it, spread it out on a plate with a squirt of color and a sprig of wonder.

Careful. The plate's hot!

Joan Reginaldo

I was born in the Philippines, grew up with all its creepy superstitions, somehow ended up in Silicon Valley afraid to put pillow cases on my pillows at night.

I blog about being a mom to an introverted kid who wants to be called Grimlock, and taking care of aging parents that are afraid of yogurt, their smartphones, and anyone not Filipino. My partner, Futurehusband, is white.

I write from the point of view of these intersections, a point of view shared by many but portrayed by few.

In terms of reading, I have so many books that they've become load-bearing structures in my house. I enjoy all genres and one of my keenest joys is to talk about books, movies, and writing.

Pet peeves:

– Migraines

– The "Reply All" feature

– People who excuse meanness as "snark"

– Asshole drivers

– The genre label "chick lit"

– Group Text

Things we can bond over:

– Animals

– Science

– Books and stories and writing

– Crafting, gardening, and baking techniques

– Twitter quips

– Tech and gadgets

The best way to contact me is through Twitter: @JoanWIP

Ernest Ortiz

Ernest is a U.S. Air Force veteran and private investigator living in the heart of Silicon Valley. He specializes in surveillance and workers comp insurance cases, and has worked throughout California, Nevada, Arizona, Colorado, and New Mexico. When Ernest is not chasing insurance cheats, he likes to watch smooth jazz concerts, go car cruising, and try insane hot sauce challenges. An aspiring writer since elementary school, Ernest is working to make his mark in the sci-fi and mystery writing world. He is currently working on a sci-fi thriller called Homing Target and a young adult dystopian called Eternal Courier, which will be out sometime next year. Ernest is a co-founder of the Black Hats Writing Group, a bi-weekly Mountain View based writing critique group, and co-founder of the recent YouTube channel Altoman5 Productions. The channel will hold weekly vlogs, comedy sketches, gaming Let's Plays, and other random content. You can read his latest blogs on his website Ernest Ortiz Writes Now, where you can find monthly updates, upcoming projects, writing wisdoms, politics from an anarcho-capitalist perspective and his short comic series, High School Life and Liberty Brew Crew. You can also reach Ernest on Twitter.

Ruth Liz Savage

Dean is pure evil, only one of his many good qualities...and I am proud/frightened to be working with him...beyond that, I've been advised to plead the 5th amendment.

Dan Tompsett

Dan Tompsett is a poet living in Kimberly, Idaho. "His poetry can be found across many internet channels and is worth seeking out," says Dean. Dan says, "All I know how to draw is a blank."

84317611R00161

Made in the USA
San Bernardino, CA
07 August 2018